# Of

# Human Telling

# OF
# HUMAN TELLING

TANYA VAN HASSELT

Matador
9 Priory Business Park,
Wistow Road, Kibworth Beauchamp,
Leicestershire. LE8 0RX
Tel: 0116 279 2299
Email: books@troubador.co.uk
Web: www.troubador.co.uk/matador
Twitter: @matadorbooks

ISBN 978 1785898 792

British Library Cataloguing in Publication Data.
A catalogue record for this book is available from the British Library.

Printed and bound in the UK by TJ International, Padstow, Cornwall
Typeset in 11pt Garamound by Troubador Publishing Ltd, Leicester, UK

Matador is an imprint of Troubador Publishing Ltd

*To everyone at ninevoices.wordpress.com with gratitude for their help and friendship*

# ONE

It was a pity you couldn't take a pill to make jealousy disappear, like you could for a headache.

It was almost a year since Stephen had got rid of her – not that he'd phrased it like this, being a man of nicely-edited and much-paraded principles – and watching him marry Beth should have been a cure. It wasn't.

Jane stared up at the departures board at Charing Cross station, fighting an impulse to jump on a train to one of the unknown and strangely alluring destinations. For a moment she saw herself arriving at an unfamiliar town, a no-longer-young woman dressed in wedding finery, a novel filling up her handbag ...

The heroine of her novel would have made a scene. As the Wharton train pulled out of the station Jane imagined the thrilled astonishment of the wedding guests, the crimson-faced groom, the weeping bride. But she couldn't lose herself in the fantasy in the usual satisfying way. An hour ago she'd run away from the triumphant church service when the organ struck up *Give me Joy in my Heart*. This was not proper heroine behaviour.

Further down the carriage a trio of younger women began to pull open glossy carrier bags and giggle over designer-label underwear. If they hoped to attract the attention of the only man in sight they were disappointed. He continued to turn over the pages of a thick paperback, apparently unmoved.

Nor could they arouse any envy in Jane. Helpful friends had suggested she was the sort of woman a makeover programme or magazine ought to take in hand, for she had one of those unremarkable faces that are sometimes featured and then revolutionised with a new hairstyle and make-up. But Jane no longer had the confidence to believe in such transformations for herself and was contrary enough to prefer the before to the after.

A mobile shrilled. Neighbouring passengers were obliged to hear at high volume how a wife ought to know when to let her husband leave, and why should the feelings of children get in the way when two soul mates had found each other? The marriage had been dead for years …

By the time you are in your late thirties you will have learnt to be less certain, Jane wanted to say, watching the pretty face. When you have learnt about thwarted desire and disappointment and compromise. But then you may never have to.

The man who had been trying to read sprang to his feet, bolted down the aisle and now stood hesitating by one of the empty seats facing hers.

'Would you mind – ?'

Jane shot him a fleeting smile of sympathy. The wedding reception would have been peppered with such talk. She opened her book to show him he was safe with her. Men always were.

A stream of schoolgirls crowded into the train.

Voices rose in competition and hyped-up laughter; a celebrity magazine was displayed for all to see.

'Angelo Arzano – a ten out of ten?'

'No *surface* damage from that car crash – '

Jane leaned forward, but could only make out a hazy image and vivid red captions. She looked back at the man opposite her, at the serious face that no schoolgirl would ever drool over. Although she guessed his height to be about average, his self-effacing manner made him appear shorter, and his well-cut suit looked new but was worn with the kind of shirt and tie chosen by a man who has little interest in clothes, or no devoted woman to choose them for him. Jane could more easily visualise him in an old tweed jacket and fraying collar. Where had he been or where was he going, looking uneasy in polished shoes and with an overnight suitcase at his feet?

She saw to her surprise that he was reading *Wives and Daughters*. Did men in the twenty-first century bother with Victorian novels with their old-fashioned social prejudices and morality? She'd thought it was only women who read Elizabeth Gaskell, or at least women like herself, without what those girls would call a life.

I read that book again last year, she wanted to say, for then he would look up and the sadness at the back of his eyes might lessen as they admitted to each other how they minded too much about what happened in books. Perhaps he too had broken down and wept at Osborne's fate.

She blinked back angry tears that wanted to fall. Stephen never read novels; he didn't need fiction to help him to understand life – or himself. He'd said it was more of a woman's thing.

And she wasn't a man's thing. She stole a glance at what she could see of the cover of *Wives and Daughters*. It showed a photograph of the appealing young actress who had played the part of the heroine Molly in a television series. She had the must-have ingredient men wanted all right, there was no missing it.

God ought to have arranged matters better than this. She wasn't the heroine in a modern novel or even a nineteenth century one, but more like Jane Austen's Miss Bates two hundred years too late: a spinster approaching forty and all that the term had once implied. It made her sound almost unpleasant.

Jane settled her plump body further down in her seat and eased her feet out of the high-heeled shoes she should never have bought. Today she'd tried to be something she was not – and what was the use of that? She was, after all, one of those Excellent Women whom men relied on to melt away without complaint when they stopped being useful.

She watched the man's hands. They were worn, like those of someone older, at home with holding a book. They had prominent veins and knuckles; reassuring, even attractive, in their ugliness.

*

She has hands like Verity. Square with strong fingers, roughened with work, how hands ought to look. Not like those other women with their blood-red painted nails and too many glittering rings.

Confused images of Artemis pursuing Actaeon, and Clytemnestra killing Agamemnon jostled through Austen's head. He'd had to switch seats in a hurry.

4

Women of that kind demanded something from him he couldn't give.

He returned to his book. Verity's paperback edition of *Wives and Daughters*. Books acted as barriers on public transport – and everywhere else.

The carriage fell silent as the last of the schoolgirls spilled out of the train. He breathed more easily, until he began to suspect that the woman opposite was watching him while he read. He couldn't change his seat a second time. The familiar reluctance spread over him and spoilt his concentration. He didn't want to get into conversation with this woman. He always found himself doing what he didn't want to do, because he couldn't manage things as other men did. Wharton was several stations further on, and the carriage was emptying.

It would be better to stop reading. He was beginning to feel dismayed by the account of the eligible widower Mr Gibson being successfully trapped by Mrs Kirkpatrick. He tucked his feet in a little closer. He would put his book away and spend the last part of the journey preparing for his coming interview at Wharton.

He'd been amazed to be invited to apply, you could almost say headhunted. He'd been certain they'd have some high-flyer in their sights already, someone they knew. It was a big jump from a smallish college in Dublin to one of England's most famous public schools. The Wharton classics department was reputed to send more boys to Oxbridge than any other school in the country. To be head of it, to have the opportunity of inspiring others with a dedication to scholarship, this was something he knew would make his life worth living.

He glanced down at the bag packed by his mother and daughter. Was it fair to drag them all the way to a small town in Sussex where they knew nobody, just because he had to get out of Dublin?

She wasn't watching him. He'd been wrong. She was deep in her book – and he wasn't an eligible widower. He was a middle-aged classics teacher with a habit of withdrawal and a past he couldn't get rid of.

But really, there was no need to fear her. She was prettily dressed but quietly so. Not covered in alarming make-up. He thought he remembered reading once – though it could hardly have been in a classical text – how women could be divided into those who spent too much time on themselves or too little. This woman didn't appear to belong to either category. She might even be someone he'd like to talk to.

It was out of the question of course. He didn't know where to begin.

The train slowed down as it approached Wharton station. He checked his watch. The woman was squeezing her book into her handbag. She must be getting out. He seized his case and scrambled to his feet.

She pressed the exit button before he could reach it, stepped out of the train and limped away from him to the ticket barriers.

Despair at his stupidity, his obstinacy, stabbed at him like an unexpectedly painful injection. He'd waited too long. He *always* waited too long.

He might have had a conversation with her – about books perhaps. He imagined asking if she liked Victorian novels. She'd probably read all of Dickens and Trollope too.

And she might have looked up with an interested, accepting face and said with unstudied simplicity, I need an author to speak to me and say things that help, they're easier to take when they come in a book. Elizabeth Gaskell must have been a wise and good woman. People criticise the Victorians for going on a bit, but some things can't be repeated too often, can they?

It might have happened like this.

But it hadn't. Nothing much ever did happen to him.

Not since that day eight years ago when the police had come to his door to tell him that his wife was dead and their only child was lying in hospital with a knife slash down her face.

# TWO

She'd been promised she would be told the results this afternoon, but it was already past four. Kate perched on the edge of her kitchen table flicking through a celebrity magazine, making futile bargains with the other half of herself, even though she knew that the one couldn't be trusted any more than the other.

*Angelo Arzano brings his family back to the UK after the death of his son in Italy earlier this year,* she read, but the words evaporated as she snatched up the telephone.

'Mrs Gidding? Clement Hunstrete, headmaster of Wharton. My congratulations. Your son has been awarded our major academic scholarship ...'

The washing machine clicked and changed to the spin cycle. Kate watched the swirl of brilliant colour through the glass. Now they could send Jonah to Wharton, and nobody would ever guess why she needed him to go there.

She flung open the French windows and stepped onto the tiny paved space which only estate agents would call a garden. Above her, wisps of cloud drifted across a sky the innocent blue of a Happy Families playing card. She should telephone Philip, but for this precious hour she wanted to relish her triumph, away from his forced enthusiasm and her unspoken guilt.

She'd tell the children first. Then there'd be no going back.

It's almost seventeen years. I have three perfect children and a husband not given to suspicion. We shall get away from here, move to Wharton. A clean road ahead. I'll be able to rid myself of the thoughts that invade my mind and the rituals I have to perform. I'll turn into the wife and mother they ought to have.

Soon the children would return, trailing back sometimes separately from the bus stop and needing food immediately before they could recover their home selves. She went into the kitchen to make tea, heard the front door open and slam, shoes kicked off, then the front door again.

'What did Dad say when you told him, did he sound pleased?' Jonah pulled away from her hug, checking out her face.

Phoebe dumped her schoolbag onto the floor and opened the fridge.

'So I'll have to leave all my London friends and live in swanky Wharton and you'll turn into a spoilt little rich boy. Mum, Gabby's staying tonight, can you give us pizzas, or give me the money for takeaways?'

'Can't you put Gabby off? We ought to have a family celebration. Go out to dinner.'

'What's to celebrate? You all go. It's a no from me.'

'We could do something tomorrow night or even Sunday,' said Teddy. 'Dad's always knackered on a Friday night. He'd enjoy it more when he hasn't been at work all day. It's brilliant Jonah, I'm really pleased.' He gave his brother an awkward hug, knocking into the table, and upsetting Kate's mug of tea.

Philip or Laurent? Sudden desolation lunged at

Kate. It's Philip's *niceness* in Teddy which stops him saying Dad's strung-up and silent after work, even though he knows it's true. But he has Laurent's eyes.

She wiped away the spilt tea with kitchen roll. Why must I go on having these thoughts? Those bloody shrinks. They don't know anything.

'Mum – are you sure you and Dad wouldn't prefer us to stay here in London?'

Kate stared at her younger son, who was concentrating on biting around the edge of an apricot jam tart.

'But of course we want to move! Wharton's a brilliant town, it's got everything. What on earth are you thinking about? You absolutely loved the school when you went to sit the scholarship exam.'

'But I like it here as well. So it's okay if you've changed your mind. I mean, the scholarship's more for you and Dad.'

Kate stood quite still.

'I don't understand why you're suddenly saying this now. Of all moments.'

Jonah shrugged.

'It doesn't matter. Can I have the piano right away or are you going to make Phoebe do her practice?'

'Don't be stupid, sit down at a piano straight after school?' Phoebe grabbed her mug of tea. 'I'm getting out of these shitty clothes. Can you tell Gabby to come to my room when she turns up? Shame I can't go and live with her family instead of this one.'

Kate and Teddy listened to Phoebe's feet clumping up the stairs and waited for the slam of her bedroom door as she kicked it shut. From the sitting room they could hear Jonah playing a scale too rapidly before abandoning it for the first difficult bars of a Shostakovich prelude.

'You might as well let her give up piano, Mum, like you did me with the trombone.'

Kate didn't answer. She stared out into the garden at that other self who had walked as light as air.

'I think Jonah was worried about the cost – you know, the fees at Wharton, even with a scholarship.'

Kate dragged her mind back to Teddy. It was unfortunate she and Philip had rowed about money in front of the children, but it didn't help to think about it now.

'That's all worked out. Anyway, it's for Dad and me to manage.'

Teddy sighed. He said casually, 'Well, if Phoebe gives up music lessons that'll save a bit of cash. When's supper?'

# THREE

Philip, returning home four hours later from a fraught meeting with a client, could hear the thump of music coming from his daughter's bedroom. The door was tightly closed. She'd have her friends in there. She wouldn't want her father embarrassing her.

'Are all teenage girls like this?' he'd once asked Kate.

'Like what?'

Turning into strangers. That was what he wanted to say, but he shrank from the words.

'*Distant –* '

'So? Why shouldn't they have their own lives and their own friends?'

He thought of how Phoebe as a little girl used to run down the stairs to welcome him when he came home from the office at the end of a hard day.

'The family's still the most important thing.'

'Philip, it's the modern world. A far cry from your stiflingly conventional and oppressive upbringing.'

He couldn't argue with her. His childhood *had* been conventional; all that living within your means and saving for a rainy day. As a boy he'd railed against its dullness and occasionally against his parents' affection. But through it all he'd been conscious of security;

years later he realised that what counted in the end was their fundamental honesty and decency, their sense of knowing where they belonged.

His wife and children – they constituted all the meaning in his life. He carried with him all the time an ideal of what a family should be; happy, growing, secure as a unit. He'd been given just that; he knew his luck. If only he wasn't sometimes too tired to enjoy it.

'Hi Dad! Want a beer? Mum's put some in the fridge for you. She's got something cool to tell you.'

Teddy. Always pleased to see you, always full of affection. Why was it that he was so much more loving than the others? Not that Jonah wasn't warm-hearted too – he was, though he was getting to the age when boys stopped being cuddly. Yet he was, in his own way, self-contained. He loved his family all right but he didn't *need* people the way Teddy did. He had so much else pouring into his life. Teddy was different – more vulnerable, devastatingly so at times, always stumbling over himself in clumsily affectionate gestures.

His wife was in the kitchen, ramming pizza cartons into the recycling bin.

'Philip? Clement Hunstrete rang. Jonah's won the top scholarship. Fifty per cent off the fees. Aren't you proud of him?'

That still leaves fifty per cent to find, Philip found himself thinking, selecting a can of beer and putting it down again. Dear God, how many thousands a year was that?

Of course he was proud of Jonah. Proud – and glad for Kate. It ought to make her happy, and he longed for her to be so. Jonah deserved it, and no doubt Wharton would give him all sorts of advantages. He tried making a list of these in his head as he opened his beer. The chance to study the classics. State-of-the-art sports halls and theatres. Other things – but he couldn't quite figure out what, at least not until he'd had a drink.

'It's wonderful news.' He poured the beer down his throat with a touch of desperation. No turning round now.

He thought back to his own education. He'd been lucky. His timid *Daily Express*-reading parents, flustered and wrong-footed when he passed his eleven plus, escaping their enclosed values into the rigorous academic discipline of grammar school. Then a place at Cambridge, where they'd visited him with the air of alarmed storks who have hatched something altogether beyond their understanding. Over the years he'd left his parents behind, but now something stirred within him, some faint feeling of loss, a little boy's homesickness.

'It was all worth it, wasn't it?'

Philip sensed the faint uncertainty in Kate's voice. He struggled for words, wanting to say the right thing, in spite of a flickering resentment that made him maladroit. He swallowed the last of his beer, and put his arms around her, aware of the inadequacy of the gesture.

'Without a doubt. It's big changes ahead then. I must go and congratulate Jonah. Are the others pleased?'

She pulled away from him to straighten the chairs around the table.

'You bet. Now we can finalise everything about the new house. Supper's in five minutes, or do you want longer?'

Supporting a family – and now this move down

to Wharton. In the hall, Philip held the banister for a long moment and then went upstairs to find his son. Sometimes he felt everything came down to him, that he carried it all. They ought to be getting some capital out of their house by selling up in London, but it wasn't working out like this. Kate had seen an advertisement for a development of two new houses built on the site of an old mansion. Five bedrooms, walking distance to the station and the school. Perfect for them, she said.

Not so perfect in price. Philip hated the idea of a heavier than ever mortgage. Wharton was fast becoming one of the most desirable towns in East Sussex. Last weekend when they'd gone to have a look round, he'd lost his nerve and then his temper.

'It's a lovely house, granted. But why take such a risk? We're happy and settled where we are.'

'We could be even *happier*' – she gave the word a strange emphasis – 'in a much better house in Wharton.'

'It's too much money, darling, too big a bite at the cherry.'

'Why are you always so cautious? Why can't you want things and try and get them like anyone else?'

'Because I'm the one who has to keep the show on the road,' he said as patiently as he could. It was an unfair argument and he hated using it.

'I could go back to working full-time.'

'How could both of us commute to London each day? What kind of family life is that?'

'I meant in Wharton. I could set up a freelance editing and translation service from home. Entice some of the company's clients to follow me.'

'Isn't that a shabby thing to do to employers who've treated you well all these years?'

'Philip, why do you always have to retreat to the moral high ground?'

Don't go back to that, he wanted to snap. It's not fair on the children. He gripped the steering wheel, allowed a tailgating Audi to overtake, and failed to keep his temper.

'We can't afford it, and I don't *want* to afford it.'

They'd driven home with his hot words smouldering in the air between them, Kate staring stonily out of the window, the children blank-faced and mute in the back seat.

'I'm sorry,' he said, as they sat in a traffic jam on the South Circular. 'I do understand you want the best for all of us. So do I. If Jonah does get his scholarship, we'll go for it. Okay?'

I'll have to work even harder, and I must do it willingly and uncomplainingly. In his tiredness he found himself thinking of Boxer, the old horse in *Animal Farm*. He recalled studying the book for his O Level English Literature, and again the pang of something surrendered crept over him. Hadn't Boxer ended up being sent to the knacker's yard? Well, the thing was done now. He would find the extra money somehow. He would have to.

# FOUR

Jonah hadn't said it was just for her. He'd said you and Dad. That should have helped, but it didn't. He hadn't meant it.

Kate undressed very slowly, folding clothes with meticulous care. Philip's stricken look lingered. She tried to brush it away. Why had Jonah come out with that nonsense about the scholarship being for her and Philip?

She'd pushed for it because the rewards would be for the whole family. Schools like Wharton needed to keep up their image of academic excellence, and the government was stepping up the pressure on private schools to sponsor clever children from less privileged backgrounds. All three children would escape the lottery that made up the capital's state system.

The extra coaching Jonah had needed in Latin and Greek had cost a fortune. She hadn't admitted to Philip how much, but it had gobbled up a substantial whack of her earnings as a part-time editor for a publishing and translation company.

French was no problem; she was fluent in it, so she taught Jonah herself. An A grade at GCSE – scholarship boys must be at least this standard. She'd made sure he was way above it. Then there was music.

Jonah had learnt the piano and clarinet from when he was seven, and played with easy competence and enjoyment. Last year she'd been able to write in their Christmas cards to friends that he'd gained a distinction in both instruments at grade six. Public schools wanted talented musicians for their choirs and orchestras.

For many hours she lay staring into the darkness, unable to sleep, her mind fast-forwarding a merciless kaleidoscope as Philip lay silent beside her. At last, early in the morning as the darkness was beginning to fade, she crept downstairs to the sitting room, and unlocked the top of the Victorian writing desk that Philip had given her on their first wedding anniversary.

One last letter. She'd be cured then.

*My own Laurent,*

She wrote, the pen a syringe in her fingers injecting the familiar release. She began to write faster, crouched over the desk in the half-light of the dawn.

*This is the last letter I'll ever write to you. It's the deal I made with myself if we got the scholarship.*

*But I'm allowed to picture you, to live with you in a parallel world. The way you come into a room, the flash of recognition belonging to fellow travellers, the ebb and flow of expression on your face. It's as if I am watching one of those French films, where fragments of reality cut into madness.*

*I imagine you lunching in one of those discreet restaurants so convenient for the Bond Street gallery, where it's politely suggested to new customers that mobile phones are not welcome, and the waiters greet you by name and show you to a familiar table. You take the girl who sits greeting gallery customers to eat there perhaps once every six months, for this is enough for the charm which never lets you down. Perhaps she too is in love with you and secretly knows there is no hope, but goes on trying, because that is the way women are made, and who should know this better than I?*

*Then there is the elegant small house in Chelsea, the rooms cool and contained, the courtyard garden with its carved stone angel, where you sit drinking chilled Chablis from tall thin glasses. You're not alone – but my mind cannot fill in the details of the face that stares into yours as you exchange gossip and small pleasantries while the colour fades from the sky. The two of you prepare a meal together, something light, exotic, using only the most unusual ingredients, and you eat it in the quiet courtyard, the scent of jasmine heavy in the air.*

*But there is Teddy. Teddy, who has Philip's long bony frame and yet looks at me with your eyes. He must never know – never even suspect. He has all your perception, but there is no reason for the truth ever to enter his head.*

*How thankful I should be that Philip doesn't read my mind as you always did. He has never had the least inkling. Why should he? Our time together was short – just enough for you to understand yourself better. He doesn't deserve to have a wife with thoughts like mine, for he is a good man. You were never that.*

*I shall be forty soon. You warned me that obsessions trap and destroy. It was the last thing you said to me.*

*I have no right to write letters with this beginning, you are not mine. But I'll never be able to stop thinking about you.*

She stopped writing and put down her pen. Her past would be left behind in London, along with the psychiatrist who knew nothing, who didn't know how to help, but who was a master at pretending to believe the words that fell from him so easily.

'Treat these intrusive impulses as if they're bubbles you can blow away from the surface of your mind,' he'd said.

Shrinks were a waste of space. She wasn't going to try that game again. What did he know of the compulsions of thwarted love, sitting behind his desk wearing an impassive face?

She stared at the meaningless words. It was to be the last letter – and like all the letters she had ever written to him, it would never be sent. She picked it up and tore it across into tiny pieces. Going into the kitchen, she dropped the fragments of paper into the bin among the rest of the day's rubbish. Beside her the fridge hummed, remorseless and detached.

On the dresser, thrust on top of a pile of papers, lay the open magazine with the paragraph telling readers about Angelo Arzano and the death of his son. But that little tragedy could never mean anything to her.

*You are not mine. You are his.*

# FIVE

*The day I killed my son began like any other.* He could start a book with a cliché like this. It fitted the man he was turning into.

Was this why Imogen had carefully positioned a file of press cuttings next to his laptop in what she liked to call his writing room, oblivious of the irony? Or was she acting out the role of the artist's muse, the beautiful, pensive mermaid on her rock, silently enduring? That was always a faultless performance.

*Angelo Arzano is a man much lauded by the literary establishment – and by himself. With his first novel Priest and Victim scooping three of Europe's most coveted literary prizes, his next book is feverishly awaited by avid readers. Church leaders and politicians have been quick to quote Arzano's work while his stylistic idiosyncrasies are slavishly copied by suburban creative writing classes …*

*But alongside success for the maverick journalist hailed as a prophetic voice for our time have come accusations of arrogance and contempt for the publishing circus …*

There he was, groomed for the colour supplements. Stark photographs, cropped at acute angles, sandwiching stagey answers to questions he hadn't been asked. Angelo crumpled up the page and threw it across the floor.

His agent, his publishers, the media: they'd invented him and dished him up to the ever-credulous public. He switched off the blank screen. He needed another drink.

In their bedroom, Imogen was sitting at her dressing-table, as she always did at the end of the day, ready to take off her make-up and brush out her dark cloud of hair from the French plait, so infinitely alluring, so emblematic of her graceful perfection. The kidney-shaped table draped in embroidered silk topped with glass and covered with expensive bottles embodied all that her background had made her – and left her without.

Her hands rested for a moment while her eyes questioned him in the mirror. He stood staring at the faultless oval of her face without seeing it, draining his glass, hearing the detachment in his voice.

'Did you want something as well?'

'You know I never drink at night. Have you said good-night to Terzo? Please Angelo, he did ask for you.'

'I was working – forgot the time. He'll be asleep by now.'

Angelo didn't tell his wife he was aware of her lie. Hadn't she done the same for him over the accident? She would go on pretending to him as well as to herself that Terzo – he went over to the window and pulled back the curtain. Outside a shadowy darkness had swallowed up the last trace of colour.

She didn't ask him if he'd written anything. She'd learnt not to, these last few months. Hadn't he had it up to his neck with half the world saying he'd find relief in his writing, the catharsis of putting it all on paper? Could it really be done by anyone of sound mind, this telling of a tale so full of shame and grief, of disillusionment and culpability?

'We don't have to stay here. I mean – ' she broke off and started unfastening her hair, watching him in the mirror. 'I know you don't want to live in a place like this. It's all wrong, with everyone knowing you. We could go somewhere else. Back to London.'

'You've always said you didn't want to bring up children in London.'

'That was when – Angelo, please don't shut me out.'

'Ever heard of the stable doors and the horse that had bolted?'

He turned to look at the gilded edges of the mirror, at his wife's neck, a drooping snowdrop angled to remind him of her careful forbearance.

'*I* could live in London – I could work better. Who knows, I might even begin to write something worth reading. Get away from this endless churning out of reviews and columns. You'd like that, wouldn't you? But on second thoughts you'd never allow it. Imogen Arzano, long-suffering wife of successful novelist, the beautiful half of the couple who live the perfect life. Your Garden of Eden.'

'It *was* perfect – for both of us, for all of us.' Her voice was very low. 'You know it was, before – '

'You've always lived in your own little world of innocence, haven't you?'

He'd got her there. He saw her flinch, the flawless line of jaw and throat stiffen. Now she'll cry, he thought, and it will be my fault. I'm a man who makes his wife cry and feels nothing. I have disappointed and then destroyed her.

He watched her open her eyes hard and wide to stop the tears, and begin to cleanse her face. Again that sense of weariness crept over him. She might have been a toy that as a small child he'd grown tired of and learnt to disregard, finding it predictable and empty of pleasure. He could own all this, be repelled by the distaste he felt – and yet he couldn't bring himself to make one move towards her.

'Have I ever said a word of blame? What more do you want of me?' She turned towards him, but remained still sitting, her voice rising with each sentence, the cream-smeared cotton wool sodden in her hand.

He looked as if from an immense distance at the face that had once promised him everything for which his soul had yearned. Now he'd forgotten what it had been. I want nothing, repeated the dull, heavy voice in his brain, there's nothing you can give me.

'For God's sake, Imogen, he has to know, he has a *right* to know. We can't go on like this.'

'You promised.'

'And where's it all going to end? You don't let him out of your sight, you won't send him to school, you can't face telling him – '

'Why should I face it?' She raised her eyes to his. 'Haven't we lost enough already?'

He stared at her wordlessly, defeated by her refusal to accept what must be their future. If Terzo learns to speak again – if he remembers!

'It's the children – ' she began again, 'the children need you even more than I do.'

She has no pride, he told himself. She'll go on clinging to what she wants to believe, shutting her eyes to the inevitable sordidness of human interface. She'll use our collective guilt and weakness and throw in the children for good measure. An unwilling admiration for her obstinacy, her childish prodigality, rose up over his disenchantment and for a moment something of tenderness crept over him. He gripped the glass in his hand, not looking at his wife, and spoke almost to himself.

'She knows I will leave her tomorrow or if not the day after. The incapacity for change in yourself as well as in other people – to be unafraid of that! Isn't it what all of us would like to grasp?'

From along the landing came the faint sound of a door closing.

# SIX

Men were only after one thing. That was what you were always told, but sometimes Jane almost doubted it.

Looking round the large draughty hall that adjoined the church, she found herself wondering if any of the men setting up the folding tea-tables were capable of being after anything – except perhaps one of the chairs with comfortable padded arms rather than those made of hard grey plastic.

'I think we're about finished,' Jane could hear the churchwarden Brian Goodacre saying as he sank into one of the more welcoming chairs. 'I suggest we leave the tea arrangements to the ladies, now that the heavy work's done for them.'

'Done for us, is it? I'd like to know where you men would be without us to run round after you – you'd be the first to complain if you didn't get your tea,' retorted Mary Silcox, his fellow churchwarden whom Jane always imagined as having a 'noble church worker' badge pinned to her bosom.

'I certainly would if it meant missing your ginger cake,' said Brian with the tact learnt during a long career dealing with touchy women in the civil service. 'There's nothing like a traditional church tea.'

Across the hall, buckets crammed with flowers

and foliage lay amongst assorted bowls, vases and blocks of green foam being distributed by a cheerful woman with liver-spotted arms. Small children were sitting round a table colouring in a poster announcing *St Michael and All Angels Summer Flower and Arts Festival in Aid of Refugees* in uneven, straggly letters. From the kitchen that led off the far end of the hall, Jane could hear the chink of china and the authoritarian voice of her mother.

'I think the small plates would be more suitable for the fairy cakes, and we must cover these sandwiches with cling film. Otherwise they will curl up and become dry.'

'Yes indeed.' Jane recognised the placatory bleat of Grace Whipple, one of her mother's surprisingly extensive collection of friends. 'That would never do. But I did wonder, Dorothy, if we might – '

'When people are being charged £5 for entry and tea, they expect to get high quality,' continued Jane's mother, who had never in her life allowed anyone to give her anything less. She appeared in the kitchen doorway carrying an iced chocolate sponge, a woman with vigorous purple-grey hair and stately proportions.

'Ah, Jane, so you're here at last. Now where would you be most useful? There are all the tablecloths to be put out or you could help Grace and Mary with the tea things.'

Jane hesitated. She didn't belong to the inner circle of church flowers and catering, and had only come along now at her mother's urging, feeling obscurely that it was easier to perform duties such as these than others that might be demanded of her. Daughters should produce admirers, then husbands and grandchildren, but Jane had done none of these things, being unattached and childless at thirty-eight and without even the successful career that might have made up for such shortcomings.

'Women ought to be able to manage men better than this,' said Dorothy, when Jane came back home empty-handed after more than ten years away in London teaching music in a school for autistic children. 'It's knuckling down to it, that's what's needed.'

'You make it sound like cleaning the bath,' protested Jane.

Why hadn't she learnt how men operated? She'd had opportunities enough. She'd been brought up in Wharton, a once quiet market town fast becoming the favoured choice in East Sussex for London commuters, and within walking distance of the historic public school which contained three hundred adolescent boys and a Common Room full of mostly male teachers. From childhood she was familiar with seeing schoolmasters cycling through the streets, sixth-formers jostling into newsagents and pubs.

Something had been missing. She'd been unlucky with the men she'd met – but no, she couldn't con herself into that way of thinking. Jane knew it was her. She remembered Stephen's complacency when he'd told her about his engagement.

'Beth and I are getting married. Isn't it marvellous? I never dreamt that I would ever meet a girl like her, but the Lord had other plans.'

Don't hide behind God, she wanted to say. It doesn't change the fact that you've strung me along and I was stupid enough to hang around hoping that God would get round to telling you – if that's what you needed – that you loved me enough to marry me.

You didn't seriously think you and I were heading for the altar, did you? The words remained unsaid, but Jane heard them. His happy confidence smiled down the telephone, smoothing over her silence.

'You had to be the first to know! London wedding planned for April. We want all our friends to rejoice with us on the day. I'd love the two of you to be friends.'

Did men honestly believe spurned girlfriends could become friends with their wives? Probably not if they thought about it but that would be troublesome and could make relationships complicated. Men were really very sensible to try to make everyone feel comfortable and that everything would turn out for the best. It would be a waste of time to disagree with them.

But the rebuff was painful enough to make Jane decide she had to move away – from London, from Stephen, and above all, from Beth. Returning to live with her widowed mother wasn't the dramatic gesture of a broken-hearted heroine, but it would do until she could face thinking about what to do with herself for the rest of her life.

If she couldn't manage men, there might be other, easier things. There was plenty of work both in schools and among private pupils in Wharton, and she didn't miss her flat and her independent living as much as her old friends – now all married with children and looking smug, or divorced and rather less so – had prophesied. Or maybe she was only pretending about that as well as about so much else.

'Perhaps you could do one of the flower arrangements,' offered the liver-spotted woman, whom Jane now recognised as Rowena Royce, someone whose delphiniums would never dare to droop. 'We need a nice welcoming display of lilies over there by the doorway into the church.'

'Something less noticeable might suit me better,' apologised Jane, giving up the attempt to look the splendid and efficient person she knew she was not. 'I'm afraid I've never really mastered the art of flower-arranging.'

'Never mind, we can't all have the same talents.' Rowena handed Jane some secateurs. 'How about putting a few roses with some pretty leaves on the windowsills? Roses almost arrange themselves.'

'I always think they're the only flowers which improve with being brought indoors,' said Jane, realising too late that this was scarcely a suitable remark to make at a church flower festival. 'It all looks *lovely*, and so different from usual,' she went on, hardly improving matters. 'I'd better do something to go on those sills right at the back of the hall, rather than anything to go in the church.'

'One of us can always tweak it after she's finished,' she heard Rowena say in undertones to one of the willing helpers, as she turned away with her scratchy bundle. 'We must encourage new blood.'

'The old must give way to the new, as the Good Book says,' said Harry Pumfret, coming up with a tray of small vases and twisted handfuls of wire netting. His bald head shone like a beacon of octogenarian kindliness and high cholesterol.

'You've done that all your life.' Winnie Pumfret whisked the tray from him. 'We'll need some bigger vases than these.'

Her round blue eyes followed her husband's retreating back with the indulgent manner of the long and happily married.

'Poor lamb, he's trying his best. Winnie, he said to me this morning, I'm prepared to come and move tables about, but fiddle-faddle among a whole load of chattering ladies I can't be doing with.'

'It's likely the majority of men are intimidated by what they see as bossy women,' observed Jane tactlessly. 'We ought to be able to manage them by subterfuge, unnoticed and beneath the surface like a submarine.'

'Harry always was the retiring sort, ever since we were first sweethearts,' said Winnie fondly. 'Some of the men are going to the George and Dragon. That'll keep them happy and out of mischief. If you don't want any more of these leaves, I'll offer them to some of the other ladies.'

'Flowers seem to develop a malicious life of their own when I try to arrange them,' said Jane, pushing an obdurate yellow rose into position. 'They know I'll give in to them.'

'My dear, you could say the same about husbands. Many's the time I've had to put my foot down or I'd have had Harry all over the place, riding roughshod over me willy-nilly. Of course you aren't married yet, you won't have learnt these things.'

'I suppose not,' said Jane, bowing her head as if to acknowledge her inferior status.

'Never mind, there's still time, though you don't want to hang about much longer or there'll be nothing but other people's leavings to choose from, and you don't want any of that, do you dear? All this nasty divorce, one in three – or was it four? – I read in my *Daily Mail* this morning, and all because people won't take the trouble to make a proper go of things.'

'Trying doesn't always solve everything,' said Jane

reasonably. Hadn't she tried her very hardest with Stephen? But then she could hardly compete with Beth, so self-evidently sweet, good and pretty that she made Jane feel stained and sour.

'A nice widower, that's what's wanted, and just the thing for you. If a man can be made to marry once, he can be coaxed into it a second time.'

'He might have grown more cunning,' objected Jane, unable to help smiling as she imagined a supersized lobster pot for catching unsuspecting bachelors. 'Or become inured to the bait.'

'Dear me, that's true enough, some do get clean away. But a virtuous wife is more precious than jewels – that's what it says in the Bible. You'd certainly be that. Mind you, men do seem to want other things these days, even the ones who should know better.'

Yes, even them, Jane silently agreed. She glanced down the aisle to the piles of hydrangea heads waiting to be chosen and arranged on the altar.

'Better to marry than to burn, as St Paul said, but people don't wait for that. Mind you, St Paul wasn't married himself, was he now?'

'I think I once heard a sermon suggesting he was a widower,' said Jane. 'Though I can't remember whether there's any evidence for it. But escaping burning does seem a negative reason for getting married.'

'That's as maybe,' said Winnie darkly. 'Always down on the women St Paul is, and where would the church be today without us? That's what I'd like to know.'

'One does sometimes feel he has a good deal to answer for,' Jane agreed, licking a bleeding finger. She found herself thinking that it was difficult to imagine how men could burn for any of the women who filled the hall, though they had at least married some of them.

Winnie wiped her hands on her stretchy trousers as if dismissing St Paul, and leant over confidentially towards Jane.

'And what does your mother think about who's come to live in one of those new houses near you? Not that it wasn't ever such a shame, pulling down that wonderful old mansion. It stood for something solid and lasting, that's what. Harry says the school should never have sold it to developers. All this about wanting the money to build fancy swimming pools and what-not.'

'It's because parents these days expect amazing facilities when they're paying such vast fees.'

'But what does the town get out of it? Desirable residences with more en-suite bathrooms than anyone needs. Why do they have to keep squashing more and more houses in, can anyone tell us that? Where's it all going to end?'

'People have got to live somewhere,' Jane pointed out. 'I'm just glad they've preserved the old lodge. I've started teaching at one of the new houses – the Gidding family. There are three teenagers, and I'm giving piano lessons after school to the youngest boy. He learns clarinet as well, but he's going to do that at Wharton next term. They have to come out of ordinary classes for music lessons and his mother doesn't want too much of that.'

'I always think that is a sign of the right kind of upbringing.' Jane's mother loomed over them. 'It shows their parents have proper ideas. Piano lessons are an essential part of a rounded education. I like to think they are a suitable family for our end of the town.'

'People always had a piano in their front room in the old days,' agreed Winnie. 'It was a nice thing to do in the evenings, having a sing-song.'

'I was thinking of rather more than sing-songs,' said Dorothy. 'I meant learning Mozart and Chopin.' She made an airy gesture with her substantial arms, as if other composers were too well known to need naming.

'The mother – Kate Gidding – says the family living in the other new house are interested in having lessons as well,' said Jane, in case Winnie should feel offended. 'I'm to call round and discuss it.'

'You don't say!' Winnie put down a bunch of feathery bronze leaves. 'You'll be teaching Angelo Arzano's children.'

'That's the trouble, I'm not used to being with celebrities,' Jane admitted. 'And I haven't read *Priest and Victim*. I know I ought to have done, but there are so many new authors we're urged to admire these days, it's difficult to keep up.'

'All those piled-up bestsellers in bookshops,' said Dorothy. 'Buy one, get one half price, as if literature were a commodity like washing powder. Or labelled For Him and For Her. I noticed somebody had switched them round some years ago when I was in Waterstones.'

'Somebody with their head screwed on tight. A crash course in romantic novels – Georgette Heyer, say – and men might learn what's expected of them. Though *not* all heroes in literature are suitable role models,' said Jane, distracted from Angelo Arzano as she remembered the less pleasant aspects of Mr Rochester or Maxim de Winter.

'Ooh, there wouldn't be anything lovey-dovey in *Priest and Victim*. More likely plenty of you-know-what instead. All that fuss there was about it in the newspapers, the vicar was very upset.'

'Probably blasphemous. I do not approve of young men writing about religion,' said Dorothy, drawing in her chins. 'They have not experienced enough of life.'

'No – though they might express some of its confusion or moral questions in a helpful manner,' said Jane, trying unsuccessfully to think of a youthful male author who had done this.

'Nor do I want unsavoury accounts of people having affairs. There is far too much bed in modern books. I do *not* want to read about such things.'

'Are there any books being written *without* them?' asked Jane, thinking that even children's books were meant to deal with grittier issues these days, and presumably sex could be described in this way.

'I don't mind a nice clean murder,' said Winnie in a cosy tone. 'It's when everything gets so complicated you don't know the goodies from the baddies, and who killed who and what for, that I draw the line. You feel cheated when you've laboured through the whole thing and you're left mystified as to what happened in the end.'

'Yes, books should have a satisfying conclusion with all the loose ends happily tied up,' said Jane, 'though that *isn't* like real life. I expect Angelo Arzano's book has an obscure or ambiguous ending.'

'Well, dear, they have to, these clever books. Something in my colour supplement there was, about it winning all those literary prizes. A frightening title and all kinds of wicked goings-on, I'll be bound. Why should I read about such things when I have to watch them on the news each night? They've two children, I've heard, but the little boy is funny in the head, and has to be kept very quiet.' Winnie looked doubtfully at Jane. 'I should think you'd have to be careful what you teach him. You wouldn't want any of those dramatic tunes now, would you? Still, there's ever so many pretty things adapted for children,' she concluded, clearly thinking nostalgically of *Jesu, Joy of Man's Desiring* or *Für Elise*.

'I think I'll go round later today, before coming back here at tea time,' Jane decided. 'It won't matter not having read Angelo Arzano's book. I'm not going to teach *him* the piano.'

'They say a lot of adults are taking it up nowadays. Good for their nerves, like those colouring books. It could be quite awkward, teaching an attractive man, when you are still quite a young woman.'

'You mean there may be temptations on the man's side? But Jane is so very sensible, not the type that men take advantage of,' said Dorothy, almost as if she regretted this quality in her daughter.

'It would be like those seventeenth-century Dutch paintings of men and women with musical instruments,' said Jane, laughing. 'They're full of suggestive symbolism.'

'Holman Hunt's *The Awakening Conscience* is more edifying,' said Dorothy, showing she had paid attention during the winter evening classes in art history. 'The Victorians knew about morality, and were not ashamed to be seen preaching it. I don't suppose there is any morality in this book of Angelo Arto's or whatever his name is.'

'Arzano – '

'However, *Priest and Victim* may be worth taking out of the library. That would not involve any risk. Or if you are going to give his children music lessons, you ought to be given a signed copy, and if so I will find the time to read it. I have always believed in keeping up with modern thinking.'

'There,' said Winnie, glancing at Jane's arrangement, and avoiding her eye. 'I shouldn't do any more to that, dear. Best to quit while you're ahead, as the saying goes.'

St Paul might have written that the church is all one body and each part is valued, but had he really understood? Jane slipped out of the church hall, imagining the early Christians huddled together and eagerly sharing all things. Had it been easier then? Had they all been high-minded and unselfish and free of jealous thoughts? They *can't* have been. But Beth is … And if you ever admitted to her what you were actually thinking she'd only smile in that irritating way and be all sweet and forgiving, and then offer to pray for you and so there wouldn't be any real satisfaction …

God has no favourites. All very well for St Paul, but it doesn't feel like that.

Then she remembered that this afternoon she was going to meet Angelo Arzano and his family, and this would be a kind of treat, a reward even, though she had hardly earned it.

# SEVEN

A good-looking man appearing suddenly in front of you is not always the enjoyable experience it ought to be. Jane had waited too long on Angelo Arzano's doorstep.

'Yes?'

The man standing in front of her looked as if he didn't want to be disturbed by anybody, however beautiful and charming. He was viewing her with that gaze of self-sufficient indifference assumed by male models in fashion advertisements. Jane took in the clipped dark hair and unsmiling eyes that were so deep brown they were almost black, and felt she should apologise for not being the glamorous woman he was entitled to expect.

'Jane Finstock,' she made herself announce in firmer accents than usual. 'I teach one of the Gidding children next door – Jonah, the youngest boy. I understood from Mrs Gidding that you needed someone for your son, and would like me to drop in to discuss possibilities. But perhaps this isn't a convenient moment?'

'I didn't say that. Come in if you like. Did she say anything else?'

'I got the impression your son's not strong just now

and you'd like him to do some music – pottering about on a piano can help sometimes. If that was what you wanted,' she finished rather desperately.

'It's what my wife wants.'

'I teach most of my pupils in their own homes, as quite a few have special needs. But some come to me. I only live in the next road.'

'I expect my wife would prefer you to come here.'

It was quite clear to Jane as she followed Angelo Arzano into a shiny white designer kitchen that he would prefer otherwise. Authors ought to be interested in people, she thought indignantly, and not isolate themselves like this. She began to feel dreary even to herself, in a way that was familiar to her and all women who are only passable-looking.

'You do have a piano?'

It was a ridiculous question. Though looking at Angelo Arzano you might wonder if he knew or even cared whether they had or they hadn't.

'My wife's family certainly made sure of that. I'm told it's of the best traditional quality.'

Jane decided to ignore the sardonic edge to his voice and try another question.

'How old is your son?'

She watched him walk over to the window and look out at the brick-paved driveway and rows of newly planted laurel hedge. A car could be heard pulling up outside.

'His sixth birthday, it was last week. Here's my wife. She'll tell you all you need to know.'

As he escaped from the kitchen she reflected that he hadn't even introduced himself to her. Had he assumed he didn't need to?

He hadn't smiled at her either, or actually looked at her at all. Of course a top class author would save himself for dramatic, highly-coloured individuals wrestling with conflicts and crises. Her life didn't have anything to offer him. It might to an author confining himself to the everyday doings of ordinary people – 'the trivial round, the common task' of John Keble's hymn that they'd sung in church last Sunday – but who nowadays would publish such books?

Coming from the hall were sounds of a murmured conversation, a child's querying tones, some sort of argument, footsteps on the stairs, a door closed too firmly.

If Angelo Arzano had an ill son to worry about, he could be excused his unfriendly manner. Attractive men always were excused everything, no doubt more than was good for them. Wasn't literature strewn with handsome Mr Nasties? Anatole in *War and Peace*, Willoughby in *Sense and Sensibility*, Mr Preston in *Wives and Daughters* – the list could go on for ever.

A woman who must be still in her twenties came in, and it occurred to Jane that she too might add to Angelo Arzano's worries. A mother who looked like a child and at the same time so extraordinarily beautiful that you didn't want to stop looking at her. She might also be the tantrum-throwing sort.

'I'm Imogen Arzano. I'm sorry you've had to wait. Would you like a cup of tea? It's no trouble. I was going to have one myself.'

'I'd love one. I've only been here a few minutes.'

Was a longing for a cup of tea written all over her face, or did Imogen have perfect manners which always said and did the right thing?

'Is Earl Grey all right? Or there's the ordinary sort – English Breakfast. Angelo doesn't drink tea, so he never thinks of offering it to anyone else.'

'Whatever you're having, please. I suppose Italians aren't obsessed with tea in the way the English are,' said Jane. 'Your husband *is* Italian, isn't he? I mean, apart from the name? Though he doesn't sound it,' she added, sensing she'd said the wrong thing.

'His mother was originally from Naples, but he spent his childhood in London.' The answer was given without any expression. 'She's returned to Italy now, and we've come back to live in England for good.'

He looks all wrong here, Jane thought. What is a man like him doing in this manicured development of family houses?

'That must be nice for holidays with the children,' she said, hating how trite she sounded.

'My own parents live in the country, in the New Forest. But Wharton is convenient for London and we needed to be in a town. My husband doesn't drive.'

Jane nodded. Imogen Arzano was exactly the type to have parents living in the New Forest. She pictured a beautifully renovated Hampshire rectory of old grey stone covered in wisteria and a drive with stone gateposts ornamented with carved pineapples or even lions. Imogen would have grown up there, nurtured and secure in its unquestioning middle-class values. Angelo Arzano seemed an unlikely husband for her, given this background.

Of course, many girls of her type fell in love with Italians whilst pursuing decorous art history courses in Florence, but they usually got over them when they returned to England. Had Imogen rushed from holiday romance into marriage? Glancing at her conventional clothes Jane thought it unlikely. Imogen didn't look as though she'd ever broken out of her mould of the well-brought up daughter. Jane imagined her at drinks parties with other girls just like herself, all waiting to make suitable marriages to well-heeled merchant bankers. She couldn't help thinking this outcome might have been more satisfactory for Imogen, and probably Angelo as well. It was difficult to see what had brought them together, though one might ask that about a good many couples, and often did.

'This is Sofia.'

Imogen turned to the child hugging a giant teddy who was standing in the kitchen doorway. She looked exactly like her mother, with the same dark chestnut hair and pink and white skin of children in old soap advertisements.

'Sofia, Miss Finstock's going to teach Terzo how to play the piano.'

'Not me.' Sofia's accusing eyes stared at Jane. 'You said I didn't have to.'

'No, darling, not you, or at least not until you're a lot bigger. Three is too young.'

'Not till I'm six as well,' insisted Sofia, 'or a hundred.'

'I wish you'd both call me Jane. Miss Finstock always makes *me* feel a hundred. Being a piano teacher has such a frumpy feel about it, I don't want to make things worse.'

'My piano teachers were usually fearful dragons,' admitted Imogen, sounding more responsive as she handed Jane her tea, 'but I expect they needed to be. I still never learnt anything. I'm surprised music teachers don't actually hit their pupils. It must be so painful having to hear all those jarring notes and wrong timing. I – we – only wanted Terzo to do a little bit, maybe half an hour once or twice a week. Sofia, darling, will you fetch Terzo for me?'

'I have to explain.' Imogen looked quickly at Jane as Sofia scampered out of the room trailing her teddy bear. 'But probably you know already – sometimes there's gossip, I see it in people's faces, I can't always tell. And God knows, it was plastered all over the tabloids. We left Italy after our other son died in a car crash. Terzo's twin. Earlier this year.'

'I'm so terribly sorry,' said Jane, her eyes filling with tears. 'I didn't know.'

'Terzo's injuries were severe, his head worst of all. He doesn't remember anything about the crash. Or that he ever had a twin. The doctors don't know if it's a kind of post-traumatic stress disorder or if it's brain injuries that may not mend. He won't speak … '

'Your daughter – Sofia?' Jane could hardly bring herself to ask. Why did such terrible things have to happen to people?

'Sofia's forgotten that she once had two brothers … She was only two, and they were identical. It was just the boys in the car with my husband and another journalist helping him with a story. We haven't told Terzo yet. There's still a chance he may recover over time or get back some partial memories. He'll be stronger then to face – what he will have to face. You'll find him very young for his age. He's closed himself off … '

A car crash. Brain damage. That explained how Winnie Pumfret had got the idea that Terzo was funny in the head.

'Music can be a way of talking to each other without words,' Jane said. 'It has a strange way of reaching into the brain where nothing else can.'

'It was my mother's idea – the sessions can be any time during the day to suit you – he won't be going to school just yet.'

Where was Angelo Arzano in all this? Jane tried to discuss possible timings of piano lessons, her mind seething with questions. Imogen was so desperate for her to start, as if she was clutching at something. Jane found herself imagining the accident, the screech of the sirens, the police cars, the rush to the hospital, the agony of the parents. She could hear the fast stream of Italian, the desperate sobbing, the last silence.

Jane was used to meeting children for the first time and the way some of them made it easy for you while others put up a defensive wall. Looking at the skinny little boy sidling into the kitchen, she knew she would have to tread carefully. He was holding a large illustrated book, which he was obviously in the middle of reading, and his expression, common to most children when dragged away from what they are doing to meet a strange and possibly interfering grown-up, was cautious and unresponsive.

'*Tim and Charlotte!* I used to love Edward Ardizzone books – have you got all the other ones in the series?'

He nodded without lifting his eyes to hers, spiky black hair falling across his face.

'I can remember the brilliant drawings – a fantastic picture in the middle showing a room full of toys, a rocking horse and a dolls' house. I always wanted a nursery like that. It's funny how certain things always stay in your head.'

44

'I just wanted you to meet Jane, darling, but you don't need to stay now. She'll be coming back in a few days to play the piano with you.'

'I'll look forward to that a lot,' said Jane. 'I promise you we'll have fun. Absolutely no boring stuff.'

She wished she hadn't said that about the picture of Charlotte. It was a s*ad* picture – a little girl surrounded by luxurious toys but nobody to play with or love. Terzo had parents and a little sister, but he looked a lonely child. Wouldn't a pet be better than piano lessons? There was no sign of a dog or cat about the place. Didn't children need the comfort and unconditional love of animals?

'You'll think I'm speaking out of turn,' she said, an idea coming to her as the door closed behind Terzo, 'but a family I know – I teach the children – have got a litter of puppies. Mixture ones, not pedigree or anything. I know they want to find homes for them. They're mostly black, a jumble of flatcoat retriever and collie, which does mean a long coat and moulting – and muddy paws.'

Her eye wandered to the newly painted skirting boards and unmarked carpets. They were unimportant in comparison with a child's needs.

'I'm sure you could have one. If you were thinking of getting a dog for the children, that is,' she faltered. There you are again, Jane, blundering in, putting your big foot in it, gentle Beth would never do that. She'd have prayed about it and then asked Stephen.

'We always had dogs in our family,' said Imogen. 'I was brought up in the country and everyone we knew had them. Horses and ponies mostly as well. They were a central part of my childhood. When everybody else was cross with you, the animals still loved you.'

'They never criticise you either,' said Jane, thinking of her mother.

'I think it would be wonderful.' Imogen's face brightened. 'Could I let you know later today? Because of being in London and then living abroad we haven't had pets of any kind, but now we're settled here everything's different – though I must ask my husband about it first.'

She would obviously have to do that about a possible puppy and probably about everything else, thought Jane. She was a wife who needed to lean on her husband and wanted him in a traditional role. But wasn't this asking too much of Angelo Arzano? Tragedy had shattered the life of this family. A man might get tired of being strong.

# EIGHT

'Angelo?'

Imogen came into the room, shutting the door behind her. 'Angelo, Jane Finstock – the piano teacher – says she knows of a puppy we could have. Did you mean what you said when we talked about it before, that we could have a dog if we were living in England again?'

He looked at her face. It was like her mother's. In a minute she would say he mustn't feel pushed into anything. He waited.

'Don't feel we have to agree to it if you don't want to,' Imogen said. Her face was as gentle as usual, but contained a look that suggested she was growing tired of always being patient.

I've forgotten what it feels like to hope for imaginative insight or understanding from her. She isn't made that way, this at least I have learnt.

I'm sick of the guilt, he wanted to shout at her. I'm drained by your endless yielding. Your ignorance, your innocence, is in effect childish wilfulness, a refusal to allow other people to be other than you wish them to be. You must release me, tell me to go, or we shall both be destroyed.

He thought of the china Dalmatians at each end of the mantelpiece in the drawing room of her parents' home, of their benevolent retrievers, bred from a long family line, lying prone in front of the Aga.

'Proper families have dogs,' he said, knowing she wouldn't perceive the irony. 'Children should grow up with dogs. Why not?'

'Then I could ring that nice Jane Finstock and tell her. I really think it would help him – make him connect with us …'

How women were prepared to try anything! They clutched at straws and expected you to believe in them.

'Yes,' he said. 'He must learn to do that again.'

All that had happened in Italy lay between them, unspoken, beyond reach. He stared again out of the window. A chilly English summer afternoon with tired grass and sullen grey sky. In Italy there would be the brilliant glare of the August sun, and old women in black would be crouched in courtyards while men drank and smoked outside cafés. By now he would be planning another book, be at that exhilarating heady stage of ideas swirling around in his head, clamouring for attention, with the empowering confidence that it could be done again. In Italy he had known the brightness of something beyond himself, a heightened awareness of all his senses. But he had turned it all into a nightmare, a place of deceit and then tragedy.

They had lived through those long weeks of police investigation following the accident which had killed their child, knowing that when at last it was over they would leave and not come back. The Italian police understood it all of course. They knew about women who were not wives and men driving too fast. What Italian would not?

Paola's name was never spoken aloud between them. But Terzo would one day remember the truth.

He turned back from the window, almost not believing that he was in this room, with his wife, in England. He'd agreed to live here. Imogen wanted to be within a reasonable distance of her parents. He owed that to her. His act of atonement.

But how futile it had proved to be! A gesture made in a mad moment when he'd believed himself capable of being a different sort of man.

Someone else was living this new life. He could want nothing from it.

'Yes,' he repeated mechanically. 'We should have a dog. It is worth trying these things.'

The voices in his brain were becoming more insistent. He saw the computer screen, the black flickering typeface covering the blank white glow. The crash, yes, his confession must begin with that, for the reader must be hooked by the opening and only violence and sex would bring the look of satisfaction to his agent's face.

*The car had been travelling too fast: everyone, even those who arrived on the scene minutes later and couldn't possibly have seen the crash, were agreed on that. They spoke vociferously, gesticulating with operatic passion, arguing over the reasons for the car's sudden spinning out of control, heedless of being in the way of the police and ambulance teams. Speed and daring were to be admired; they were, after all, Italian. But not when it put the lives of bambini at risk. That was not to be forgiven. In other countries, yes, where children were less loved, more carelessly treated. Not here in Italy. Wasn't their sacred innocence the beating heart of the family?*

# NINE

'I've been telling my granddaughter it's the oldest kind of tree in the world, but she knows I've a way of making things up.'

A woman and a girl of around eleven or twelve had emerged from the lodge and came up to Jane as she hovered on the corner, looking up at the brilliant green of a ginkgo tree in their garden. The woman had untidy white hair but was probably only in her early sixties, and the long-legged girl with a brown plait and a jagged mark down the side of her pretty, friendly face must be her granddaughter.

'I've been visiting your neighbours,' explained Jane, coming out of her reverie, 'and I know the Gidding family as well, in the other house. I'd been wondering who'd come to live in the lodge – I've always loved it.'

'And so do we, that's for sure,' agreed the woman, in the sing-song accent of someone originally from the south-west corner of Ireland. 'Not that it's ours – it's owned by the school. We've our home back in Dublin rented out. There's only the three of us here, so the lodge is a fine size, though as we're all different generations one day we'll be wanting separate floors, like in *After Henry* – that was on the television now, you'd be remembering that as a child maybe. We're just off to see the flower festival at the church, would you be coming along with us? I'm Nora Kinsale and this is Ellen. My son's too busy poring over *The Odyssey* – so tiring to think of all those endless adventures, and in August too, which I'm thinking is a very worn-out month.'

'Dad didn't want to come with us,' put in Ellen. 'He said it wasn't his thing and he's not good at pretending. That's what he always says when he doesn't want to do something.'

'Now that's men for you,' said Nora. 'Keeping themselves safe. Does your husband do the same?'

'I'm not married,' said Jane, wishing she didn't sound embarrassed. 'My name's Jane, Jane Finstock, and I live with my mother just down there.' She pointed to the small tree-lined cul-de-sac leading off the road they were walking down, containing respectably dull Edwardian houses.

'Austen is one of those unsociable widowers,' explained Nora. 'Coming into a church full of people, especially women, would be purgatory to him. He's more suited to a quiet service, the one at eight o'clock.'

Had it not been for her fondness of what she called a civilised Sunday breakfast, Jane's mother would have preferred to attend this early traditional service, given that the words of Cranmer's Prayer Book resonated more strongly with her than the modern language of the service later in the morning. Now Jane could imagine her mother with that familiar glint in her eye, and decided she'd better not mention Austen.

'I suppose one shouldn't really go to a church service to meet people,' she said, thinking how often she'd done exactly that.

'Or to *not* meet people,' said Nora. 'Though it can be a relief to go to a service where nothing is demanded of you by other people.'

'You can just concentrate on God,' said Jane vaguely, who felt she wanted to want this more than she actually did.

'Tell me that anyone manages that without their thoughts wandering and I'll not believe you. It's a miracle if I get to the end of the Lord's Prayer ... *kindle a flame of sacred love on the mean altar of my heart* ... you'll be knowing that line in the hymn?'

In London I was usually busy trying to kindle quite different sorts of love, thought Jane. It hadn't worked with Stephen. The familiar sense of being somehow lacking once more crept over her.

'We've been making up a soap opera about some of the people in the *Ancient and Modern* hymn book. The people who wrote all the hymns, I mean. Granny says she read about it being a good way of getting through the boring bits of church. Our chief villain is Bianco da Siena, but he has an accomplice who kills people off for him, Augustus Montague Toplady. Horatius Bonar's the detective – like Hercule Poirot, only not so fat – last week he saved F. Pratt Green from being smothered with a pillow after changing his will.'

'I used to think that Anon wrote all the best poems when I was young,' admitted Jane. 'I was quite disappointed when I discovered what it really meant, as I'd imagined exactly what he was like. Bianco da Siena sounds a perfect monster of wickedness.'

'You could add an episode one Sunday,' said Ellen in a kind voice.

'I'd love to. Are you going to have tea while you're

visiting the church? I was in there earlier on, and I spotted some tempting cakes. Not that anyone goes just for them,' Jane ended rather unconvincingly.

'I don't see why not,' said Ellen.

'No, I don't either,' said Jane, laughing. 'There's also an art display with some marvellous paintings – and others which are quite pretty in their way.'

'Will they be of vases of flowers or cats on cushions?' interrupted Nora. 'Not even the most encouraging vicar could get away with describing *them* as ground-breaking or powerful.'

'There are rather too many of those,' admitted Jane. 'The school holidays is late for a flower and arts festival, but it was arranged to attract summer visitors to the town, as well as local people – being a historic building we get a lot of tourists coming in.'

'And don't we have a saying that we feel closer to heaven in a garden than in a church, so it's a fine thing to bring the two together,' said Nora. 'Have you done one of the flower displays, will we be looking out for it?'

'I'll probably find it's been changed or dismantled altogether,' said Jane. 'It will be a lesson in humility. You tell yourself it's ridiculous and petty to mind about such things, but how often you do!'

'T.S. Eliot – or was it somebody else? – said that to survive humiliation is an experience of incalculable value,' said Nora thoughtfully, 'but I'm wondering if he knew what he was talking about? Or maybe he was meaning more noble or greater experiences than the humiliations and pinpricks of daily life. Men don't always grasp these details, or notice the small sadnesses attached to them.'

'It's the little experiences that make up most of life,' agreed Jane. 'Aren't we told that God minds about even the smallest things?'

They had reached the church and she caught sight of her mother, who was by no means one of life's smallest things. She was standing by the heavy wooden doors, wearing a silk summer dress in a print of purple daisies.

'I met Nora and Ellen as I was coming away from the Arzano family,' said Jane, as she made the introductions.

'Are you a piano teacher? You're not very like one,' said Ellen, examining Jane with a critical expression.

'Imogen was telling me they were looking for someone to teach their child piano,' said Nora. 'You can tell yourself you're an answer to prayer.'

'Mrs Arzano might not have prayed about it,' commented Ellen. It was clear neither she nor her grandmother suffered from any inhibitions.

'No, indeed, one does feel it is too frivolous a matter. Like praying for a parking space. I believe the practice is quite common in America,' said Dorothy, giving the word a sinister emphasis as though anything might be expected from such a place. 'Still, it's important to get someone who's good and Jane is certainly that.' Dorothy sounded sure of this at least, if not of any other gifts her daughter might possess.

'Have you read *Priest and Victim*? Will you feel obliged to, if you haven't already, with Angelo Arzano living next door?' said Jane hastily to Nora.

'We've a copy in the house, but the story of the covering up of sexual abuse within the establishment and the church all in the context of a massive novel might not be one for the summer holidays. I've a mind to tackle it in the autumn. Austen tells me it's a harrowing read.'

'I think I heard that some of it is from experience. He does look locked into himself, though he could have other reasons for that.' Jane fell silent for a moment, thinking of the tragedy behind the outward appearance of the celebrity author with his beautiful wife and children.

'The title might be from the hymn,' suggested Ellen. 'You know, the one you like, Granny, with the bit about sweeping across the crystal sea.'

'*Thou on earth both Priest and Victim in the eucharistic feast,*' exclaimed Nora. 'That makes it all right – there is room for *all* of us there.'

'And are you musical as well?' said Dorothy, declining to unravel this line of thought. She turned to Ellen, who was peering into the church, where groups of people were exclaiming over the displays, whilst trying not to look as though they were in a hurry to get to the tea.

'I have to admit,' said Ellen, 'that I can't sing at all, at least nothing anyone can recognise. My worst thing would be one of those karaoke evenings. I once tried learning piano but I was so bad I stopped after two lessons, or rather the teacher stopped me, and you couldn't blame her.'

'She gets it from me,' said Nora, stepping forward eagerly into the entrance and almost colliding with a trailing fountain of buddleia. 'My husband always told me I was tone deaf. But listening to other people gives me a lot of pleasure. It does usually anyway,' she added, as if remembering various charity concerts she had attended in the past and even anticipating those she might have to endure in the future. 'I always sing out of tune but I do love the well-known old things we're told to dismiss as sentimental.'

'Granny! You mustn't say that. You're always singing hymns about the house, the ones without too many alleluias anyway. They're definitely in tune – at least *I* think so. And it doesn't matter anyway. If God minded about people singing in tune, he would have made everyone able to.' Ellen's last sentence came out accusingly. It was evident that God's failure in this respect was a running sore with her, and people should be reminded of it.

'*Music, the greatest good that mortals know, and all of heaven we have below,*' said Dorothy, apparently not wanting to be outdone, and showing that she too could summon quotations at will. 'Though I cannot say I agree with Joseph Addison, because we have so many other riches of heaven here below.'

She fell silent, and Jane could see she was thinking of good food and well-cut clothes from her favourite department store.

'Beautiful paintings and flowers would be among them.' Nora stopped to admire a massive display – or perhaps installation would have described it better – of dahlias, glass and silver paper, entitled *Revelation: The Vision of St John.* 'You must both of you come and have tea sometime with us, in spite of our lack of musical talent, or even because of it.'

'It was a compliment really, when I said you weren't like a piano teacher,' Ellen assured Jane. 'Do you know any Greek or Latin?'

'I don't think I got beyond declining *hic, haec, hoc.*'

Jane tried to remember it, and then began to laugh. 'I never did discover what it meant.'

'Dad's the new head of classics at Wharton,' Ellen explained. 'But don't worry. Granny and I are rubbish.'

'All I remember from my blessed convent is turning the inscription on the front of *The Approach to Latin* textbook into *The Approach to Eating*,' said Nora.

'Dad's all right about people coming to tea. But sometimes he forgets and goes out.'

'*Souls of men, why will ye scatter, like a crowd of frightened sheep?*' quoted Nora, not altogether appropriately. 'But I can promise you my son will not scatter away from *you*. Does next Sunday sound a good time?'

'We shall look forward to it very much,' said Dorothy. 'Tea on a Sunday afternoon is a very pleasant occasion, and one which is unfortunately going out of fashion, like so many things.'

She smiled graciously at Nora, to indicate her appreciation of new neighbours who understood the importance of maintaining little courtesies and civilised traditions. Jane saw she had noted the mention of a son, who might be both eligible and available.

Jane sighed. She watched her mother move away to examine a giant thistle arrangement mystifyingly entitled *Doubt and Faith*. Soon she would remind Jane that it was high time the unbecoming cardigan she was wearing was sent to a charity shop.

# TEN

He was called Terzo, which was wrong as he wasn't a third boy, and his middle name was Roland and that was wrong too. There was nothing roly-poly about him, not even when he was curled up on his bed reading – and he was *always* reading.

Just now he was looking at the illustrations in *Five on a Treasure Island*. Terzo knew the Famous Five stories were meant for older children, but he had the whole collection on his shelf. They'd belonged to Mummy when she was a little girl.

The puppy was coming this afternoon. The lady with brown hair who liked books and who was teaching him piano was going to bring him. Jane was nice and he thought learning to play some music might be okay. She was someone who wouldn't ask him anything difficult. But he wasn't sure about a puppy. He'd have to look after it, and this was worrying because he might do something wrong and hurt it when he didn't mean to.

Terzo had known about the puppy for days; he'd overheard his mother talking about it – 'exactly what he needs, it might just make the breakthrough'. You heard all sorts of things when you were lying in bed and everyone thought you were asleep. But sometimes you listened to things and then wished you hadn't. They lay like enemies next to your head on the pillow.

It was better when he was alone. All those questions! They made his head hot and confused, as if he was running away from something in the dark and couldn't see the way, or even what exactly he was running away *from*. Some things he understood, while others remained muddled and shadowy, so that he felt he was lost in a wood of unexpected shapes and foggy outlines.

His parents came into his room with Jane, who was carrying a bundle of black fur. His mother was looking at him with that expression on her face which made him feel she wanted something from him. But what was it?

'Look, darling, you can stroke him. He's feeling lonely without his mother.'

He put out his hand, watching her face. He saw that it lit up, as if she was pleased. Timidly, he patted the puppy's head, looking at the dark eyes and the heavy, silky ears. It was shivering and making little whimpering noises.

'I won't stay,' said Jane, 'now he's safely delivered. He was very good on the way here in the car, but he looks pleased to be with you in his new home. Have you thought what you're going to call him?'

Terzo looked at the puppy as it rolled over onto its tummy on the bedside rug, its legs waving at him, the underneath of its paws soft and pink. He must try and think of a name. That was what Mummy and Daddy wanted.

On the bookshelf next to his bed were rows of his old books, the spines scuffed and peeling. There were dogs in some of them. He tried to remember, but his thoughts kept flickering, light then dark, like his torch when the battery was running out. His fingers traced out letters on the duvet.

'Darling – '

His mother's voice was shaking. His father didn't move. He'd made a bad mistake. Their faces told him. He fought a longing to shut his eyes to make everything frightening go away. He looked desperately at the bookshelf and pointed.

'*Moorland Mousie* – Granny gave that to you after our last visit, didn't she, darling? It was her favourite pony book as a child.'

Still his father didn't say anything. Didn't he like Granny's books? Terzo turned his head away, his thoughts falling into muddle as he watched Jane slip out of the door.

I couldn't say thank you. He plucked at the corner of his duvet, wanting her to be still there.

His mother leant over to kiss him. She'd picked up the puppy and was holding it towards him. Her face felt wet.

'Mousie's a lovely name. Give him a last stroke, and we'll put him into his bed in the kitchen. Sofia wants to play with him, but she let you have first turn as he's really your dog. The two of you might take him into the garden after tea. Have a rest first.'

Rest. That meant he could stay in this room. He was always resting. All that time in hospital when the days spilled into the nights. Mummy or Daddy by his bed. They were never there together. The nurses said that was because of Sofia; one of them had to stay at home to look after her. But it felt wrong.

Sofia was his sister, he knew that. He stared at the illustration in his book of Julian, Dick, George and Anne, with Timmy the dog. He could have said he'd call the puppy Timmy. He hadn't thought of it in time. Sofia had the same shiny hair that Anne had in the picture, parted at the side and fixed with a slide, but it wasn't the same colour. Sofia's was dark, like his own.

He peered closely at the drawing, then reached for other books on the shelf – *Five on Kirrin Island Again*, and *Five Go To Demon's Rocks*. The pictures showed the Famous Five looking just the same. There was Julian, the brave big brother; dark-haired Dick who was almost as clever but not quite; George with short curls who wanted to be a boy; and Anne, who was pretty and good at cooking.

He liked it when Mummy read the books to him. The children never got any bigger, they never changed. You knew exactly where you were with them. They managed things for themselves; they outwitted villains all on their own. Things always came right, and they ate potted meat sandwiches, macaroons and drank ginger beer and never had bad dreams.

It was a good room to be on your own in. You could lie and stare at things, taking in each detail, even though you knew everything so well that you could shut your eyes and see it all in your head. There were his curtains, which were made of a white material, with four different sorts of fruit painted in bright colours. Terzo started at the top where the material was bunched together and let his eyes travel down the fruits. An orange, with a little leaf at the top. Then a lemon, acid-yellow with pointy ends. Then some funny-looking fruit which might be a melon, cut in half with rows of seeds, which Terzo liked least of all, so he didn't look much at that. The pear was last, fatter and greener than real life pears were. When the sun shone the fruits glowed against the white; they had magic powers.

On the wall was the picture that Mummy had given him. It had a bashed-up old frame and she'd told him it had been in her bedroom when she was a child. It showed a small boy in a little sailing boat, all alone except for the stars and seagulls. The colours must have faded, because the sea and sky drifted into each other in a greeny-blue mist and there were pale purple reflections in the water. It looked soft and dreamlike, as if the boat was gliding through it, leaving no mark.

There were some words underneath in old-fashioned squiggly writing: *Dear God, I'm sailing on thy wide, wide sea, please guard my little ship for me.* Slowly and carefully, Terzo let his eyes trace round the curving letters. He knew every extra flourish and decorative twirl.

Mummy said he could choose some posters for his bedroom, but he didn't want anything else. It would make him feel muddled, and stop him seeing things as they were. He wanted to look properly at what he had, so that he knew every little detail. He stared again at the picture, the puffed-out grey sail, the glowing yellow lamp on the mast. The boy in the boat had dark hair like his own. He kept him safe when the bad dreams came.

# ELEVEN

'Mother, I am *not* interested in meeting Austen. It's no use you making that face.'

Austen – no doubt supercilious and knowing his own worth as a sought-after widower – would give her the usual bored appraisal swiftly turning to distaste. Meeting a new man was like pulling a cracker: packaging and novelties on track for the rubbish bin.

On the other hand, Nora was one of those women whose uncritical friendliness made it impossible for anyone to be ill at ease in her company. She liked the look of Ellen too. Jane loved being with children and it looked as if she wasn't going to have any of her own. It was another secret grief, but not, said the stern voice in her head that always sounded like her mother's, one that other people wanted you to go on about.

'You have let yourself go – you have *always* let yourself go,' declared Dorothy on Saturday morning, giving a vigorous rub with the duster to the grand piano in their sitting room. 'You need to smarten yourself up if you're going to get anywhere. You might find something nice in Nortons. One should make more of an effort with one's appearance if a man is present.' She stood back to admire the polished surface, and patted her cable-knit cotton cardigan. 'Remember, fine feathers make fine birds.'

'You can't make a silk purse out of a sow's ear,' said Jane, speaking more carelessly than she knew she ought to have done.

'Now Jane, you can always find a proverb that appears to contradict another. But it's merely looking at both sides of the question so matters can be resolved on a higher sphere – dialectical truth, I believe is the correct term.'

'The double-sidedness of things does have a way of creeping up on you.' Jane suspected the irony would be wasted on her mother but didn't care. 'It's a kind of nemesis for all that black-and-white thinking when you were young.'

Dorothy picked up the silver-framed photograph of Jane's father and began to dust it with a widow's efficiency.

'It's your Christian duty to look as nice as you can. It gives pleasure to other people, especially old people, and that's very important.'

It was difficult to argue with one's Christian duty, though Jane was aware that the phrase acted as a kind of umbrella for her mother. She unfurled it to cover any inconsistencies in her own point of view.

But Jane indulged her whenever she could. Organising other people's lives was the happiness of Dorothy's, and the death of Jane's father last year had left her short of material. Giving in over small matters went some way towards compensating people for all the things you couldn't do or be for them.

'Don't fall for one of those boxy jackets,' Dorothy lectured her as she was leaving. 'Such horrid little garments. They do nothing for the figure and are quite unsuitable for anyone who has a bottom.'

A cloak of perfumed air enveloped Jane as she went through the swing-doors of the town's luxurious department store. On the first floor a young male shop assistant was undressing a pink mannequin that was lying prone on the thick carpet. A little old lady averted her eyes and scurried away to the safety of the nightwear collection.

'Do you need any help?' a salesgirl asked, after Jane had wandered fruitlessly around the ladies' fashions, and ended up in the petite section. The young man had now unscrewed the arms off several more mannequins and was wrestling with a pile of body parts, reminding Jane of various cubist paintings she particularly disliked, where people were fragmented in disturbing and distressing directions.

'Thank you, but I'm not quite sure what I'm looking for. I'll know it when I see it, if you understand what I mean.'

'Something new for the autumn, something fancy? Of course not all the new season's collections are in yet, seeing as it's only August. Still, there's some lovely coordinated outfits in aubergine over here. That's very fashionable, just now.' The girl looked doubtfully at Jane. 'They say it's a colour that suits everyone.'

Not if you have a bottom, Jane wanted to say. She had already observed that most of the new autumn clothes were conspiring to be deliberately disagreeable: dirty oranges and yellows and an especially deadening muddy purple.

'I'd like blue or green if only I could get it. I wonder why designers seem to copy each other's colour choices when you'd think they'd try to be different?'

'Oh *well*,' said the girl, beginning to lose interest.

'We had a lot of those pastel colours in the summer. There's some loose-weave jackets, real quality fabric, over in the reduced section – they might appeal. Very forgiving they are.'

'Thank you, I'll bear that in mind,' agreed Jane, sidling away as her eye caught a display of jumpers and cardigans. What would happen if she waved her hand carelessly towards them and asked for one in each colour? 'They'll look perfect on you, Madam! You can carry off anything!' Then the girl would wrap them up in tissue paper and Jane would leave the hot, scented shop and gesture grandly at a taxi to take her home. When they arrived she wouldn't fumble in her purse for the fare while the driver sighed in his mirror, but hand him a crisp note, and he would open the door for her and carry the designer label bags to the front door. Keep the change, she'd say in a lordly manner, and he'd look pleased and say he wished more ladies were like her …

Containing cashmere, the labels said. She'd heard somewhere that once you'd tried cashmere you never went back to ordinary wool. Perhaps it was an advertising slogan that had slid into her unconscious mind. She began to finger the jumpers, and selected one in silver-grey. It might be setting her on the path to extravagance but its light, silky softness was perfect for the end of summer.

A skirt flecked with luminous pinks and turquoise and with a stretchy waist looked as if it would go nicely with the jumper. Jane imagined the comforting swish of the material over her legs, a reward for having to undress and face the discouraging sight of the backs of her thighs in the angled mirror, made even more hideous by the cruelties of fluorescent lighting.

'Getting on all right, are you? You need high-heeled shoes to make a proper statement,' warned the salesgirl, hovering by the curtain of the changing room.

'I'm afraid statements aren't exactly my line,' apologised Jane, struggling out of the clothes and pushing her feet into her scuffed flat shoes. 'But could I have this skirt and jumper, please?'

She paid the bill, conscious of the girl's disappointment. I ought to have chosen a scarf to add what beauty editors call a hint of exciting colour at the neck. No doubt they suggest it draws attention to the face. Would Stephen have chosen me if I had made these little efforts?

Hesitating for a moment on the pavement, she caught sight of herself reflected in the shop window, thrown together and ungroomed, like a badly wrapped parcel, amidst the other busy women shoppers. She tested the soreness she'd carried about for so long. How much did it still hurt?

'Ooh, have you been having a naughty afternoon?'

Winnie Pumfret's inquisitive blue eyes peered into Jane's carrier bag with its glossy rope handle. Clinging to her arm was Mabel, one of the elderly ladies at church who always made Jane think of a malevolent carpet beetle.

'We're just popping into the restaurant upstairs,' said Winnie. 'Mabel does so love the treat of going out to tea.'

'Yes, they have gentle background music and you can watch everyone else enjoying themselves,' said Jane, and then remembered that Mabel was deaf and uninterested in anyone's pleasure except her own. She found herself thinking of a particularly unpleasant story about a man waking up and finding he'd turned into an insect.

'Why don't you join us, dear?' Winnie smiled kindly at Jane. 'You look quite worn out.'

'Thank you,' said Jane, 'I should have liked to, but I ought to get to Waitrose before it runs out of the Danish pastries my mother likes. Not that it ever does,' she added hurriedly, as if a Waitrose manager might be listening.

'Do just tell us how you got on with Angelo Arzano?'

'He's certainly very good-looking,' said Jane, feeling she must say something of interest to make up to Winnie for not joining the tea party and sharing the burden of Mabel, while not quite liking to use another word to describe Angelo's undoubted sexual attractiveness.

'Handsome is as handsome does,' said Winnie, knowing better. 'And what did you think of the family?'

'I talked more with his wife Imogen. She has beautiful manners and she *is* very beautiful too. So are the children, Terzo and Sofia.'

'I've learnt something about them.' Winnie glanced at Mabel and lowered her voice. 'My sister was on the telephone to me last night, in on the whole story she was. She always knows everything about anyone famous. The Arzanos used to live in Italy, right down in the south, she said, and there was a dreadful tragedy with their child being killed. Those Italian roads are something shocking. Five years old he was. Terrible what some people have to go through, isn't it? It quite turns you over to think of things like that happening.'

'Yes,' said Jane slowly. 'Imogen Arzano did tell

me. Terzo's twin brother.' She saw again Imogen's lost look and the childish squaring of shoulders. 'You can't imagine how people ever get through the days enduring such grief. It must be with them at every moment, almost too much to bear. But they have to, with two other children to care for.'

'Another little angel in heaven,' said Winnie. 'When my sister was telling me I remembered about Tobias and the Angel. I've always thought it was the sweetest story – it ought to be in the Bible proper and not just in the Apocrypha, shouldn't it? He was called Toby you see, that's short for Tobias, isn't it? Toby – such a lovely old-fashioned name.'

Jane stood still on the pavement as Winnie and Mabel disappeared through the glass swing-doors. All around her, shoppers hurried past with bags and trolleys, but she didn't see them. She saw only a small boy with dark, shuttered eyes and dusky hair falling over his face.

When she arrived home, she realised she hadn't remembered her mother's Danish pastries after all.

# TWELVE

'I had high hopes for this cake,' said Nora, bringing out an iced sponge on a chipped pottery plate, and stepping carefully over a tortoiseshell cat asleep in a pool of sunshine. 'But it's let me down and gone lopsided. I'm telling myself it'll taste the same.'

'It could be the uneven temperature in the oven,' said Dorothy, 'or the rack might not be quite level. I believe even a slight tilt can make all the difference.'

'The unreliable oven and the crooked rack! Would that be making a good illustration in a sermon?' Nora seized a large knife and began to cut the cake rather wildly.

'Cooking is always a useful resource in preaching,' Jane observed, enjoying the picture of enterprising vicars holding up steaming kettles and packets of self-raising flour in front of their congregations. 'I suppose comparisons are especially memorable as food's so important to us.'

'To young and old alike,' said Dorothy, watching with complacent pleasure the large slices Nora was cutting.

It was Sunday afternoon, and the three women were sitting comfortably on the paved terrace in the lodge's garden. Nora glanced up with a tolerant smile at the sounds coming from the house.

'Here is Austen, timing it with masculine cunning. Isn't it remarkable the way men know to a minute when the tea is being poured?'

'There is a lot deal to be said for a man who doesn't get in the way when meals are being prepared,' excused Dorothy.

'And a consciously domesticated man could be tiresome in his own way,' said Jane. 'He'd always be finding fault, noticing that your ironing wasn't as perfect as his or pointing out the thick coating of dust on the lampshades.' She stood up as a man appeared at the door that led into the kitchen, hovering there uncertainly.

'Don't you be getting up now,' said Nora to Dorothy, laying a hand on her shoulder, and looking affectionately at Austen as she made the introductions.

Jane registered an ageless quality about him which she had once read was a characteristic of horologists. Austen Kinsale didn't make clocks, but immersion in classical antiquity had possibly had the same effect. His hair was the colour of conkers that have lost their fresh rich brown and might soon be streaked with grey; he could have been anything between thirty and fifty. It's all right, Jane told herself, he's not a Stephen. She could relax.

He sank into a chair opposite Jane, with a smile that was both wary and uncertain of a response. At the same moment she realised she'd seen him before. Or was it someone very like him?

He was – and Jane couldn't think of a better way to put this – very ordinary looking. Hundreds of men like him poured out of the station every evening, an endless trail of commuters pumped out like dirty washing water. As she thought of the stream of worn faces and hunched shoulders draining away with briefcases and raincoats to their homes in the surrounding Victorian terraces, it suddenly struck her that he was the same man she'd seen on the train the day of Stephen's wedding. The man who'd been reading Elizabeth Gaskell. He'd sat down in the same self-effacing way.

'Your mother's been telling us that you're the new Head of Classics at Wharton.' Her life so far had taught her it was both the safer and easier course to talk to men about themselves, though it might not be an infallible rule for all of them.

'Yes, I am,' he said, but looking doubtful, as if he might not be doing this after all. 'I hear you do some part-time piano teaching there.'

'Just recently I have been. Most of my work is private lessons. I don't actually know the school very well, other than the way everyone living here knows it. Since it became day as well as boarding, it's very much part of the town. I'm only in there for three afternoons locked away in a little teaching room in the music block.'

'You make it sound like prison visiting,' said Nora. 'I hope the boys you teach don't see it as that.'

'I'm sure some do,' said Jane, laughing. 'But they're very good-tempered when I nag them about practising. Next term I'm to become a sort of auxiliary house tutor in one of the boarding houses for a couple of evenings. It's thought expedient to have at least a token female about the place.'

'They must all have a matron, who would be female,' protested Nora. 'But I expect it would be a good thing to have some other motherly types around for the younger boys.'

'So long as they are of a mother's age,' said Dorothy.

'Remember adolescent boys are prone to strange urges, especially with females a little older than themselves. One would not wish to encourage anything of *that* nature.'

'Is it *Tom Brown's Schooldays* and episodes involving Flashman and young domestic staff in your mind now? Are you telling me there's a danger of anything like that at Wharton?'

'Mother, that was in the nineteenth century.' Austen sounded resigned. 'Public schools have changed out of all recognition since the time of Dr Arnold of Rugby.'

'There may have been goings-on in the past,' pursued Dorothy with a certain grim satisfaction. 'But no scandal has hit the local press in recent years, unlike some other public schools. The headmaster has succeeded in managing that at any rate.'

'I've been told it involves patrolling the corridors making sure the boys do their prep and aren't slaughtering each other. That sounds quite safe and will certainly have its funny side. Does every boy at the school learn Latin?' Jane asked, noticing that Austen was looking down at his feet, perhaps fearing that his mother was going to admit to a love for the Billy Bunter books or other school stories now considered politically incorrect. All that caning of the Fat Owl of the Remove ...

'Yes, they do Latin their first year, and quite a reasonable percentage keep it on. Not many do Greek of course. But it's a big department and I'm fortunate – thriving classics departments are few and far between these days.'

'Classics is without doubt the best training for the mind,' said Dorothy, repeating one of her favourite precepts. 'I believe you are an Oxford man?'

Jane put down the piece of cake she was about to eat, knowing what was coming. Only that morning her mother had read an article in *The Sunday Telegraph* about the doubtful value of vocational courses and now she considered herself an authority on higher education.

'These are cucumber sandwiches,' said Nora, proffering a plate. 'Aren't they an essential part of tea in the summer?'

Jane saw that they were generously filled but no attempt had been made to cut off the crusts. Thankfully, her mother was too preoccupied with Austen to notice. She was looking at him approvingly as he confirmed that he'd taken his degree at Oxford, evidently deciding that his lack of aptitude for small talk could be forgiven. Her mother didn't expect unmarried men to be good-looking – that would be asking too much – but she never grudged any effort in forwarding Jane's prospects.

'Ellen has gone next door,' Nora explained. 'I bumped into Imogen in Waitrose. Her husband went up to London yesterday, something to do with a column he writes, she said. I'm hoping Imogen will bring the children to join us for tea – Ellen's gone to encourage Terzo. Imogen thought he might be shy about coming.'

'Your granddaughter is a kind girl,' approved Dorothy, 'and that is unusual these days when children are brought up to think more of their own pleasure and success than their duty to others.'

'Duty! A grand word, that's for sure. I wonder now, would children today know what you meant if you used it?' Nora looked vaguely down the garden, as if imagining the good and dutiful Victorian children who had once played there. 'But most of them are kind enough – or would be if they thought about it. They don't always consciously set out to be unkind, they're just thoughtless.'

'They have been brought up to be too busy thinking of themselves,' pronounced Dorothy. 'If ignorance is not an excuse in the law of the land, then neither should it be when it comes to morality. It all boils down to selfishness in the end. Parents should be taking more trouble to instil some sense of right and wrong into their children.'

She drank her tea in a brooding manner, as though it contained some vital moral precept, which should be carefully imbibed and digested.

'It may only be possible to do that by example,' said Nora. 'And then we are put on the spot. How often we older generation resort to the saying, do as I say and not as I do!'

'There is still a strong tradition of moral teaching at Wharton,' said Dorothy. 'In a small town like ours where the school dominates, it can have a major influence. The current headmaster – Clement Hunstrete – is a woolly-minded creature, but the chaplain I believe conducts himself with unimpeachable integrity. He was at school here himself.'

'Martin Darrow, you mean? Yes, I knew him by sight at Oxford – we were more or less contemporaries. He was very well thought of.'

Austen delivered this statement in a precise, schoolmasterly manner, and Jane half expected him to list the relevant dates of their college years or to state that Martin Darrow had been 'a good man'.

'He has never married, but devotes his whole life to the school and the welfare of the boys,' said

Dorothy, putting down her teacup. 'One has to admire such dedication, although it is a pity as he would have made a very reliable husband. Of course, there are unfortunate stories in the lower class of newspapers about vicars, but a chaplain in a public school would not have the temptation of being closeted with adoring female parishioners. His wife would be safe from that danger at least.'

'There might be others,' said Jane, embarrassment hurrying her into unguarded speech.

'He is certainly not a marrying man,' said Dorothy, throwing Jane a warning glance. 'In my day it was perfectly acceptable for men to be unmarried. They were often excellent uncles and extremely useful socially. Nowadays everybody calls them gay. People can't think beyond bedrooms, a very lowering state of affairs.'

'Yes, it's a pity all right, the way people are classified according to sexuality,' said Nora. 'People are so much more than that, and life *contains* so much more!' She made a wild sweeping gesture with her arm, and knocked a plate onto the ground. The tortoiseshell cat opened a reproachful eye and stalked away, expressing indignation with a slow wave of its tail.

'We are becoming more like the apes in the way it permeates every aspect of life and dominates our thinking,' continued Dorothy, apparently unable to bring herself to use the actual word. 'That does *not* feel like progress to me. Something has gone very wrong with the Ascent of Man, whatever that Bronowski man may have said.'

'I've seen Martin sometimes at concerts in the school chapel,' put in Jane desperately. The conversation had strayed into perilous territory. Her mother had the appearance of an ocean liner, launched and invincible, but might be steered into safer waters. 'He makes me think of those saints in old master paintings – all pale beauty and godliness. Not that good looks are important or always appealing,' she added, lest Austen feel she was drawing unflattering comparisons. 'An excessively handsome man who never got dandruff or a spot would be unnatural, or even untrustworthy.'

Her mother adjusted her weight in her chair, while Austen shrank back as if abashed by this edict. Jane looked down at her plate, her thoughts falling away in confusion.

'Have another sandwich,' said Nora.

'I met him when I came over to be interviewed,' Austen said, after a pause. 'It was a piece of encouragement at the time. I wasn't sure if I'd be coming here myself.'

His Irish accent, Jane noticed, was much less pronounced than that of Nora or Ellen. His years at Oxford would have ironed out the distinctive lilt that was so captivating in his mother and daughter. Nor did he share their easy manner.

'I sat opposite you on the train once, back in the spring,' she said, before she could stop herself. He wouldn't remember her – men never did – but for some unexplored reason she was curious.

Austen looked at her in some surprise, and then hesitated slightly. He might have said something, but at that moment Ellen came into the garden with the Arzano family. Imogen smiled at them all, and presented Nora with a gingerbread wrapped in clingfilm.

'It's not made by me. My mother sent it, she makes wonderful cakes.'

'It's lovely to see you all here,' said Nora, 'and it's also lovely that as everyone has met each other already, I needn't make any introductions. I so often get them wrong.' She looked at the trio of children. 'I've done a tray of much more interesting tea for you three. I'll add some of this delicious gingerbread to it. Ellen, why don't you take it down to the bottom of the garden, where the willow is?'

'We're so lucky,' she continued, when the children had disappeared, 'that the lodge has got the lion's share of the old Victorian garden. There's an L-shaped wild bit, with one of those huge willows. Just the thing for swinging on, and getting away from annoying grannies.'

She handed Imogen a cup of tea, giving her a reassuring look. 'They'll be fine, you know. There's nothing like pottering about in a garden.'

'My mother is a devotee of *The Secret Garden*, as I expect you've guessed,' observed Austen. 'She believes gardens have restoring powers.'

'And what's so outlandish about that? There are endless precedents for the special qualities of gardens in myth and legend, and in the Bible as well. Not that they're a cure-all. It's more like the opposite when it comes to a sore back from too much digging.'

'Ah, you need a hot bath for that,' said Dorothy. 'There's nothing like it for all kinds of aches and pains.'

'Hot baths and boiled milk have been standard remedies in our house ever since I was a child,' Jane said, laughing and turning to Imogen. 'Everything could be cured by this combination, and Vaseline for every kind of sore patch. Was it the same when you were young?'

'My mother was always there when I needed her, so

I must have had a perfect childhood.' Imogen looked down the garden, her beautiful face tense and watchful.

'I'm hoping I'll meet her one day soon,' said Nora. 'I'll be asking her how she makes this delicious gingerbread. Were you saying your parents live within reach?'

'Yes, near Lymington, in the New Forest.' Imogen paused, and flushed slightly. 'I haven't seen so much of them in recent years.'

'Perhaps I should have asked the Gidding family to join us,' said Nora, refilling Dorothy's cup. 'It would be grand to have all the neighbours together. But it might have been hard on their boys, Austen could be teaching the poor things next term. You'll be thinking I could have asked Philip and Kate on their own, but I've an idea they're more *drinks* sort of people, if that's the right way of putting it.'

'You're suggesting they are more modern in their way of living,' said Dorothy with a hint of disapproval.

Could people be divided up into different categories like this, Jane wondered, or were there some who were capable of appreciating both forms of entertainment? She began to imagine grouping the people she knew into one of those Venn diagrams with intersecting circles, remembered from her schooldays. She and her mother fitted without question into comfortable tea parties. Imogen, being so much younger, ought to belong to the drinks group, but there was a nebulous, insubstantial quality about her that made her seem not quite right for that, despite her perfect manners. It looked like age had little to do with it. It was more down to temperament and taste. Austen quite definitely fitted into neither group; she pictured him, awkward and shy, isolated outside the Venn diagram. She must have known the mathematical term for this once …

'I think there's nothing more pleasant,' she said as she leant back comfortably in her chair, 'than sitting in one place and not having to move from one group to another, like you have to at drinks parties. Or having to pretend not to notice that the person you're talking to is looking over your shoulder to see who they can talk to next.'

'This is when Austen should chime in gallantly and say he's sure nobody would ever look over your shoulder in a bid to escape,' said Nora dryly. 'But as he never goes to drinks parties of any kind we can't expect him to understand how it is.'

'I'm certainly not very good at those occasions,' said Austen rather stiffly. 'Or perhaps at any other.'

'Your mind is on more important matters than the idle shrieking that goes on at so many social events,' approved Dorothy. 'People should stand up for the right to be themselves and say what they mean.'

'That might have alarming repercussions if taken to excess,' observed Nora, apparently interested in this line of thought. 'But it could be an enjoyable relief for a time. What would happen if we all allowed our natural inclinations free rein? Lots of dreadful things said out loud.'

'Or the nice ones not said,' said Jane.

'It's like the three sieves.' Ellen appeared beside them, and turned to Jane and Imogen. 'Granny told me her aunt used to go on about three tests you had to make before you said anything. They were: is it true, is it kind and is it necessary? You had to think of those three things before you spoke – they're the three sieves. You and your brothers didn't take any notice, did you, Granny? If you ask me, nobody would ever say anything if you did it properly.'

'An excellent maxim,' said Dorothy. 'I'm surprised I haven't come across it before. I must remember to send it to the editor of our parish magazine.'

'Sofia's making a bed for Mousie, and Terzo and me have fixed a swinging seat from the willow branches. They want everyone to come and admire. They want you especially.' Ellen smiled at Imogen. 'But please finish your tea, they're perfectly all right for a bit. Semolina – that's our cat – is with them. Sofia's been telling me about your new puppy. D'you think we could introduce him to Semolina?'

'I'll make some more tea for us all while you try out the willow seat,' said Nora, as Imogen floated off with Ellen, looking like a rare and fragile flower. Jane watched Austen's gaze following Imogen down the garden, his face enigmatic. She jumped up.

'I'll come and help.'

Nora's kitchen was an extension of Nora – haphazardly colourful and untidy enough to be relaxing. Jane leant against the worktop and started to tell Nora about what had happened when she'd brought Terzo the puppy.

'It can't be a coincidence, can it? Imogen said he didn't remember about Toby.'

'On one level he may not.' Nora looked at her. 'But getting the child a dog was inspired. Mending will take time. Longer than you think.'

'As it did with Ellen? Over losing her mother, I mean?'

Jane asked this uncertainly, for what had happened

to Ellen's mother was still a mystery, and she didn't want to put her foot in it.

'Ellen was only three when my daughter-in-law died. Too young to remember very much.'

'Was it illness?'

'She worked for a drug rehabilitation project, and was stabbed to death by an addict. She'd picked up Ellen from the nursery and was on her way home … when they found Verity's body, Ellen was strapped in the buggy, a knife slash down her face but still alive. Of course the man was mad, off his head from the drugs. He killed himself hours later.'

'So you've looked after Ellen ever since then?'

'I'm thinking it's one of the advantages of being a widow. You're free to do what needs to be done and that can't always be managed with a husband in tow. They've a habit of wanting more than their fair share of attention. I went to stay with Austen and Ellen, the other side of Dublin. Getting back to work was the best thing for Austen … '

'And Ellen's face … '

Nora stirred the tea, her expression hidden.

'They said they can do something about it when she's older.' She picked up the teapot with an abrupt movement. 'Let's be taking this out before it gets too stewed. I'm wondering what sort of conversation your mother and my son have been having. Do you have a suspicion the three sieves will have reduced them to a companionable silence?'

# THIRTEEN

'Are you expecting me to come to tonight's doings at Wharton or not?' asked Philip, glancing out of the hall window to see if it was raining. On wet days Kate was prepared to drive him to the station. Otherwise he walked and had proved that the estate agent's description of it as a 'twenty-minute leisurely stroll' was less mendacious than expected, though 'brisk walk' might be nearer the mark. Today there was a hint of drizzle, but not quite enough to make him feel he should ask for a lift.

It was just after seven o'clock in early September. Phoebe – with a sullen face that disturbed him – had started at her school two days earlier, but this evening at Wharton there was to be a start-of-term chapel service and a get-together for new parents and staff. Philip hadn't meant to sound put upon, but he knew that a note of martyrdom had crept into his voice.

'Of course I am. You want to be there, don't you? I imagine all the other parents will go together.'

Kate handed him his briefcase, much, it occurred to him, as she might hand a schoolbag to one of the children or handbag to a guest who'd outstayed her welcome. He recognised the technique. It was one of her ways of hurrying people up.

'It's a tricky day for leaving work early, even if I do a bit of juggling.'

'If you come straight from the station, I'll meet you with the boys outside the chapel. Remember we do need to be there by six. Not much fun for the boys to be late on their first day.'

Philip tried to ignore the tartness flavouring the words. He made an effort.

'I'll be there, work and trains permitting. At least we should get a drink at the bun-fight.'

'It's not a bun-fight, it's a reception. There's to be a talk by the headmaster and a chance to meet some of the teachers and other parents. It'll be in that beautiful room, the one that used to be a ballroom, with the Turner painting.'

'Not to be missed then.'

He glanced at his image in the hall mirror, already the resigned and squashed-into-dullness commuter. He kissed his wife on the lips because he'd always done so and he loved her. It was family ritual and he was, above everything else, a family man. But did Kate still expect it of him? Did she even want it? He couldn't always tell with her. She was distant at times, preoccupied with doing things, getting things, looking at him with eyes that had nothing of her inner self behind them. He sensed she wanted him out of the house, away from her own life, as if the real business of the day couldn't begin until he'd gone.

A month of commuting had been enough for Philip to learn the small manoeuvres that made it tolerable. He was beginning to know his fellow travellers; he'd learnt which ones talked, opened papers too wide, spread their feet beyond unspoken limits.

One quartet of men he was careful to avoid: a group who had presumably been doing this journey for years, for they had the bovine vacuity of farmyard animals herded at regular times. They sat together, exchanging trivia and in-jokes. Philip took pains to stand at a different end of the platform.

But not too near a pair of much younger men, both with the clear faces of rosy schoolboys in a children's storybook. He'd fallen victim to them just once and learnt his lesson. Their effusive friendliness to other passengers was like strong sunlight shining in your eyes; it made you want to turn away your head. You couldn't stop their flow of words, any more than you could silence a wind-up toy, except by stamping on it. Philip took avoiding action; he feared he might be invited to an evangelising men's breakfast.

The girl in the pale green jacket was in his carriage again. A quiet girl with a composed face. Philip approved of her. She didn't spend the journey sending and receiving texts or doing her make-up or exchanging accounts of evenings out. A slow, secretive smile at him, and that was it.

Today she was absorbed in a glossy textbook, painstakingly marking passages with a pencil. *Art of the Romantic Era*, Philip noted. A student at the Courtauld Institute perhaps? He had noticed that she always went off down the Strand in the direction of Somerset House, so she might be studying there. No, it was too early in the morning, and she was a little older and definitely more tidily dressed than the average arts student. A lecturer perhaps; he could imagine that. He pictured her talking calmly to a roomful of students, her chin lifted slightly, her almost white fair hair framing her face. Hadn't Anita Brookner once lectured there, when she wasn't writing those novels his wife read so avidly? The disappointments of life, Kate had flashed back, when he'd asked her what they were about, and he'd wished she didn't want to read books like that.

This girl didn't look unhappy. She looked restful. Something more than that. Contented with herself – keeping her own counsel – at ease with the world! An interesting-looking girl, with a strange attractiveness about her he couldn't quite analyse.

Nor should he. His mind shifted to his sons starting at Wharton. Thank God they wouldn't have to pay for Teddy as well. Two years in the sixth form at full fees couldn't have been thought of if it hadn't been for his godfather's legacy. They'd never spent the lump sum that Neil had left for Teddy's education, but Kate had a point. They might as well spend it now. How did they know Teddy would actually want to go to university?

Neil. His best man and then his eldest child's godfather. They'd been at Cambridge together but afterwards their paths had divided. Neil had begun a high-flying career in commercial law in the City, while Philip had opted for family law in a small firm off the Strand. Then, before Teddy was old enough to go to school, Neil had drowned off a Cornwall beach attempting to rescue an unknown child carried away by a rip-tide.

\*

From the other side of the room, among the throng of parents sipping wine, Kate watched Philip returning to her side with his third glass. She was drinking nothing. She didn't want the distraction.

All boys had been taken to their houses to be given timetables and to choose sports options. Kate imagined them being allocated cupboards and pegs in cloakrooms, and shown which desk was theirs in the prep room. She was glad to have them out of the way for the moment. She wanted to make the most of this opportunity. She eyed the various members of staff, distinguished by their academic gowns, noting the red or white silk hoods that denoted Oxford or Cambridge degrees. A man in a dog collar. He'd be the school chaplain. No thank you.

In one corner she could see their neighbour Austen Kinsale standing with a colleague, and a group of parents. He looked stiff and ill-at-ease. She didn't see any point in bothering to go over and greet him; she could speak to him any time at home. Teddy would probably be taught by him; he wasn't able to do Latin or Greek at A Level, having not done any at his comprehensive in London, but he'd opted instead for something the prospectus described as classical civilisation. It included what Teddy called all the interesting things, like the art, history and literature of the ancient world without the slog of learning the languages. Kate thought it was probably the easy option for less academic boys, but hadn't argued with Teddy's choice. She knew they'd been fortunate to get Teddy into the sixth form at Wharton, had been allowed in at the back door, thanks to Jonah's scholarship. It would be better not to push their luck too far. Other people might think she never knew when to stop, but she did. Not like that pain of a woman behind her.

'The name is Ra*bet*,' went the insistent whine. '*Not* Mrs Rabbit, but Mrs Ra*bet*.'

Piano Jane, as Kate thought of her, wasn't here. She was starting duties in one of the boarding houses and was presumably there now. Kate didn't remember which house it was; Jane had mentioned it but it wasn't the one Teddy and Jonah belonged to, and anyway they weren't going to board, so she hadn't listened. Jane was all right so far as it went and all that, but they had nothing in common. In fact, Jane was really rather a bore.

Meanwhile, there were more important people she wanted to meet. The name badge on the jacket-lapel of a man standing close by caught her eye. Jonathan Laird, director of music. He would be worth talking to. Jonah was ready to take his clarinet grade seven exam; this would be her opening gambit. Gripping Philip's arm, Kate prepared her socially confident smile.

# FOURTEEN

Phoebe let herself into the house, pleased to see that the car was missing which meant Mum was out. No annoying inquisition then. She slung her school bag onto the hall floor and kicked off her shoes.

Phoebe liked having the house to herself after school. It happened quite often, with Teddy and Jonah having a much longer school day. They often didn't get back until five or six, while she finished at half past three and got the chance to mess about in shops on the way home. Sometimes Teddy didn't have any afternoon lessons and came back early too, but this was okay. Teddy never gave you any grief.

The fridge was full of the usual things Mum bought in bulk each week plus the carcass of last night's roast chicken. Phoebe picked a bit of white meat off the wishbone and examined the yoghurts on the top shelf, arranged in the rows that Mum was so obsessive about. She took a mango one, and decided against cutting herself a slice from a huge slab of Taleggio cheese. Mum had a habit of going crazy over some new product she discovered, buying it all the time like she couldn't stop.

There were several unopened packets of chocolate digestives and Jaffa Cakes in the cupboard, but she needed something salty. She chose a packet of barbecue-flavoured crisps, and poured herself a glass of water. Everyone knew you were meant to drink at least eight glasses a day for your skin. It was a drag when you weren't thirsty. She and her friends Renny and Char were seeing how long they could keep it up, but right now Phoebe was beginning to get bored of wanting to go to the loo all the time. Renny and Char were keeping a tally of how often they went and said you ought to hold on as long as you could. That meant you built up muscles in the right places which got you better sex.

They talked about sex most of the time, all of them except for the losers. You couldn't expect sad people like Millie Heath to join in, looking the way she did. Thighs like tree trunks and that disgusting acne all over her face. She'd never pull anybody, because whoever would want to have sex with her?

'Is that music club you're always going on about full of dummies who can't get any other social life?' Renny had asked, and Millie didn't even come back at her.

The other girls said that Millie always tried to make friends with new girls coming to the school. Phoebe had thanked them for the warning, but she hadn't needed it. In Phoebe's experience there was always a Millie in pretty well every class and in every school. They stuck out.

Sometimes Phoebe and the others asked to copy her maths homework, because Millie was always way ahead with that, and maths was something you could get away with not doing yourself. Millie had her uses in this way, and put on that numpty smile when you asked her. The trouble was she didn't know when to back off afterwards. Just because someone could get their head round quadratic equations didn't give them a right to be your friend. Phoebe and the others had to suggest going to Starbucks or New Look in front of her, or even say yeah, she could come along. Then they'd make sure they all went to Topshop and Café Nero instead. Was she stupid or what?

From the kitchen window, Phoebe caught sight of that Year Seven girl with the cross-stitch mark on her face turning into the drive. Ellen, she was called, like something out of an out-of-date story, though as Ellen was that way herself, it suited her. Look at the way she was wearing her uniform exactly as the school said, you'd think she was still at primary school.

There was Teddy as well, so it was one of his early days. He always said hi to Ellen. Probably that was because she was only eleven; Teddy never said anything much to any of Phoebe's friends. He just avoided them, like they had the plague or something. Renny had asked her if he was gay, and Phoebe couldn't work out if she minded this question or not.

'Kind of young for you, isn't she?' she said to Teddy, when he came into the kitchen, where she'd settled herself with a mug of tea and *Grazia* magazine.

'She's all right,' said Teddy, but showing by his glance at her that he'd caught her meaning. He hung his school jacket over a chair more carefully than usual. 'It's tough starting all over again with friends – they were in Dublin until July.'

'What of it? We've had to start again. It's easier for her, starting in Year Seven. Everyone's the same. There's only me and a couple of others new in Year Ten.'

'There's only half a dozen new in the sixth form at Wharton, and they're mostly Chinese, all geniuses at maths and science. I'm just saying it can't be much fun not having a mother and there being only her. Not exactly a proper family life.'

'She mightn't mind. I don't go for all this bullshit about family life. You can keep it, if you ask me. Have you found out about her mother then?'

'Yeah – done in by some street nutter when Ellen was a baby.'

'Shite. So it's like Ellen doesn't remember her?'

Phoebe finished her tea as she digested this. She was often angry with her own mother. Sometimes she felt like she hated her guts, but still, she was *there*. Phoebe couldn't for a moment imagine what it must be like when there wasn't a mother in the picture at all.

'She said she can still remember what she looked like, but that could be because she's got a photo by her bed. I can't remember anything from when I was three, can you? But I reckon it's important to her to *think* she does. Her dad never talks about her. Oh, and Nora told me she was always trying to help other people.'

'People always blah on like that about someone who's snuffed it.' Phoebe's mind flickered to her own grandmother. 'I thought mothers-in-law always hate whoever their son marries. Look how Gran's always bitching at Mum.'

'Nora's different from Gran. She never has a go at anyone. Ellen told me some story about her accidentally pulling down a corner cupboard full of old family china when she was a little girl, and all Nora said was how it was a good thing as she'd always hated those tea cups.'

'You've nosed out a lot in record time.'

'Yeah, well. It's harsh for her having only a grandmother, however much Nora tries to make up for it. There's her dad,' Teddy sounded unconvinced, 'but then he's at school all day and Saturday mornings as well.'

'That geek!' Phoebe stood up scornfully and switched on the kettle. 'D'you see much of him at school?'

'Only when I have him for class. civ. lessons. I guess he stays in his classroom all the time,' said Teddy, picking up the bread knife and sawing through a packet of Jaffa Cakes. 'Almost all the other teachers you see around the place, telling you to tuck your shirt in or get a haircut, but you never catch sight of him.'

'Not much of a loss.'

'No – I can do without having my next-door neighbour breathing down my neck at school. Especially as I'm the worst in the set. Not that we see anything of him here either, do we? He must hide away at a desk all the time, buried in Horace.'

'Who? Oh, don't bother to tell me, I don't want to know.' Phoebe poured boiling water into her mug, squashing a teabag against the sides.

'Just some Roman poet, nobody reads him now. Unless they're like me and have to. Actually, Kinsale's okay if you're in the right mood. He's just a bit of a one-off.'

'A loser, you mean?'

'Not exactly.'

Teddy struggled with his thoughts. He wasn't going to repeat a jibe he'd overheard – Austen's lost it. That was Ollie Benson for you. Funny one minute, cruel the next, like those amazing caricatures he was always drawing.

'It's like he's got his own world and stays in it. He's a good teacher though. People respect him all right. You'd think he'd have trouble keeping order, but he doesn't.'

'He probably doesn't notice when people are taking the piss.' Phoebe was beginning to be bored. 'Anyway, aren't they all boffs at Wharton? Does Ellen have to learn Latin and Greek at home as well? She looks like she does. And Nora.'

'She'd most likely give it a go if she thought it would please her dad. It's funny how she protects him. They both do.'

Teddy stared out of the window as he considered their neighbours, comparing them in his mind with the families he'd known in London. Those households had been much more like his own; mother, father, children jostling together. He thought of the lift shares to after-school activities, educational trips and foreign exchanges, his mother shouting at them to do their music practice. You were never still because you had to be learning something and improving yourself as otherwise you'd be left behind.

It hadn't occurred to Teddy then that there was any other way of life; this was how things were and you got on with it, even if you didn't much like some of the things you were made to do and didn't get anything out of. But Ellen lived in a different sort of set-up altogether, where there wasn't any of this busyness and setting goals. She was given time to drift about and think for herself. It made her come out with things that were nothing like the random stuff that most people (including him) said as a matter of course.

Having time might, in the end, make you more

interesting rather than less, he thought, because then you had space to consider all the things you didn't know instead of hiding behind the ones you did. It was what people didn't know, and how they imagined things and puzzled over them that drew you to them, not what they did know.

He was glad the Kinsales were living next door to them, because it made him realise that families needn't all be the same. Ellen might be only eleven and Nora getting on, but actually he liked talking to them. He hadn't given it much thought, but if someone had asked him why, he might have said it was something to do with the way they treated each other.

A picture flashed into his mind of how he'd first seen Ellen the day they'd moved in. A kid with long brown hair hanging over half her face watching them from the lodge window. He'd given her a quick wave to say hello, and she'd made a hesitant answering movement before turning away.

Or it could be that Nora came up to his idea of what a grandmother ought to be. Dad's mum and dad were scared of anything new. But Nora enjoyed things even if she was too old for them herself and was pleased to see you doing them. The way her nose wrinkled up when she smiled made you feel she liked you.

She doesn't want you to be any different from what you are, he wanted to say.

'I bet they love stupid stuff like that,' said Phoebe, lobbing her used teabag into the bin. 'Some people haven't got a life and never will have.'

# FIFTEEN

She *had* to have a cool phone.

This Saturday was the Year Seven disco. She'd heard that some of the girls texted each other while they were dancing with boys, to compare notes on how they snogged. She'd be the only girl in the year without one. Could you even *go* to a disco like that?

Smartphones cost a fortune, but everyone had them. Everyone except her. Granny said you shouldn't ask people about things to do with money, and that it was very bad manners indeed to ask what people earned or what their possessions cost. It was obvious to Ellen that either Granny was ridiculously strict on this particular point or that almost everybody had no manners, because the price of things was what people talked about all the time. Clover, in the same class as her, who always had the latest and coolest of everything, had told her exactly where you got the best deals.

She didn't want to ask Dad about a phone. She hated asking him for things, because it made him look sorry, as if he was thinking he ought to have given them to her without being reminded. He never spent any money on clothes or stuff for himself. Apart from books. Ellen had to admit there were far too many of those in the house.

Dad had never loved anybody like he'd loved her mother. He couldn't talk about her but Ellen knew he was remembering her all the time. She couldn't wipe away Dad's lost look, but she could keep everything the same in Wharton as it had been in Dublin. There were ways of making sure that Dad wouldn't want to live with anyone else. Not giving him trouble was one way.

Ellen ran a finger with its bitten nail down the scar on her face and frowned. Dad belonged to her and Granny. She wasn't going to let that change.

Teddy. The thought came to her as she stared out of the window. He was someone you could ask about things. He wasn't at all super-cool, but he had an iPhone; she'd seen him talking into it on the way home from Wharton. Phoebe and Jonah had them too; Phoebe had one that was shiny white. She and her friends were always hanging around in the town centre after school, tapping away at their screens, taking selfies, giving each other knowing looks and laughing.

Granny was busy in the garden digging holes ready for the bulbs they were planning to put in, so Ellen called to her that she was going over to ask Teddy something. That was one of the good things about Granny. She never said, why are you doing this or that, she just accepted that if you wanted to tell her things you would.

Fridays were Teddy's early days, Ellen knew, so he'd be home by now. She was in luck; he answered her ring on the doorbell. That was a relief. Kate was scary.

'You're absolutely the person I need,' Teddy said, holding open the door for Ellen to come in. 'I've been struggling to get my head round Black Figure and Red Figure vase painting. I bet you know all about them.'

That was just like Teddy. Lucky, lucky Phoebe to have him for a brother.

'I like the vases with Achilles and Ajax on them,' she said, 'but I don't know any other stuff about them. I could test you though, from the book, which vase is which I mean, from the pictures.'

'I might just get you to do that one day, if your dad threatens us with one of his gruesome tests. I'll remember your offer then. It might be a bit of a non-starter today, I haven't even got the basics into my head. Did you want a drink or anything?'

'No thanks – Teddy, you wouldn't have an old smartphone you don't use any more?'

He was silent for a moment, giving her his funny Teddy look meaning she didn't need to explain things.

'I could have. It might take a bit of time to find. My room's a tip – according to Mum anyway. But I'm sure I've still got it. You're meant to take them to a charity shop but I guess I shoved it away somewhere for now.'

Dear, darling Teddy. She'd known he would help.

'Yes please. You see, I only want to look as though I've got one, for the disco tomorrow night. I can say I've run out of battery when it doesn't work. I don't need a real one.'

'It won't do your image any good, having a fake. Why don't you borrow mine? I'll show you how it works. You can give it back to me on Sunday.'

Ellen hesitated.

'It might get damaged. I'd be worrying all the time. Anyway, you'll want it yourself.'

'Have the old one then. I'll dig it out and bring it round – is tomorrow okay?'

She got up.

'Yes. It's brilliant. Thank you, Teddy. Will you do one more thing?'

'I might.'

'Don't tell anyone.'

He gave her another look.

'Of course I won't. You don't need to remind me, no point in fussing our families about stuff they haven't a clue about.'

When Ellen got home, Granny was rummaging in one of the kitchen cupboards.

'I've a rush of blood to the head,' she said, pulling out some soft brown sugar. 'Shall we be making some fudge? It's so long since we made any I've forgotten when it was.'

'It was when we had to boil it all up again because it didn't set,' said Ellen. 'Don't you remember, we decided we hadn't got it hot enough. Can we really do it now? Shall I get out the weighing scales?'

'Do you think Terzo would like to come and make it with us? It'd be a good thing, wouldn't it, for him to get out and about more. Imogen says he might be starting school after Christmas.'

For a moment Ellen was silent. Making fudge with Granny was *her* treat. She liked Terzo, he was sweet and she was sorry for him ... but then Granny smiled.

'Or will we be being cosy and having just us?'

That decided her. It was enough that Granny understood and felt the same way she did.

'I'll run over and see if he'll come. And Sofia.'

Ellen was about to ring the doorbell of Terzo's house when she heard a man shouting, and the sound of someone rushing down the stairs. Bad timing. She shrank away, and was out of sight when the door was flung open. Terzo's dad came storming out. Ellen didn't think he would have seen her even if she'd still been standing by the door, because his face was angry and shut in and his eyes had that look of not seeing anything. She waited, staying quite still, as he slammed down the drive, and disappeared round the corner.

What should she do now? Would it still be all right to ring at the door? She hovered uncertainly for a moment and then decided that she might as well. Poor Terzo and Sofia having such a stressy dad. She knew that things were hard because of Terzo's brother dying in the car accident and Mr and Mrs Arzano weren't telling Terzo yet because they were waiting until he was quite strong again.

Hearing this had made Ellen feel sad for days, and she could see Terzo's mum and dad might feel sad all the time. But that didn't make it okay for Angelo Arzano to get angry and slam out of the house like he hated it.

Imogen opened the door to her, and immediately Ellen was sorry she'd decided to come, because Imogen's eyes were watery red. She'd been crying.

It was embarrassing when grown-ups you didn't know very well cried in front of you. You couldn't hug them or ask them what the matter was, even when you wanted to. You had to pretend not to notice. So she asked Imogen if Terzo could come and help make fudge and Sofia too if she liked, and Imogen looked really grateful and went to fetch them right away. When she came down the stairs with Terzo and Sofia following behind her, Ellen could see she'd washed her face so it had gone back to being beautiful. It was unfair how some people looked awful for ages after crying while others could just wipe it off.

'We'll make a real lot,' she promised, as their feet crunched acorns on the drive by the lodge with a satisfying squish. 'You can take some back for your mum. And your dad,' she added, though to be quite truthful she didn't think he deserved any. It was difficult not to grudge giving things when people were so horrible.

'My granny is quite like you, but you're even older,' Sofia told Nora, smearing butter round a tin with a piece of screwed-up greaseproof paper. 'Does that mean you'll die soon? I don't want you to.'

'I'm not nearly as old as I look,' said Nora seriously, and Ellen saw her turn away to reach for another wooden spoon so that Sofia and Terzo wouldn't see her laugh. 'Now who's going to do the next bit of stirring?'

Ellen got up and took the spoon.

'I will, or you'll say, "then I'll do it myself, said the little red hen". You always say that when nobody offers to do things. I must say the little red hen in that story was a bit of a goody-goody as well as a right martyr, always saying that.'

'She was clever and rescued the lazy old cock and mouse,' said Sofia, her intent face lighting up with pleased recognition.

'And she tricked the greedy fox. I can see your granny has read you the same book,' said Nora. 'She and I would be having lots to talk about.'

'Me and Terzo are going to see Granny and Grandpa on Saturday,' said Sofia. 'Mummy always drives, because Daddy won't.'

'My dad goes by train whenever he can,' said Ellen,

seeing Terzo's anxious face bent over the greased tins. 'He's always wrapped up in Ancient Greece and forgets where he's going, so he's safer on the train.'

'You can give your granny and grandpa some of the fudge when you go,' suggested Nora. 'Let's decorate one of these cake boxes and make it look pretty. Now, will we try dropping a bit of this mixture into a saucer of cold water and see if it sets? I've an idea it's meant to go cloudy if it's ready. Or is it the other way round?'

It was only much later, after Terzo and Sofia had gone home, with two paper platefuls of successfully set fudge and a cardboard box with daisies crayoned all over it, that Ellen was free to put the nicest pieces that were left into a box for Teddy.

He called in the next day with a package. She handed him the fudge and he grinned his thanks. Seeing his face like that was the best feeling ever.

Afterwards she went up to her room and examined the phone. It was silver and there were user instructions with it and a charger. It looked exactly like the one she'd seen Teddy using. Then she saw that he'd scrawled a number and a message on a scrap of paper.

*Dear Ellen, this old phone was pay as you go but still has some credit and works fine. As it's turned up again it's going spare. You can keep it – it's yours! Teddy x*

# SIXTEEN

Angelo considered his wife's profile as she drove the Volvo estate and found himself thinking of his mother-in-law. Judith had the flawless classic beauty of Ingrid Bergman in *Casablanca*. In another twenty years Imogen would look exactly like her.

Or not. How could you live through this past year and not show something of it on your face?

But then had Judith's life been as uncomplicated as Imogen persisted in pretending? Imogen and her brother Charlie had been small children when Howard had switched his lucrative career in insurance from London to Hong Kong, leaving the family behind. Two decades of living apart and everything that meant. Now he and Judith presented themselves as having as solid a marriage as any other couple living in Hampshire comfort and subscribing to *The Daily Telegraph*.

Angelo knew about expediency and concealment – his childhood had been shaped by them – but he was impatient of Imogen's denial to everyone, herself included, of the truth behind her father's move to Hong Kong. Wasn't it obvious he'd wanted to leave Judith, and he'd chosen a pleasant – to himself – way of doing so? Whether Judith had ever tacitly acknowledged this was another question. Angelo imagined how it had been: Howard's career must come first; lots of wives have to live without their husbands for months on end – look at the navy – and she could always fly out and visit. He wondered how often she'd actually done so.

Had Howard asked Judith to take him back when he retired, had he put himself through emotional scenes of reconciliation? No, that wasn't his father-in-law's way. Judith and her tribe tidied up their lives – and those around them – into neat boxes of a manageable size. He could hear it all. Just a little difficulty, to be sorted out by a little holiday and if we just try a little harder, we shall all know where we are.

Here he was, strapped in for a weekend of it. He'd lived in such a way and done things that had brought him to where he was now. Nothing could change that. His guilt, wherever it lay, made no difference.

*I have taken away her innocence.*

For it was for this that he'd married her – he with his dirty childhood had fallen in love with her untainted freshness, her artless confidence in a middle class world where your mother kept you safe and you knew who your father was and abuse was something that couldn't happen to you, only to other people whom you wouldn't ever meet.

His son was dead. What sort of father was he that he backed away, afraid to love his surviving children? And didn't they rightfully belong to his wife first and foremost? Hadn't he forfeited any right to their love?

*Leave them to what remains of their innocence.*

The motorway stretched out before them, shimmering grey silk in the heat. He was aware of an urge to wrench open the door and fling himself out of the car. He needed to get away from this life that he'd created, away from the man who was trapped in this killing machine that was built like a tank.

Was it to be wondered at, that he almost hated himself and the woman next to him and the car that was carrying them every moment closer to where he dreaded being? It had been given to Imogen by Howard and Judith on that first numbed visit when they'd come back from Italy. Imogen should have the safest and most reliable car possible, they'd said, not looking at him. It's something we can do for our daughter.

*If you hadn't been drunk and the boys' seat-belts had been fastened they wouldn't have been thrown out of the car like ragdolls.*

Always that gap between what was said aloud and what he heard.

*

'Why aren't we there yet?'

Imogen glanced at her daughter in the mirror.

'We'll be able to see ponies soon, darling, when we turn off the motorway. You look out on one side and Terzo the other.'

She relaxed her hands on the steering wheel. Think of ponies, of her old home in the New Forest, of her parents together again after their years apart. Don't think of anything else. Especially not of Angelo, sitting beside her with the look on his face she'd learnt to dread.

He used to tell me how beautiful I was. Was it all he loved about me? Am I nothing else in his eyes?

She found herself thinking that she *was* nothing

else. She was beginning to be afraid of him, of her own thoughts, of the life she was now living.

She saw carloads of families passing them on the fast lane, the husbands driving, the wives sitting by their side. Did they ever fear their lives might shatter, that people and feelings were so ephemeral they might change or disappear without warning?

'Terzo,' she made herself say, 'open up the coolbox. It's time you and Sofia had a drink. Could you pass one to Daddy?'

It was essential not to think of things that were too frightening or difficult to grasp. They were on the last stretch of the journey now. She saw the familiar landmarks of her childhood and felt herself breathe, like a crumpled garment pulled from the tumble-drier. Late summer trees among patches of rough dry grass and streams where small children paddled and fished. Groups of ponies grazed undisturbed. Foals with spindly legs and startled dark-eyed heads clustered close to their mothers. Above them the sky was a children's picture book blue.

\*

If only Howard would decide to get settled at his desk and do something lengthy like his tax return, so she could get on with preparing lunch by herself. He had a habit of coming in and out of the kitchen when she was cooking, to fetch a drink, to remind her of something, or really, she couldn't help thinking with a half-smile, simply to interrupt her listening to the radio. Men didn't like you to enjoy anything more than their conversation; this is what it amounted to.

Judith never resented the other women who must have filled various roles in Howard's life throughout their thirty years of marriage; they'd shared the burden of looking after him. There were even moments when she could imagine herself laughing with them over his peculiarities. Did that mean she was past feeling threatened? Judith didn't know. Only that there was no point in thinking too much about these things, it never did any good.

He'd written to her after recovering from a stroke, telling her he wanted to retire from the Hong Kong office and to come home. He hadn't been an ideal husband, he said; he blamed himself that in some ways she'd had a rough deal. But there was still plenty of life ahead for both of them, and he'd come to see that being with her was what he wanted most of all. She was strangely touched he'd put it like that. He'd never been demonstrative to her. It must have been difficult for him to have used these words.

There was never any question in her mind. Was it all to be forgotten, to be for nothing, those thirty years? She remembered the early days when they had been setting out on their life together. They'd been friends and companions then, and satisfied lovers. The coming of the children, first Imogen, then, two years later, Charlie, had caused her to transfer her attention and energy to her children. They'd bought Forest House as a family home for them all, and kept the London flat for Howard during the week.

It had been then that they'd grown apart, each of them with a separate set of priorities. She was absorbed by the house and the children; he was increasingly absent. She hadn't argued when he'd taken the job in

Hong Kong, but she'd refused to go with him. During the years that followed she'd got on with her life, the house, the children. They'd become detached from each other, as he, by withholding all confidences, had effectually rejected hers. For Howard did not want to communicate; he wanted to live for himself, to be allowed to do his job. His tidy life in Hong Kong had been congenial to him; the boundaries had been clear.

Her eyes rested on the view of green fields, fringed with yellow gorse, hot and fierce against vivid wild fuchsia. Across the water meadows she could see groups of grazing cows, their reflections cobalt and burnt sienna in the marshy ground, and beyond to the changing blues of the Solent.

During those years of desertion she'd stiffened her backbone and managed, telling herself it was just a matter of self-discipline. Getting on with what needed to be done and not giving in to self-pity. 'I'm used to it,' she would say when friends asked her how she was coping on her own. It was true; she did get used to it.

But it was the return of Howard that had given her the necessary strength when her beloved grandchild was killed. She needed to be strong for her daughter. Howard's coming home made the continuing exercise of self-discipline possible. She didn't think she could have got through this year without him.

For life shifted and turned around, savage and consuming as spring tides. Howard restored to her, and then, only months later, Toby taken away. How entirely different the working out of a marriage and a life were from the expectations you had when you first set out. Could anyone safely predict their path?

She piled Demerara sugar onto the cooked ham

joint and put it into the top oven to caramelise. A family favourite going right back to Imogen and Charlie's childhood. Later she would pick generous bunches of mint and parsley for the potatoes, large floury ones with gleaming golden butter at the bottom of the dish, just as Howard liked.

It was in these apparently trifling aspects of marriage that satisfaction could be found. The big things might not be talked about but they lay quiescent enough. A companionship furnished and made comfortable by details. Folding up Howard's pyjamas on his bed, making sure he didn't overtire himself playing golf, cooking him his favourite Welsh rarebit which she'd never learnt to like herself.

\*

Terzo leaned out of the bedroom window that he and Sofia shared when they stayed with their grandparents. The tree that came right up almost into the room was no longer covered in pink blossom. Instead there were coppery leaves, shiny on one side. He stretched out an arm to touch their silky softness. In the spring when he and Sofia had stayed here he had lain in bed staring at the wafting pink petals clustered on dark branches. He could imagine himself floating on the billowing softness, as if he was on a cloud in heaven.

Mummy had been staying with them then as well. Daddy hadn't been there, except at the very beginning. Mummy said he was busy in Italy. It hadn't meant much to Terzo. All he could remember about Italy was being in hospital, a confused, dreamy time of people appearing and disappearing. Doctors and nurses would look at him and take his temperature and ask him questions which he couldn't answer. That was because he'd been in a bad car accident which had hurt his head and made him forget things, so that people and places were strange and new. At other times they were half-familiar, like things from a dream, or shadows coming at you out of a mist that turned into the people you recognised.

Then they were all in an aeroplane coming to England and Mummy and Daddy had brought them to Hampshire, to this lovely old house where Mummy had lived when she was a little girl. She'd told him how she had loved the pink tree, but it didn't reach up to the first floor then; it was only a young sapling. Terzo thought it was the most perfect tree in the world, and loved it even more than the huge and beautiful one in the middle of the garden with a wooden seat which went all the way round its trunk, so that Sofia could sit on one side and he on the other and you couldn't see each other at all. The tree was called a liquidambar and Terzo liked saying the name to himself, because it so exactly suited the warm richness of its leaves.

The house was made of red bricks that glowed like a friend when the sun was on them. Terzo felt it was in some way alive; that it knew and loved the people who lived there. He could almost feel it breathing and welcoming him in, so that he wanted to lay his head against the sympathetic walls and stay quite still.

The garden wasn't all tidy flowerbeds, but had lots of huge bushes, some of them covered with flowers, and interesting leaves, pink-veined or striped with different sorts of green and yellow. Old flaking croquet hoops straggled over the mossy lawn, and there was a bench with wooden slats that dug into your back, and deckchairs with the material faded and thin. In the corner there was a summer house, where the mower lived, and where you were meant to put back the croquet mallets and balls, only nobody ever did.

His grandparents were exactly as they should be. Grandpa was always pottering about minding his own business and he didn't fuss you. He let Terzo start the mower for him and had taken him to play golf, but hadn't minded when Terzo didn't want to go on with it. He'd just said that golf wasn't everyone's cup of tea, and life was too short to waste time doing what you weren't cut out to do.

Granny was never, ever cross, not even when Sofia had broken a glass, and crunched all the bits with her shoes on the hall carpet. It had taken ages to clear up all the glass and they'd had to make sure that every single bit was picked up because of Gladstone and Salisbury. It would be dreadful if they got any stuck in their paws.

Thinking about Gladstone and Salisbury made him remember Mousie. He was pleased now that he'd chosen Mousie for a name; it was more interesting than calling dogs after old prime ministers who most people had never heard of. But he loved Gladstone and Salisbury. They were comforting and safe and never jumped on him. They waved their tails lazily and spent almost all their days snoozing in front of the creamy Aga, so you'd think they'd be baking.

'Aren't you *ever* cross about anything?' Sofia had asked Granny about the broken glass. Granny had kissed them both and said, 'never with you two, or with Mummy either.' She didn't say Daddy or Grandpa, Terzo noticed. She must have meant them though. He reminded himself that he'd only ever heard her put on a firm voice when annoying people rang up and tried to sell things to her over the telephone.

They were going home tomorrow. Daddy had to go to London to write things that made people angry and shocked them out of complacency – wherever that was. He'd heard Mummy and Daddy fighting about it and Mummy had cried. He'd seen Dad soon afterwards and his face had worn an expression which Terzo often saw on it. He struggled to understand what it meant, but he found that thinking about it made him feel frightened in a muddled way, so he didn't know what he *was* afraid of.

Terzo leaned further out of the window. He was beginning to feel dizzy. He screwed up his eyes as tight as he could. Air and noise and broken colours swirled about him. The familiar terror was coming for him. Now it was swallowing him up and a voice from somewhere screamed for a boy called Toby.

# SEVENTEEN

As Jane turned out of the Wharton school gates, she saw that the man walking ahead of her was Austen Kinsale.

Since the day of Nora's tea party, she'd only caught sight of him a few times. He was always hurrying into his classroom. If he'd noticed her, he certainly hadn't said hello.

Now the awkwardness of her situation made her hesitate. Should she call out a friendly greeting, which would mean he'd be obliged to walk home with her, when this was probably the last thing he wanted to do, or should she slow down so he would go safely out of sight? There were groups of boys behind her and she didn't want to get entangled with them. But if Austen turned round for any reason and saw her, it would look as if she'd been deliberately avoiding him.

Of course this was what did happen, and Jane was only glad that the fading light made her confusion less evident.

'Hello,' he said, looking neither pleased nor displeased to see her, or possibly trying to remember who she was. 'I didn't realise you were just behind me. Are you walking home? We might as well walk together.'

Not the warmest of invitations. Jane trudged

beside him in the damp September evening. At the end of a long day of teaching, who would want to have to exchange pleasantries with the part-time piano teacher? Especially one as dull and worthy as she must look, carrying her National Trust tote bag full of dog-eared music books. It was unfair that after having looked forward to seeing him again, she should meet him in such unpropitious circumstances, and when she felt she looked more than usually unattractive.

'I'm only going as far as the church,' she said at last, as their conversation – if it could be called that – seemed in danger of dwindling away into complete silence. 'The autumn discussion groups start this evening. I'm early, but I'll be able to help put out the chairs and make the tea and coffee.'

How very dreary that sounded. Just what a woman like me would be doing. She remembered Austen sometimes went to the early Holy Communion at the church, and guessed it was probably to avoid having to talk to all the female do-gooders at the main service later in the morning. She began to feel resentful that the burden of their conversation was falling entirely on her.

'Who else goes to these discussion groups?' Austen broke the silence, sounding slightly more interested. 'I believe I noticed a leaflet about them.'

But you didn't think of going to them yourself, thought Jane, with a flash of annoyance.

'It *is* mostly women and retired people … it's asking a lot of younger men to come out in the evenings after a long day at work,' she said, thinking this might be equally true of younger women.

'Women are better at joining in with church activities

and may have more to offer,' observed Austen in the dry manner she'd noticed him using at the tea party. 'Though that doubtless sounds like an excuse. Will your mother be there? I imagine she would contribute interestingly to any discussion.'

'She likes to sort things out – so long as people don't quote the bits of the Bible that she disapproves of.'

'You mean she knows that some of the customs can be justifiably relegated to history but it's her prerogative to decide which ... what's on the menu tonight?'

'An examination of the meaning of Advent, so we are well prepared when it comes,' said Jane, conscious that this description was hardly enticing.

'A spiritual alternative to the secular countdown to the Christmas season, as advertised on the covers of all the women's magazines at this time of year?'

'Before the New Year issues promising magic ways to fight the Christmas flab,' agreed Jane. 'It's all what everyone knows already and it's practically identical every year, but I suppose it's comfortingly predictable.'

'Do you always want to be well prepared for things?' asked Austen, looking at her quizzically as they paused to wait for the traffic lights. 'Advent's a couple of months away. It's like the boy who's always done his prep. One sometimes longs for him to be like everyone else.'

'I once heard a sermon that compared the church year to a dog burying bones and then digging them up when the time is ripe. It's the unearthing of things which helps us to appreciate the theological meaning.' Jane spoke shamefacedly, aware she did not always feel all that she ought to feel at Christian festivals, or actually at any time.

'That's an interesting way of putting it,' said Austen. 'I do find solace in the rhythms of the church calendar.' As she turned to him, she saw his face alter suddenly, like a field lit by unexpected winter sun. 'Do you have to put out these chairs or whatever, or have you got time for a drink? My mother has taken Ellen to a poetry-speaking competition at her school, so I'm not expected home yet.'

'I should like that very much,' said Jane, surprised but pleased. 'Will you be obliged to report any Wharton boys you find drinking? Ought we to go to a pub where we're unlikely to see any?'

'Luckily I'm short-sighted. I can legitimately not see them, or not recognise them as Wharton boys. It works best that way. Shall we go in here?'

They were passing a brightly-lit pub which was unfamiliar to Jane. She hadn't been in any of the town's pubs since she was a teenager. She remembered the hours of sitting stiffly with a drink she didn't want and a boy who was already losing hope.

'What would you like?' Austen asked her, when they had found a table and were sitting at right angles on an uncomfortably upright padded corner bench. 'A glass of wine? Gin and tonic?'

'A glass of white wine would be lovely, thank you.'

Glancing around the room while Austen went up to the bar, Jane saw that the man sitting by himself at a table with three empty glasses beside him was Angelo Arzano. *Priest and Victim*. The words came into her head without warning. His startling and distinctive good looks were the same as ever, but all at once she saw him, not as the hard and successful man she'd met, but as a victim, alone and defeated.

She averted her gaze quickly in case he looked up, but at that moment he sprang to his feet and hurried out of the door.

'I hope it's not too sweet for you,' Austen said, as he came back with their glasses of wine.

'Actually, I'm happy with anything,' admitted Jane. 'The first drink I ever had was Babycham. I thought it was delicious.'

'And I have to confess I still like eating jelly babies,' said Austen, smiling at her. 'Our dreadful secrets are out in the open.'

'I never finished telling you that day we had tea in the garden,' said Jane, the discussion about drinks suddenly making her think of the champagne she'd missed on the day of Stephen's wedding, 'I'm sure I saw you once in the train from London. You were sitting opposite me reading *Wives and Daughters.*'

'Oh – that,' said Austen, eyeing his drink. He looked guarded, as well he might, Jane reflected, though some men would feel flattered by the idea of a woman noticing such small details as their reading habits.

'I was surprised. Men don't usually like Victorian novels.' Jane realised she was drinking too quickly and speaking almost at random. 'I know your mother loves them.'

'She has a line from literature for every one of life's situations, which could have made for an unbalanced upbringing if she'd limited herself to particular poets or authors. Too much of Kipling, say, could have been wearing.'

'She told me she was made to learn poems by heart as punishments at school,' said Jane. 'Verses from the Bible as well. It must have given her a store of riches and wisdom for later years, words to turn to in both good and bad times – '

Austen jumped up.

'Let me get you another drink.'

Jane sat back. He hadn't liked it when she'd said that about the comfort of poetry in bad times. Perhaps he was afraid she would ask about Verity. Not that she would; he was obviously a man who kept his sorrows to himself, and this was surely something to be applauded. She'd come across too many men who were looking for an endless drip-feed of sympathy. She wondered what colour jelly baby was Austen's favourite.

She tried briefly to invent a daydream of Austen taking her arm as they walked to the church or asking her out for another evening. But she knew it wouldn't happen. Everything about him told her he wasn't a man who ever did ask for things, at least not for himself. He'd been too knocked about, lost too much. Reading between the lines, his father had been difficult and uncommunicative. The brother whom he'd been so close to had died when he was a teenager, and then years later his wife had been killed in horrifying circumstances.

Another man might have found a different way of recovering, by flinging himself into a replacement relationship. Austen evidently hadn't.

Nor was he going to. She must content herself with being a friend of the family. Hadn't Stephen told her she was born to be an aunt? Except that being Stephen, he hadn't remembered she didn't have any nephews or nieces, and as she was an only child she wasn't going to have any in the future either.

So there was no reason why she shouldn't ask Nora

and Ellen – and Austen too – if they'd be interested in coming to see *The Watsons*, due to be released in cinemas next month. Yes, she would drop a postcard through the door suggesting it. Not yet – she'd wait a few days. A casual postcard would be less pushy – and easier for her to ask and him to refuse – than telephoning.

When Jane arrived at the church hall, she saw that her guess as to who would be attending the autumn discussion groups was largely correct. Looking round at the circle of faces, she recognised the usual stalwarts of the church, what one might even call the vicar's groupies.

The hall was chilly and Jane saw her mother's friend Grace sitting huddled in her winter coat. It had a large fur collar, and she had a matching muff on her lap. It couldn't be real fur of course; Grace would be too worried about upsetting people. This looked as though it was pretending to be bear, for it was immensely thick, a rich brown flecked with black. Jane imagined it being worn in some Russian film and Lara's theme tune from an old *Dr Zhivago* film started running through her head as Omar Sharif trudged through endless whiteness.

The vicar was handing round some sheets of notes and apologising for the draughts. 'The heating will soon warm us up,' Jane could hear his genial voice saying as he nobly took off his own coat. Rowena Royce was leaning forward across an elderly deaf man to discuss the flower rota with Winnie Pumfret, whose eyes were darting about eagerly to note new arrivals. Harry stared stolidly in front of him, stirring sugar into the cup of tea on his lap.

Jane sat down on the vacant seat next to Grace,

which she would have expected to be occupied by Mabel. The two women lived in neighbouring flats, with Grace's timidity appearing to encourage Mabel's despotic rule. She noticed her mother enthroned in one of the more comfortable chairs, her lips moving portentously as she read the vicar's notes for the meeting.

'It is so *very* good of the vicar to take all this trouble,' Grace said, stroking her fur muff. 'I do hope he had a *hot* meal before he came out. Though there is this nice tea and coffee.'

'There is always that,' said Jane. 'But an ability to drink tea or coffee at all hours of the day can't still be an essential part of a vicar's role? It must have been trying for clergy in the past if they didn't like either of them or only the rarefied and expensive kinds.'

'That would never be true of *our* vicar,' fluttered Grace, for whom the clergy were a higher class of men to be treated with almost as much reverence as God, 'or even if it was once, he would have fought against it. Such a *lovely* man, so understanding.'

'Was Mabel not able to come this evening?' asked Jane, knowing that Grace was rarely allowed out without her tyrannical neighbour.

'The doctor visited this morning and told her she was on no account to go out,' confided Grace. 'I didn't like to leave her alone, but she insisted I came so that I could tell her about it tomorrow. She likes to know who makes the effort, and I can take the vicar's notes for her to read at home.'

She made a self-deprecating gesture, as if to pre-empt the criticism she was convinced was always coming her way. 'She will understand them much better than I do, even though I'm here and able to hear it all at first hand.'

'You have all the benefit of listening to the vicar in the flesh,' said Jane, relishing the expression, which sounded somehow unsuitable for the occasion. 'I'm sorry to hear Mabel's not well,' she continued, more to convince herself than Grace. It was difficult to dredge up sympathy for Mabel, who had spent her life demanding too much of other people's time and attention.

'She hasn't been in good health for a long time, ever since her husband died. Though I believe she had a very wearisome time with him,' said Grace, who having found her own husband unsatisfactory liked to believe other women belonged to the fellowship of suffering wives.

'She had her troubles, but it's always a blessing to have a man around.' Mary Silcox leaned over, her expression changing to one of doubt as her eyes wandered over the meagre scattering of husbands in the hall.

'Oh, I'm sure we manage quite happily without them,' said Jane, the glasses of wine mixing with a scarcely acknowledged hope inside her.

# EIGHTEEN

Nora picked up the envelope with its Dublin postmark. She stood for a moment in the hall, cluttered with bags of books, anoraks and coats slung over pegs and a collection of umbrellas they hadn't yet managed to lose.

She took the letter into the kitchen and sat down at the table, amid the remains of breakfast, and opened the envelope to take out the sheets of thick cream paper with strong decisive writing in black ink. Not at all the illegible scrawl doctors were popularly supposed to develop from their years of writing prescriptions.

*My very dear Nora,*

*It must be three months since you left Dublin, and during that time I have thought of you and wondered how you are getting on in commuter-belt England. If I know anything of you, you will have made the best of everything. You always did. I feel sure you have set up a happy home with Austen and Ellen.*

*No doubt you will hear soon from other old friends of my news, if you haven't already done so. I don't know why I should assume that my concerns are important enough to set people talking (I'm wondering if you've taken to email now?) and getting them to make that long-delayed phone call, but the old cliché that bad news travels fast is usually true.*

*My wife has left me. There, I've written it down, and every time I do so it gets easier. If I'm honest, I can't say I blame her, nor am I surprised. The other old cliché about doctors' wives dying young is probably true too, only it's not just dying they do these days, it's running off.*

*I suppose I did know in some part of me that Finola wasn't happy. But I was busy. You know how it is. She said I'd neglected her and she must take her chance of happiness while she could, with a man who actually spoke to her like a human being. A sit-com come to life, you might say.*

*I think myself it was the thought of my retirement now only a year away that made her take the plunge at last. For better, for worse, but not for lunch. An old joke with a sting.*

*How much I miss your endless, uncritical friendship. If only you were still here in Dublin! Would you ever come back?*

*Your old friend who admires and misses you more than you can imagine,*

*With love as always, Conor*

The empty house felt absolutely silent. Semolina slept on her cushion as still as a cat in a Flemish old master painting; outside, the early autumn air was muted and soft with dew. Nora put down the letter and gently traced the signature with her finger. She'd received letters from him before – at times of bereavement, thank you notes for suppers, brief news in Christmas cards – but nothing like this. Nothing with this undercurrent of strong feeling repressed, of something that might be more than friendship.

What was Conor saying to her? *With love as always.* Was he hinting that if she was still in Dublin he would 'turn to her' for more than the comfort of an old friend? Had he sensed that unspoken attraction which she'd hidden so carefully; could it be possible he'd felt something of the same for her?

As she read the letter again, her eyes swam and she found herself reaching out for him, as if expecting his solid, quiet comfort to be actually there, as it had been for so many years.

He'd seen her through everything, she'd always thought, the big and the small, during the years of bringing up her two boys, Francis and Austen. When Francis, an epileptic since childhood, died of a fit when he was nineteen, it wasn't her husband Everett who helped her through the grief of losing their eldest son. It was Conor Devlin.

Falling in love with your doctor was such a hackneyed cliché! You're just a silly woman who has read too much of the wrong kind of romantic fiction, she told herself in a fierce inward voice. She tried never to think of him except as their family doctor, a most trusted friend. Conor Devlin was married, had four children.

She was still trying a year later when Everett's drinking caught up with him. He'd developed liver cancer and even he couldn't win that argument. She nursed him with a devotion which afterwards surprised her. The admiring love she'd once felt for him had died a long time before.

Why hadn't she left him? How could she answer this question, seen in the faces of well-meaning friends – and sometimes asked outright? It was easy now, in her sixties, to say she should have done this or that. At the time she'd struggled to make the home as happy and secure a place as she could for their sons; when Francis died she had no choice but to see it through.

For Austen's sake partly, but also for Everett's. He'd never been a man for friends of his own; there were only his colleagues at the university where he lectured in philosophy, and these he only spoke to out of necessity. He had her and Austen – and alcohol.

In sickness and in health! What a huge, terrifying responsibility! Romantic love wasn't enough in the end; you needed more or the human spirit faltered under the demands made upon it. Grace in the form of pity and tenderness might well be given to you on a daily basis, but it wasn't given in advance; there was just enough to feed the day, and no more. Would she have lasted the course without it?

Certainly not in those last few terrible months. He'd been a man of immense intellect and capacity for study, but none of that served him as death approached. As she crept about the bedroom, seeing to his needs, making him as comfortable as she knew how, he would lie inert on the clean sheets still brooding over the great philosophical conundrums which had filled his mind during his life and taken his attention away from his wife and sons.

After Verity's death, she'd seen less of Conor as she no longer lived in the same part of Dublin. But nobody could displace him in her mind as the kindest man she'd ever known. Who else made her feel that she was being listened to and understood so completely? Who talked to her as though he wanted to talk to nobody else just then?

When you'd struggled with a difficult husband, you longed to have your faith in men restored. He was one of those men who women might well turn to in their confusion or unhappiness, and perhaps many women had done so.

It's not a possessive love or one with any end in view, she assured herself. There's no harm or shame in loving someone in secret.

This news about Conor's wife was almost inexplicable. She'd always thought of Finola as one of those women who enjoyed the comfortable position that her husband's career gave her and not so selfish that anybody describing her as a nice woman would be actually lying. How could Finola not have been happy with him?

The late September sun was lighting up the shrubs in the garden. Nora could see the anemones Ellen had planted out. Flowers that made her think of Imogen in their frail, crushed beauty. Beyond them there was the willow where Ellen and her new friend Clover had made a den for Terzo and Sofia whenever they came over, which was almost every day.

When she thought of Terzo, Nora's heart tightened with love. Playing peacefully in the garden with Sofia and Mousie was giving him back the glowing outdoors look that children ought to have … and then there was the music-making with Jane. She breathed a prayer of thankfulness. Terzo was going to get well again.

Her thoughts strayed to Jane, with her clear blue-grey eyes entirely free from self-consciousness and guile. At a time when every other woman coloured her hair, Nora thought Jane's natural brown hair infinitely more appealing.

But it was her expression that made her distinctive; it contained a trusting generosity that also held something of ruefulness. It was as though she was always wanting to say, if only I could make things better for you, I would if I knew how!

'Jane isn't curious but really interested,' Ellen had remarked. 'It's quite a different thing.'

Jane was a darling; Nora knew this when they first met on the day of the flower festival. It must be impossible for any woman to be with Jane for an afternoon and not want her for a daughter-in-law. Men overlooked her – she was the sort of woman they would pass by, not noticing her quality – but Nora thought it inconceivable that Austen could spend time with her and not fall in love. She must go carefully and perhaps opportunities might present themselves, little things that would bring them together.

And Ellen. Nora knew she couldn't leave her. She'd been as a mother to her since Verity's death. Verity's own parents had divorced young, and both were absorbed in second families. They'd never found time to take much notice of Ellen, even when Verity had been alive. There was no absolute love and security for Ellen there.

In the first few years after Verity's death, Austen had been shattered and silent. Now he'd built a wall of reserve around himself. He might be forty years old, but he was still the son she longed to protect and heal.

You couldn't take their suffering away from your family, or bear it for them. In the end they had to walk alone through life, as did every human being. All you could do was to be there; to watch and pray as the hymn put it.

That was what being a mother meant and always had been, since the very beginning. Hadn't the Roman Catholic Church always understood this so much better than the Protestant? No wonder the Hail Mary, the best loved prayer of Catholics all over the world, ended with the plea for the Blessed Virgin to pray for us sinners, now, and at the hour of our death.

One day Austen and Ellen might not need her to be here. She stared out at the bright grass, silvery with dew. The leaves on the beech trees beyond the garden fence were beginning to turn orange and gold. Squirrels were busy on the lawn, gathering acorns that scattered everywhere from the great oak tree on the drive.

*For everything there is a season, under heaven.*

Very slowly she picked up the letter and went upstairs. She wouldn't write back to Conor just yet. She'd give herself the weekend to treasure his words. Then on Monday she'd write to tell him how sorry she was to hear about his wife, putting into her letter all the comfort and friendship she could.

She'd remind him that her life had to be in Sussex, she needed to stay with her son and granddaughter. But that might not be for ever … it would be grand if he could come over to see them … Wharton wasn't a million miles away from Dublin.

As Nora climbed the stairs she found herself thinking that had Finola made this decision a year earlier, before the Wharton job had been heard of, things might have been very different. But then, she reflected wryly, Finola had never had the least sense of timing.

# NINETEEN

Ellen and her new friend Clover had meant to get out of school ahead of the main rush, because Clover was coming to tea with Ellen, and they planned to loiter in the shops on the way home. But then Ellen couldn't find her locker key and by the time they'd hunted for it and discovered it had been in the lining of her jacket all the time, they were trailing out of the school entrance behind everyone else.

'There's that poisonous Year Ten gang,' said Clover, when they reached the newsagents near the bus stop. 'They stare at everyone like they owned the place.'

Ellen spotted Phoebe Gidding among the swarming crowds of girls opening packets of sweets and cans of fizzy drinks. She was laughing at something – or someone. A girl in an outsize anorak came out of the shop empty-handed and walked away by herself. Ellen stared down the road after her.

'She looked like she was crying.'

'I bet those others were bitching at her. They always are, that lot.'

'D'you know her then?'

'I've seen her about. Millie somebody or other. She's always on her own. It'll be because of her weight.

I know what those Year Tens are like. We'd better move. It's not our business anyway.'

It was fun going round the shops trying on clothes with Clover. She was so stunningly pretty and looked so amazing in everything she tried on that Ellen half expected a model agency scout to spring out of nowhere and sign her up on the spot. They spent ages looking round Accessorize, and Clover bought a scarf and a silvery necklace with pink sparkly bits all over it for herself which looked fantastic against her black skin, and a pack of scrunchies made of brightly coloured threads for Ellen.

'For your plait, see? You want to draw attention to your hair.'

Clover was like that; tough on the surface, but always carelessly generous and brushing it away when you thanked her.

When they got home, Nora gave them a tray of goodies to take up to Ellen's room.

'You get brilliant food here,' said Clover, helping herself from a plate of roughly-cut flapjacks and sprawling coconut biscuits decorated with cherries. 'Mum mostly gets in bought stuff. She says she's got more exciting things to do than slaving away in the kitchen.'

'Your mum's cool. I like her a lot,' said Ellen. 'I guess she doesn't have time like Granny does. We're getting a chicken thing later. Actually, it's the same as we had last night when Jane – she's that really nice lady who does piano playing with Terzo next door – came to supper.'

She paused, remembering leaden quiches and cakes that sagged in the middle. If you were being truthful, you had to admit that Granny's cooking was a fairly hit and miss affair, more a matter of luck than following a recipe.

'Things go wrong when Granny's making things for church get-togethers. She says little devils get into the cooking. I asked her what she meant, but she just laughed and said it served her right for trying to impress people.'

'What's wrong with that? You have to impress people all the time, or you don't get noticed.'

'Yes,' conceded Ellen. 'But I suppose it might be different in church. I mean, you shouldn't show off about things you can do, at least I don't think so.'

'Sounds stupid to me,' said Clover. 'I thought we're meant to feel good about ourselves? Mum says if you see something you like you should go out and get it. She does too.' She looked at Ellen. 'Promise you won't tell anyone? Mum's going to move in with Dickless Rickie this weekend. So she says.'

Clover's mum and dad had glamorous jobs in television and advertising. Clover said they were always fancying other people. Her mum had a boyfriend called Rickie whom she'd met when she'd worked for Sky. Clover said she was sick of the way her mum made jokes about that. There was a never-ending list of ways you could make puns about being lifted sky-high.

'It's enough to put me off watching Sky altogether,' grumbled Clover. 'But if it wasn't Rickie it'd be somebody else.'

'They might be worse,' said Ellen, wishing she could think of something better to say. She could see she wasn't being much help.

'Me and Kit call him Dickless. Though he can't be

or Mum wouldn't be moving in with him.' Clover let out a scornful laugh. 'So? Grown-ups are after new kinds of sex all the time, they get bored of having it with the same person. If they can get spicier sex somewhere else they're going to go for it.'

Ellen said nothing. Clover didn't expect to be believed about everything she said; she just liked hearing herself say it.

'It's okay about Mum and Dad splitting up,' Clover had asserted to the other girls at school. 'I get more treats and presents.'

Everyone had nodded. They knew Clover was only kidding herself, and trying to kid them, and knew that she knew this too. But it didn't do any good to say things out loud. That made them real. It was safer to go on pretending.

When she'd first started at the school, Ellen had been wary of Clover. Scared was nearer the mark. She'd thought that Clover – along with some of the other girls – looked down on her because she didn't have all the latest clothes or even any of them. But she'd been wrong. Maybe because she'd been too busy worrying about what Clover was thinking of *her* to see what *she* was really like.

'It's just Mum and Dad shelling out to keep us out of their hair. Then they don't feel guilty about being such crap parents,' she'd said to Ellen.

Hearing this shocked Ellen; it was awful to see your family in that way and for a moment she didn't like Clover as much as she'd thought. But then she guessed Clover minded about her parents underneath and talking like this was her way of dealing with it. That made everything okay.

She remembered this now with a rush of gladness that made her go warm and happy inside. Clover wasn't going to go on pretending. She pushed the plate of flapjacks towards her.

'But what'll happen to you and Kit?'

'During the week we'll be with Dad, and go to Mum's some weekends. Not every weekend though because of Rickie's own kids. He has them sometimes on Sundays, Mum says. I don't see why I should have to share my weekends with *them*.'

'Not much fun for Kit either,' said Ellen. Kit was Clover's younger brother and still at primary school.

'He doesn't care – they're nearer in age and play computer games all the time so they don't have to say anything.'

'Will you mind terribly having to go there?' Ellen asked cautiously, not wanting to provoke Clover into thinking she pitied her.

'They fuck you up, your mum and dad.' Clover shrugged, pulled out her new scarf and looked with satisfaction at her reflection in the mirror. 'Oh, don't make a teacher face, it's from a poem. I should have thought you might have known that, the way your granny's always reciting things.'

'How does the rest of it go?'

'I only remember that bit,' admitted Clover. 'I got it off a boy I used to know. Self-obsessed parents messing everything up. We've got a right to our own lives, haven't we? Oh God, I forgot about your mum. Sorry, Ellen, that was out of order.'

'It's all right.'

'Actually, it's not all pants. Mum's promised she'll take me with her next time she goes to her beauty and grooming place in London. Why don't you come too? They might be able to do stuff for your cheek.'

'I don't mind about it that much.'

'Yeah. Makes you look different. You could see it as an asset to play up to. Gives you attitude. Anyway, Mum says even though she's moving in with Rickie she loves me and Kit more than anyone else in the world.' Clover looked challengingly into Ellen's face.

'Of course she does.' But even though Ellen made her voice as convincing as she could, she didn't really believe this. If Clover's mum really did love her and Kit more than anyone else, then why was she going off with Rickie? It didn't make sense. If children were everything to their mothers, then why did so many mothers want something more? Some mothers even went off with the husbands of their friends. It was incredible anyone could do that sort of thing to a friend, just because of sex. Was sex really so totally overpowering you couldn't help yourself? Was having it with the person you wanted to have it with so important you stopped minding about making other people unhappy?

It wasn't just mothers of course who did these inexplicable things. Fathers did them just as much, maybe even more. Not her own father; he was different. He'd loved her mother too much. He still did.

'Who's this Jane that came to supper? She after your dad?'

'Of course not. She's Granny's friend, not Dad's.'

'So? That wouldn't stop her. Not that she's likely to get him, if she's that big-bummed one you said hi to in the street the other day and then gassed on for hours. A bit nutty, like your granny isn't she? In an okay way,

I mean,' Clover added. 'Talking about books and stuff and wearing uncool clothes.'

Why hadn't she thought of this before? That Dad might want Jane just like Rickie wanted Clover's mum. Jane was fat and comfortable, not someone who wanted a boyfriend. And Dad wasn't like Rickie. Not at *all* like Rickie, Ellen told herself fiercely.

'Dad never wanted anyone else after Mummy died. He would *never* think of Jane in – in the way you said.'

Clover was giving her the withering look she'd practised until she'd got it pretty near perfect.

'Come *on!* What did I just say about grown-ups wanting sex all the time? Mind you, I suppose if he did fancy her moving in, he wouldn't want your granny around any more. He'd have to boot her out. Pack her off to Ireland.'

A sick feeling started inside Ellen.

'He wouldn't. Granny's always lived with us. Since … you don't think that could actually happen?'

'Yeah, I can see it'd be harsh on you. Your granny's like your mum really, isn't she?'

'Even if you're right, and you aren't, you absolutely aren't, Jane'd be fine with Granny being here.'

'Dream on. What woman's going to put up with their partner's mum nosing in on them? Your dad wouldn't have any say in it. Sounds to me he doesn't have much say in anything anyway.'

'I could tell Dad I don't like her,' Ellen said suddenly. 'Just in case.'

'Waste of breath. You said you did like her – and you're the world's worst at porkies.'

'Not if she hurts Granny – or Dad.'

'Keep your knickers on. Jane looks the sort you can

get rid of, no problem. There's better ways to do it than having it out with your dad. I'll show you.'

There was a silence during which Ellen wished that Clover wasn't there, because she had too many new and alarming things to think about. But she would have to do that later, when she was lying in bed before going to sleep so she might just as well listen to Clover now. Clover knew about things, didn't she?

'I wish Phoebe Gidding didn't live here,' she said at last, going over to the window. In the fading light the leaves of the ginkgo tree were a mysterious opaque green.

Clover lolled on the bed and stretched out her legs to admire their shape.

'Isn't it worth putting up with Phoebe for the sake of having Teddy? Isn't he your boyfriend?'

Ellen could feel her face going red.

'Don't be silly.'

'He texted you at the disco, didn't he? So you're going out with him. As good as.'

Ellen busied herself with drawing the curtains. Teddy couldn't be her boyfriend. She wasn't that stupid. He was just nice to her, like he'd be nice to anyone. But even as she was thinking this, she knew part of her was pleased that Clover was looking at her with new respect. She also knew that although she hadn't thought of Teddy as her boyfriend – or only in a don't-be-stupid-it-isn't-going-to-happen kind of way – Clover putting it like this was *making* her think differently about him.

'Has a boy ever tried it on with you?' asked Clover, swivelling her legs off the bed.

Ellen stiffened. Your first kiss from a boy should

be a beautiful romantic experience. Hers was a creepy, nasty secret.

It had been when she was seven, running down their street, on the way home from the corner shop. She remembered the cold terror when the tall, stringy figure stopped her. He'd caught hold of her and said, 'give us a kiss then, go on, just one kiss.' She'd been so scared she'd done it, shivery and disgusted at his weasel's face pressed up against hers.

Glen Tollerton, he was called. He was one of the gang leaders of the teenagers who hung around the shopping centre and the play area in the park, bored and aimless, bullying small children and sneering at old ladies. She'd kissed him on the cheek, and then he'd put his tongue into her mouth. It was wet and disgusting, like a slimy slug wriggling into her. After that he'd let her go and she'd raced home, and torn up to the bathroom to wash out her mouth again and again.

She'd never told Granny. She wasn't sure why. It might have been something to do with her being a grown-up, and somehow you didn't tell that sort of thing to grown-ups, even ones like Granny. Granny would have minded dreadfully for her; she had to save Granny from feeling like that. But for ages after, she'd gone on feeling dirty …

It was funny, but she suddenly found she quite wanted to tell Clover about it. She could see Clover would know just how scary and gross it had been, and how it was she'd never told anyone, even though it wasn't such a big deal really when you thought about it now. Telling people about what got to you was part of being a friend, and even though the way Clover dealt with things sometimes surprised Ellen, she could be relied on to understand what Ellen had felt about the Glen Tollerton business.

She could still picture Glen quite clearly, his white pimply face looming over her, and those staring pale blue eyes. He must have been about sixteen then. The same age Teddy was now. No, she wouldn't say anything about Glen to Clover. She didn't want him taking up space in her mind, and never, ever would she allow herself to think of him in connection with Teddy. She frowned at the pattern of William Morris lilies on the curtains. Even remembering about him for a minute spoiled everything.

'Forget it,' said Clover, who never minded when Ellen clammed up and who was beginning to look bored. She flicked open her phone. 'Here, have you heard this song? Did I tell you I got their autographs when I was in London? Shall we decide which of them we'd most like to snog?'

# TWENTY

'Do you know why Jane hasn't come?' demanded Ellen, craning her neck round at the congregation on the first Sunday in October.

Nora was staring at a pomegranate among the glistening piles of grapes, confused images of the horned god Pan with his pipes swirling about in her mind and becoming mixed with the cries of Persephone being snatched away from her mother. Then she remembered that she was not in Ancient Greece but in a Victorian church and these were modern children playing their part in the annual harvest service.

'I expect she went to the early morning communion service.'

'The same as Dad,' said Ellen. 'I wonder why. Thank goodness he didn't invite her back to our house for breakfast afterwards.'

Nora turned to look at her granddaughter's face.

'Would you have liked him to?'

'Absolutely not. We don't want her bothering us all the time. She's not family.'

Terzo was sitting dreamily between them, apparently lost in his own interior world, but now he touched Ellen's arm, his face an anxious question.

Ellen flushed and said quickly, 'I don't mean you. I'm really glad you're here and that you're coming to lunch.'

Nora didn't pursue it. There was something in Ellen's manner which worried her. Then there had been that strange overheard conversation earlier in the week. She'd been upstairs ironing and listening to the radio when the telephone rang. Ellen must have picked it up because after a minute Nora could hear her saying, 'He's not back from work yet. After that he's taking his new girlfriend out to dinner. Shall I tell him you rang? No? Goodbye then.'

'Who was that?'

'Someone trying to sell something,' Ellen called from downstairs. 'Nothing important.'

'Oh dear, we ought to have brought something for the two of you to take up,' Nora said now, watching a small boy dumping an overgrown marrow, so distended that it must be inedible, on the altar steps. She peered at the pile of offerings which were destined for the town's drop-in centre for street sleepers. An abundance of baked beans. Well, tins and packets might be more practical than fruit and vegetables which needed to be prepared and eaten right away. Nora, who had spent the previous evening peeling and coring windfalls kindly given to her by Rowena Royce, and whose fingers still stung, could not but sympathise. Naturally, she was thankful for the picture-book beauty of apples on trees, and there was nothing like home cooking, but there were times when she felt equally grateful to Marks and Spencer's food department.

Nora had asked Imogen if Terzo could come with Ellen to the service. The more he ventured out of his home in small excursions without his mother, the better he would be able to face school when he started going. It would also give Imogen a peaceful morning with just Sofia – since Angelo was once again away on some unexplained business – before they all had lunch together in the lodge.

'Such a sweet sight, the children taking up their gifts,' whispered Winnie Pumfret from the pew behind Nora, as they stood up to sing the first hymn *All good gifts around us.*

'It is that,' Nora agreed, but her thoughts had strayed to Conor's letter. She'd read and re-read it. She was no longer at the age when love letters were carried around in pockets or placed under pillows, but she could see every line in her mind's eye. Conor. Years of loving him. The old, old ache because she couldn't have him. *Accept the gifts we offer for all thy love imparts, and, what thou most desirest, our humble, thankful hearts.* Not having Conor – was that one of the gifts she must always be offering?

A bird-like woman with a thin neck and sharp, jutting chin read the lesson from the Old Testament, announcing the chapter and verse almost disbelievingly as if it could not possibly be the right choice and she wanted to disassociate herself from it. *The people are to go out each day and gather enough for that day* she read, finishing on a triumphant note as if she'd laid an egg.

'She's like a stressy hen,' Ellen whispered.

'You're right there, one of that breed whose name I can't remember, the kind we saw in the bird sanctuary place we went to,' Nora agreed, in too loud a voice.

'Let's decide who else here looks like a bird or an animal or a fish,' said Ellen to Terzo, making him laugh.

At the announcement of the next hymn Ellen made an agonised face.

142

'I hate this one, it's got that awful vengeful *and thine angels charge at last in the fire the tares to cast.* Don't sing it, Granny, will you.'

As the vicar began his sermon, Nora straightened her back against the unyielding wood of the pew and tried to concentrate. The story of the virtuous workers in the vineyard grumbling when everyone got paid the same turned everything upside down and in a way that Nora approved of. Sitting at the back of the church there would be Ben, the gentle giant who lived in a local hostel for adults with learning difficulties, and was probably even now eyeing the basket of crusty cheese scones and currant buns that Winnie Pumfret had baked for coffee-time in the hall after the service. She always made extra, especially for Ben. There was the anxious, fussy goodness of Grace Whipple, majestic Dorothy Finstock in her tweed coat, even the woman who looked like a hen. God's grace given simply because he wants to give, falling on everyone, not because they've earned it.

Soft walls and ever-open doors. The phrase from some long-ago sermon came back to her. This was how a church should be, perhaps even, in a very imperfect fashion, the way this one was. Her jumbled thoughts swooped all at once, synchronised like a murmuration of starlings. Wasn't it about accepting God's generosity for everyone, herself included?

Terzo, watchful and intent, was leaning against Ellen, her arm around his thin shoulders. She must have misunderstood what Ellen had said on the telephone. And Conor – he would always be there for her to love, even though she couldn't be with him.

As the vicar and the choir processed down the

aisle during the final hymn, she began to think of the chicken now roasting in the oven for lunch, and to choose which vegetables they would have with it. She and Ellen could make a crumble topping for some of those apples, a suitable autumn pudding using the fruits of the earth. These were more fitting thoughts on which to end a Harvest Festival.

# TWENTY-ONE

Teddy hadn't minded moving out of London in the way Phoebe had, but he was surprised to find how much he liked his new school.

It being a posh private school wasn't great; he'd had to keep it from his mates at his comprehensive, and he'd worried he would stick out at Wharton or not find anyone there he liked – or who liked him.

But after a few weeks he found that schools – and people – were pretty much alike under the surface trappings. Okay, there weren't any girls at Wharton, but the boys listened to the same music, drank the same brands of beer, watched the same films. When he'd tried to explain this to some of the other boys in his year, they didn't know what he was on about. Why did he have this idea they'd like be from an alien planet because they were at a private school?

There were some arrogant bastards who went around making life hell for anyone who caught their eye, but that mostly happened lower down the school. Teddy was thankful he was in the sixth form where bullying rarely got physical. There might be verbal abuse from a handful of shits who thought they were God's gift and above the law, but he knew how to keep his head down. They'd left him alone so far.

Nor did it add up either about public schools being exclusive clubs for the upper classes. Or at least this one wasn't. There were stacks of boys there on scholarships, and although Teddy guessed that many of these came from homes where they could afford to cough up the full fees, some of them were from housing estates with parents earning peanuts. One of the very brightest boys was black from a one-parent family, and he was more popular than anyone else in his year. Teddy had to admit the charges of snobbery and divisiveness within private schools didn't wholly add up.

The guy who did know what he meant was Oliver Benson. He'd arrived the year before, but was having to repeat the lower sixth, having, as he said, cocked things up. He'd been at a state school before that, so he understood what was different and what – unexpectedly – wasn't. Other people's crackpot perceptions and prejudices are their concern, he said, with the look of knowing his own mind that Teddy wished he had himself. Ollie had a way of laughing at just about everything. He was able to hold his own with everybody and anybody. He was cool.

Another thing Teddy liked about Wharton was that there were so many boys from abroad. Loads of Chinese. They jabbered away to each other and got takeaways to share in the evenings, and were all brilliantly clever, as well as playing the piano and violin like musical prodigies. Teddy wasn't sure if he was going to get on with them, but now he was learning a few expressions in Chinese just for fun, and one boy was teaching him how to play the mouth organ. He'd promised to bring him back a special one from

Shanghai after the holidays. Then there were boys from Africa, India and Pakistan, and other countries all over the world that he'd known hardly anything about until now. Some of the boys thought nothing of speaking three or four languages; Teddy felt they were a whole lot more clued up about the world and even the UK than he was.

Here at Wharton there were teachers who talked to you like equals. Even though some of them were off-the-planet weird, used extreme language, or threw your crap essay at you, they were never boring and faceless. You felt you were alive when you were with them, and occasionally the stuff you were studying took on some life too, rather than just something you had to churn out in an exam. Teddy supposed teachers in private schools were allowed to be eccentric or even borderline cracked, and looking at it all round he thought it was a good thing.

He could see Jonah was pleased with Wharton. No surprises there; he'd liked their London school too. Jonah kind of bounced along in life. It was funny this way he had of getting the best from whatever he was doing or wherever he was. He got on with everyone, not just at school but at home. Mum was never on his back the way she was with him and Phoebe.

Mum was always moving on somehow, not just other people but herself as well. Like you weren't quite what she wanted you to be, or weren't becoming it fast enough. Maybe she wasn't like that with Jonah because he always *was* what she wanted him to be.

And Dad, well, he was always too tired to bounce anywhere. He didn't pick you up on stuff like Mum, but he snapped at nothing sometimes, and he didn't always answer you when you asked him a question. He just went on staring into space thinking about work, which was the be-all-and-end-all to him these days. He didn't look as though he enjoyed anything any more, which wasn't like he used to be, back in London. He'd got tired then, but he'd looked happy, and he was cool in his own way; he'd joshed around and joined in when they all argued at mealtimes.

Mum said that commuting was bound to be grim until you got used to it, but Teddy thought it wasn't just the commuting. Dad had always worked long hours when they lived in London. He was like that; he had to wear himself out. No, it was something else.

Even admitting this to himself made him feel uncomfortable. Teddy didn't really want to think about it because, when he did, he found himself worrying it was something to do with Mum (or the way Dad felt about Mum) that was making Dad look like he was holding on, but only just.

Parents shouldn't load their problems onto their children. They ought to be able to sort things out themselves; that was what being grown up was meant to be about. In London he'd had friends from broken homes who'd been dragged into rows, made to take sides. His best mate had told him how his parents would get at each other through him, slipping in snide comments, or asking questions about what he'd been doing with the other parent, like it was a sort of competition. Then his dad's new partner had tried to turn him against his own mother. As if having taken his dad away wasn't enough, she had to take him too.

It was sick that people who once loved each other could stick knives into each other like this. The idea that his own parents … Teddy turned over another page of *The Aeneid*. All around him in the school library boys were silently getting on with their work. You could go on day after day living your life and nobody, not your friends, not your teachers, not even your family knew what was going on in your head.

He needed to talk to someone. There hadn't been anyone special he'd talked to at his school in London, though there were teachers who you felt were on your side and would have done their best. There was the school counsellor, but she talked at assemblies in crap textbook language, as though all teenagers were a predictable species she'd studied. When people tried too hard it was a turn-off.

Here at Wharton there was the school chaplain – Teddy liked the look of him. Mum hadn't. She had a thing against God-botherers.

Ollie said Martin Darrow was a legend and that it was shite he was leaving at the end of term. Ollie hadn't explained further. Teddy thought he could guess the reason for that.

So there was nobody who he could ask about Ollie. Ollie, who was beginning to disturb him in a way he didn't understand – and which threatened to change his whole life.

# TWENTY-TWO

The invitation to a party at the home of Stephen and Beth came at a bad time.

Jane, opening an envelope addressed in girly handwriting, presumably Beth's, glanced at the printed invitation card. Drinks and eats from 8pm at their house in the smart end of Fulham, with an email address for replies. At the top was a scrawled message written by Stephen: *Time you came out of hiding in Sussex – plenty of room to stay the night if you need to!*

This was friendly enough. It was also exactly like him. He probably hadn't noticed she'd missed the wedding reception, but he always knew how to say the gracious word. She guessed that the party was being organised by Beth to show off their new home and wedding presents, with various rejected girlfriends included among the mass of friends invited because this was less trouble than having them to dinner.

She ought to go. She'd turned her back on her London friends for too long, and one thing might lead to another. She could hear her mother saying it.

But just at the moment she felt too despondent to want to be led anywhere – especially not among a collection of happily married couples and the inevitable sprinkling of single women and non-marrying men.

Wharton drinks parties, chats with mothers of pupils and church teas didn't constitute a very satisfying social life. A date with Trevor Faversham, the head of the art department at Wharton, had been a fiasco never to be repeated. The nights were closing in, and so were her horizons. Even her mother was out at her evening class expanding her horizons as she liked to put it, learning about the Bloomsbury group.

She'd seen Austen quite often because Nora was always asking her to drop in for tea after she'd been with Terzo, and that turned out to be a day when Austen finished teaching early. He was usually at home and he always *looked* pleased to see her. That must mean something; she didn't think he was the kind of man given to social pretence. They'd become friends ...

But he hadn't made the effort to see her *by herself* – not since their drink in the pub. That was what counted. And even Nora's kindness didn't make up for Ellen's chilling politeness.

Worst of all was reliving a phone conversation just before the Harvest Festival weekend at the beginning of October. She'd telephoned Austen, a spur-of-the-moment thing, to ask if he'd come with her to Mozart's *Requiem Mass* being performed in the school chapel on the Sunday.

She hadn't been able to speak to him. Ellen had answered the call, sounding quite unlike her usual self, cutting her off as though she'd never met her in her life while at the same time taking care to inform her that Austen had a new girlfriend.

A new girlfriend. Well, of course he would have. Had there been many others? She remembered Austen watching Imogen in the garden, his expression inscrutable.

In the pub she'd thought she was seeing the real man emerging from a careful camouflage of colourlessness and anonymity. How could the man who'd sat with her and confided that he liked jelly babies be the same person as the one who hadn't returned her phone call?

Had Ellen told him she'd called?

Another woman would ignore being snubbed by the daughter of the man she was attracted to. Jane knew she wasn't, and could never be, that other woman. She hadn't telephoned again.

Something had happened to make Ellen hostile like this. She was such a darling. The soreness inside Jane became more painful as she prodded about for explanations, growing cross with herself. It shouldn't hurt like this. It wasn't as if Austen had ever said anything to her that he might not have said to any friendly female neighbour.

He'd come to hear the Requiem, though. She'd seen him across the nave, head bent, his face in shadow, apparently lost in the devastating emotion of the music. *Kyrie Eleison.* He'd have been thinking of Verity.

Sitting down at her laptop she tried to summon up the enthusiasm to write a grateful acceptance to Stephen and Beth's invitation.

The ringing of the telephone rescued her as she'd finished her struggles and clicked send.

'Jane?'

It was Austen. He sounded even more diffident than he did face to face. She smiled, all at once happy again. Austen calling her was like a pat on the back for doing what Dorothy would call her social duty. People like Beth would say God was rewarding her.

'Are you busy on the sixth of December?'

Surprise kept her silent for a second. He'd never responded to the postcard she'd dropped through the door about going to see *The Watsons* and now he was asking her about a day ages away. It sounded horridly familiar. She glanced at the invitation card lying beside her laptop. Yes, it *would* be. Not a reward from God after all.

'I'm going to a party in London in the evening.'

'Oh, I'm sorry.'

'I've only just accepted the invitation – ' She let the sentence hang, though without any real hope he would press her.

'I've some tickets for the new Alan Bennett play. I was hoping you'd come.'

She'd been brought up to stick to a first engagement even when a better one came along. Not for the first time Jane wished she hadn't.

'I'd loved to have done. If only you'd rung five minutes earlier. Was it very difficult to get tickets? I read they sold out for the first season within days.'

'I must have been lucky. Another time then.'

He didn't sound disappointed enough.

'Another time would be lovely,' she repeated drearily. 'Thank you for asking me.'

There was a pause during which both of them seemed to have retreated into distant acquaintances.

'I was sorry about *The Watsons*,' she blurted out, before he could ring off.

'*The Watsons*? The film, you mean? Did you see it and not like it? I believe my mother took Ellen.'

So he had forgotten her postcard.

# TWENTY-THREE

Imogen sat half-heartedly doing a few stitches in her tapestry, not listening to a television documentary about the rise and fall of politicians, which she'd put on because she was learning to be ashamed of the ignorance which hadn't mattered before her marriage.

Imogen had never been interested in politics and cared even less. But she hoped that one ex-prime minister in particular would fall into disgrace because that might stop Angelo's outbursts of rage whenever his name came up. What use was a man who contributed to the destruction of peace in your household?

But of course this was only one of many surface angry streams which overflowed and spread over their joint lives. The real issues lay deep, deeper than these things that Angelo talked about with so much passion.

The front door slammed and Angelo stalked into the sitting room. For a few moments he stood glowering.

'What are you watching this for? That man was deeply dishonest while he was in power, obsessed with what he fondly imagines is his place in history. A power-mad bastard with delusions of being God, and the great British public didn't see it.'

Imogen continued to push her tapestry needle into

the footstool cover she was making. The design showed her mother's favourite type of old-fashioned tea roses, pink and cream amid green and bronze leaves. She'd begun it in the summer as something to occupy her in the evenings, which were so often spent alone. It was beginning to feel like a child's comfort blanket.

'He got away with his lies then and he's still lying through his teeth today. We're left with his legacy – a worse-than-ever mess in the Middle East and a people who can't believe anything they're told by the men who govern them.'

'Is it truly as bad as that?'

Imogen knew she sounded feeble but she never argued with Angelo when he talked about politics, and especially not when he began lashing himself into anger. He knew so much more than she did, was so much cleverer than she would ever be. He was her husband; she thought as he did. She just wished he could think it more quietly. Especially when – but she would never admit it – he'd been drinking. She could smell it from where she was sitting.

'It's a hell of a sight worse, because nobody can be bothered to grasp the real implications of what's happening. People will believe anything if they're told it in a certain way.'

He was looking at her as if he wanted to strike her. His face, which had once looked at her with love, almost with worship, was swamped with anger – and something more which she couldn't define.

'The country lies down and accepts the loss of its liberties. When did Europe last do that, do you know? A waste of a question. Barbara Cartland didn't write about fascists and Nazis.'

'Of course I know about things like that,' she said, stung by his tone. 'I do think about them. Mummy and some of her friends went on one of those marches in London.'

'Quite.'

'They disagreed with the government.' Imogen spoke in a low voice, trying to remember what the march had been about. 'You know they did.'

She struggled to hold back tears. Why did he have to speak of her parents with that dismissive contempt? Was it to punish her? All at once she felt very tired. Tired of never getting it right. Tired, some dim perception was beginning to tell her, of being the wrong person.

Angelo snatched up the remote control and switched off the television.

'I'm not going to your parents' tomorrow. I can't do it.'

'But it's all planned. We fixed it up for this weekend ages ago. We can't just let them down. Mummy and Daddy are looking forward to seeing the children, they'll have prepared lots of things already. You know what Mummy's like.'

'I know exactly what she's like. I said I'm not going. You go with the children. I'm going to London for a few days. Or longer.'

'Angelo, if only you would try … if you would wait until – '

'I can't go on waiting. And as for trying – for God's sake, there are things that are past it.'

He took a quick step away from her towards the door. A bluebottle thrashed with frantic and futile whirring against the curtain.

'What will I say to them?'

'Whatever you like. Make up some excuse. Or try the truth for a change: I can't stand going there and being part of their Home Counties complacency.'

'You didn't always say that.'

'Didn't I? Perhaps you hadn't learnt then how good I am at lying.'

There was a jeering note in his voice, as if he wanted to hurt her. Suddenly she couldn't bear it any more.

'If that's what you want to do, you'd better get on with it.'

He stared down at her wordlessly. The incessant buzzing of the bluebottle was sending waves of pain through her head. She saw again the sharp shift of mood that had been so much part of him since they had come back to England. An angry restlessness punctuated by outbursts of savagery turning abruptly into a swollen silence. Then there might come the bleak kindness which frightened her worst of all.

'Do you think I'm ever free of it?' he said at last, speaking more gently. 'Can't you see what it's like going to your parents' home and reading the expression in their eyes?'

She couldn't speak. Toby, always Toby. The grief would kill them both.

'I'll call you from London,' he said, not looking at her. 'Tell the children something, that I have to go and work, anything. Just let me go, can't you?'

She didn't cry, not even when, some twenty minutes later, she heard the front door close. She sat absolutely still. This couldn't be happening to her, to Imogen Arzano. He's gone, she told herself, holding the tapestry in numbed hands that no longer belonged to her. Her mind shied away from his words, lingering in the wounded room.

She stared down at the familiar design, traditional and predictable. Some of the roses were nearly finished; they were coming along well. If she made more effort she might complete the whole thing by Christmas. Her mother would be pleased with it. *Darling, you have worked hard! When you were little you always sulked when I did sewing with you!*

She was twenty-six and she had two children living. She'd made a mess of her marriage. Thousands of women did the same, but Imogen didn't want to think of them just now. They couldn't help.

Vaguely she registered that the bluebottle had fallen silent, was perhaps now lying dead on the carpet. From his bed in the kitchen she could hear Mousie whimpering in his sleep. The roses dissolved into a blur of pink and green.

She wiped her sleeve across her eyes just as she'd done when she was a child. Tomorrow she would pack the car and drive down to her parents' house. What else was there to do?

*

Walking swiftly through the night streets to the station, carrying a bag of clothes and his laptop, Angelo breathed in the smoky autumn air. Faint traceries of cloud swirled over the oyster moon.

Wait, she'd said.

He *had* waited.

Waited for Terzo to recover his memories of that

day and tell her about the crash, about Paola, what Paola had done.

Waited for her to grow up.

She didn't know what she was asking of him. If she'd known how close he was to – he swerved abruptly, disoriented by the unreasoning fury still gripping his body.

'London, please,' he said to the man in the ticket office.

'A return ticket?'

The man's hand lay poised over the machine. For a second Angelo felt himself hesitate. Then he spoke in a voice that did not seem to be his own, but was firm and steady.

'No. Single.'

As he pushed the ticket into his pocket and walked on to the platform to wait for the London train, the beginnings of release pulsed slowly through his body. He was alone. This was how he wanted to be. How he had to be.

# TWENTY-FOUR

Kate hadn't yet fixed herself up with a job. As she sat on the train to London in late October, she decided it was unreasonable – though Philip, to do him justice, had said nothing – to start working so soon.

The move to Wharton had been a big emotional upheaval, much more than she'd expected. Getting the new house straight ate up her time. So many things from their old house didn't fit; she spent days altering curtains, rearranging furniture, buying extra things they needed.

There had been all the school stuff for the children too. Private schools took it as read you were happy to shell out for vast quantities of uniform and sports equipment, and even Phoebe's new uniform at her comprehensive had been expensive enough. The amount of money they were getting through was staggering. Kate reminded herself and Philip – who had spent even longer than usual poring over the last bank statement – that most of it was a one-off and wouldn't be repeated. It just added up to a lot because it was all coming at once.

Today she was going to look at a leading musical instrument shop, to check out clarinets. Jonah needed a better one. She might order it. But that wouldn't take her all day. She would have almost a couple of hours to spare before she needed to get the train to come home.

She reached into her bag and felt the pad of paper. No more writing it all down, it doesn't help for long enough, nothing does. If I could see him … No, not that. To be somewhere near, that would be enough …

I will plan what to give the children for Christmas, she tried telling herself, to distract her mind from where it was going. But that brought her back to Philip again. Phoebe's fifteenth birthday had caused enough hassle with her wanting the latest iPad and Philip, normally so persuadable where the children were concerned, saying it ought to be a joint birthday and Christmas present.

'It isn't good for anyone to have everything they want. It might actually make them less happy.'

'It's not like you to come up with philosophical claptrap like that. I suppose you read it in *The Guardian*?'

'Look at it another way then. By Christmas there'll be some new and infinitely superior version launched which will make the current model instantly obsolete and worthless.'

So Kate had bought Phoebe a stack of bits and pieces instead; make-up, a belt with a huge jewelled clasp, designer jeans, a camisole, a mock-suede embroidered jacket. When you added all that up it didn't come to much less than the wretched iPad.

The business with the iPad had made Phoebe sulk briefly, but she'd looked pleased enough with the other presents. She hadn't wanted a party at home, but instead had gone out with a group of friends to the pizza place in the High Street. Philip had been disappointed, but Phoebe was like all other teenagers and wanted to have her own life. She'd been quick to make new friends and judging by some mid-term tests she'd brought back yesterday was doing well at school. So much for Philip fussing that it was invidious to send the boys to a fee-paying school and Phoebe to a comprehensive, however high it scored in the league tables.

Happiness – or what passed for it – could be bought, couldn't it?

It had been wrong to come. Kate knew that, as soon as she turned out of Bond Street. She hesitated at the corner. She couldn't pretend even to herself she was doing a little shopping in the area. Women like her didn't shop in these exclusive establishments; they went to John Lewis in Oxford Street. So why was she here, loitering on the pavement, her shopping bag and the new clarinet in its case hanging heavily and expensively on her arm, her heart beating faster than it should?

Because I have to test myself. I shall make myself walk past the gallery.

She began to walk slowly down the street.

There was a different gold plate on the door. Kate stared at it blankly. It looked as if it had been there some time. *Deakin and Worth*, she read. She'd never heard of them, whoever they were. There must be some mistake. She stood looking dumbly at the engraved inscription. She hadn't been here for seventeen years. Not since the day he'd told her they had no future together.

'You don't know me.'

He'd said it to her, staring not into her eyes, as he did when they made love, but at something else only he could see. He held her against him, keeping a space between them.

'I know you've wondered. Tried not to believe it.'

*He's gay, He's gay, He's gay.* The words went round and round in her head, making no sense. Had she wondered? Only in tiny, terrified moments. She knew too much about avoiding unwanted thoughts that landed in your head.

'I can't go on pretending to myself – and you. I love you – Oh God, Kate, it's not in the way I need to love –'

*I love you, I love you, I love you.*

'I've cheated you,' he said. 'I've used you. I'm no good to you. Go back to your husband. For God's sake, for your own sake, for my sake, keep away from me.'

She walked away from him then and never saw him again. Not even when, some weeks later, she found she was pregnant, and realised that in the madness of her obsessive affair with Laurent she'd missed taking her pill. She'd disappointed Philip by not wanting children yet, but if this was Laurent's baby it would be all she would ever have of him.

She'd married Philip because his straightforward, disciplined character made her feel safe. He came from a Yorkshire background which seemed to her then to be honest and worthwhile; hard-working, unpretentious people who lived quietly within their means and put money by for their summer holiday in the Jersey hotel where they went every year. His sister Elizabeth, who was already married and lived in a neighbouring road in Ripon, came from the same mould.

Kate's own parents weren't solid; they were paper-thin, like stereotypes on reality television. They'd taken themselves off to the hot sun and pleasures of Spain, to fritter away their lives playing bridge, drinking and bickering. There they remained, and Kate had ceased to expect anything from them. They had always avoided anything disagreeable or facing up to upsetting facts and they weren't going to change now.

'A perfect little boy.'

The midwife gave her the baby. Kate lay exhausted after her labour, looking dazedly at the tiny being lying on her breast.

'My beautiful and wonderful wife – ' Philip bent over to kiss her.

Kate didn't speak. Tears trickled down her face.

'Darling, you've been so brave. I can never tell you enough how proud I am and how happy.'

I'll never know if my child is Philip's or Laurent's. This is my punishment. I married Philip without loving him as he deserved to be loved. And within months I gave my soul to someone else. I must give Philip more children.

Phoebe was born a year and half later, and then, after much the same gap, Jonah. All three children, as they grew up, looked as though they belonged together. Teddy even had Philip's fair hair. Only someone who remembered Laurent's expressive almond-shaped eyes might have wondered.

But they never would, because she'd taken care to cut herself right off from his world. The gallery off Bond Street, the little mews house in Chelsea, the Sicilian restaurant where they'd eaten. She had to keep to her rules because if she didn't then Teddy would grow to look like Laurent, she would come back to the house and find that his fair hair had become dark.

She was fenced in, safe from other people – as safe as she knew how, from herself. Writing – word after word, letters, lists. Secret rituals of reassurance which nobody would ever find out about.

They said affairs always ended in tears. But they *ended*. People moved on, whatever that stupid expression meant.

She hadn't. She couldn't.

Was it because Laurent was so different from anybody else she'd ever met, and would ever meet, so much more vivid and bright? No, it was something in her which could not let go, could not change.

'You're making progress,' said the psychiatrist. He'd put on his satisfied all-knowing expression; another successful case on his books.

She swung round, and walked with frightened steps back towards Charing Cross and her train. She'd got the clarinet, hadn't she? She wouldn't think about anything else, not until she could get home and check that everything was safe, that nothing had happened to Teddy.

The carriage was only half-full, Kate noticed with relief, as she stepped onto the train just as it was due to leave. A girl with white-gold hair and dressed in a green jacket walked down the aisle and sat down opposite her.

There was a rash of this particular shade in the shops this autumn. It went well with the girl's smooth creamy skin and pale pink lips. She had a face that made you want to go on looking ... and it held an odd expression.

The girl was studying her. Not even covertly either, in the way women did as a matter of course, but almost insolently, assessing each detail. Kate averted her eyes, mentally veiling herself from the scrutiny, unsettled and annoyed. She pulled out a paperback novel from her handbag.

She needed to finish reading it so she'd be able to contribute to the book group discussion tonight. Not that half the other women bothered to get through the chosen book. For them it was window-dressing, an excuse for getting together. The discussion invariably got sidetracked into people's personal lives. Sometimes – when the book chosen was fantasy or sci-fi, both of which Kate despised – this was more interesting. Since most of the other members had sons at Wharton, it was also a convenient way of keeping up with what was going on in the school.

She read several pages before it seeped across her mind she'd seen this girl before, more than once. Hadn't it been near their house? An image of green slid across the surface of her memory and then disappeared. Maybe she lived in one of the neighbouring roads. She'd be able to find out if they walked the same way home.

But when the train stopped at Wharton the girl didn't get out. Kate hurried out of the station, deciding she must have been mistaken.

# TWENTY-FIVE

It was nearly December, and the trees in the New Forest were already stripped bare, their dark branches and tracery of twigs etched against dying autumn skies. Only a scattering of oak leaves clung on, shrivelled and brown, waiting for the winter storms.

Each day, Imogen took her children out for a walk. When she'd been a child, this routine was like eating a proper breakfast or washing your teeth before you went to bed. It was one of her mother's rules of life.

As she watched Sofia and Terzo make dams in cold, muddy streams and throw sticks for Mousie, Imogen listened greedily to their excited shouts. Coming back to her old home wasn't running away. It was the best thing she could have done.

For it was here that Terzo had started to speak again – and that almost as soon as they arrived. He'd run into the garden followed by Sofia and she'd heard – quite clearly – him calling Mousie. Then the two children were chasing each other round the liquidamber tree and Sofia was giggling and Imogen knew that Terzo was getting well at last.

She and Charlie had brought the family dogs to the same patch of forest. They too had fallen off the old rope swing over the pond and soaked their clothes;

gone home with mud-caked dogs and squelching boots. Now Charlie was in New York working for an investment bank. Did he walk with his girlfriend in Central Park and remember his uncomplicated childhood?

She'd turned her back on her happy world of sailing and tennis clubs and parties in homes that were somehow all alike. She'd written off her childhood crowd of friends as boring simply because of the way they spoke. Charlie's friends were suddenly callow schoolboys, chinless wonders with nothing to say except, Good shot Imo! Even Rupert, Charlie's best friend who told jokes all the time, had become dull and predictable.

Had she really been as blind as that? Yes, she had, for she'd met Angelo, and after that she hadn't been able to think at all. He took up every inch of her mind; fierce physical attraction and worship of everything he said and did combined with triumph when he married her.

She'd seen him first at a publishing party. Dark, restless eyes, helping himself to one glass after another, talking too fast.

'Have one of these,' she said, and fell in love before he'd said a single word to her.

She was one of a team of girls serving champagne and canapés, her first job when she'd come to London after leaving school and finishing her Cordon Bleu course. Upmarket waitressing and cooking was what girls like her went into; it was how you met the right people.

She met crowds of them at dinner party after dinner party. None of them made her heart beat faster

– until she saw Angelo. Angelo worked for a London paper as an investigative journalist and was already frightening the establishment. He was known to be ruthless, pushing past lines others drew for themselves, drinking and smoking too much, sometimes callous, and always demanding more of life and people than they could give him.

'I'll marry you,' he said as he undressed her in his flat later that evening. 'Hell, why not?'

He was drunk. She didn't care. When Angelo made love to her she was no longer the correctly brought-up boarding school girl, running true to her mother's Sloane Ranger breeding line. She'd stumbled into a paradise her mother had most likely never known.

They were married six weeks later. No white dress, no wedding in a pretty Hampshire church, no photographs to remind her of the day. Angelo was drunk again but she still didn't care. He'd stop drinking when they settled down.

He won't need to drink so much in Italy, she told herself when they left England with their twin boys and Sofia. In Italy he'll get away from all this hysteria over *Priest and Victim*. She was still in love with him. But she was starting to be nervous …

When she'd arrived in Keyhaven with the children, Imogen was sure her mother would insist on sorting out her future, exactly as she'd done throughout Imogen's childhood. But did she still want her to? Imogen didn't know. She was wonderful with the children, firm and standing no nonsense, which was necessary just now with Sofia behaving like a prima donna. Nothing but attention seeking, her mother said, and swept Sofia away to plant tulip bulbs.

Imogen had time to herself now, plenty of it, but she found herself unable to make use of it. She couldn't concentrate. A dithery aimlessness consumed her, making her unable to think coherently. She would tell herself she must make plans, but hardly knew where to start. She was like food taken out of the freezer that must sit about until it defrosts.

Each day crawled by in slow motion. In her numbed state of mind, Imogen restricted decisions to small matters: which clothes to put out for the children, whether to take them to the forest or along the coastline, what they would have for their tea. The questions in her life were shadowy cliffs hanging over her that she couldn't see any way of climbing to reach a different view.

At the end of her fourth week in Keyhaven, Imogen drove into Lymington with her mother's food shopping-list. She went into Waitrose, rejected half the items requested and bought several days' worth of ready meals. Her mother didn't approve of convenience food and never bought it. Cooking from scratch was inseparable from civilised living. It was why she'd pushed Imogen into that fashionable cookery course when she'd left school.

*You've always lived in your own little world of innocence*, Angelo had thrown at her.

She didn't *need* to please her mother, to please anyone.

She loaded up the bags of food into the back of the Volvo, shut the tailgate, and got into the driving seat.

She could go anywhere she wished, but there was nowhere she wanted to go, nothing she wanted to do or see. There were old friends from the past whom she could look up – 'I couldn't resist dropping in while I was down, it's so dreadfully long since we saw each other' – and she would smile as though she was still the same Imogen, and everything that had happened since she'd married Angelo could be put to one side. She couldn't do it. She could imagine the startled faces, the over-effusive welcome to cover up embarrassment, the straining to find common ground.

So much of friendship was convenience: people doing the same things at the same time. Girls formed friendships in their hunt for men; young mothers banded together for support in coping with their small children. Before she and Angelo had gone to Italy she'd been part of a London circle where the trauma of childbirth and sudden responsibilities of motherhood offered immediate intimacy and made barriers tumble down.

But now she was a pariah among young mothers; she no longer belonged to the jolly club where you discussed and joked about the shared experience of raising children while messing up each other's houses. It was impossible not to be aware that other mothers avoided her when they could. Her presence cast a shadow of fear and embarrassment in their fun-filled and chaotic lives; the aura of loss clinging to her reminded them that their children were mortal and not everything was Prosecco and party bags for all.

She twisted the gold band on her finger. It felt loose and frail. So slight a thing, a marriage, a life. It slipped off without a sound.

How different would she look without it? She stared down at her hands which she had once been so proud of. Small, well-shaped with very clean and

171

carefully polished nails. She'd always taken trouble to keep them perfect.

She dropped the ring into her handbag and opened the car door. She would walk down the High Street and wander into all the little shops that were difficult to go into with children. That was what she really wanted: to be alone in a town, anonymous in a crowd. Here she wouldn't be the beautiful wife of Angelo Arzano, the mother whose child had been killed, the woman who couldn't hold the love of a man.

She locked up the car and wandered down the hill, past shops and offices. Her parents' solicitors, Flimwell and Farr, she noticed, had moved into superior premises. She felt glad for Rupert, Charlie's old friend, who she knew had joined the firm on leaving Durham. Unambitious, kind-hearted Rupert, who hadn't wanted anything more than to be a hard-working local solicitor. He'd be there for the rest of his life. His colleagues would welcome him at the golf club; his clients would come to rely on him and trust him with family secrets. He might even be the senior partner one day, a big fish in a small pond. He'd known who he was.

The bookshop was bright and inviting. Christmas books stacked up at angles; gimmick and joke books clustered around the till. People needed humour at Christmas. It was when everyone had heart attacks and murdered their relations. Buy One, Get One Half Price, Best Xmas Presents, Recommended Reading.

Nothing she wanted to read.

If I was the right sort of wife, I would be surreptitiously putting *Priest and Victim* into prominent positions on the shelves. She hesitated amongst display tables. But then there isn't any point. It's still selling well two years on without any help from me. Here it is, being promoted as fiction for the thinking mind. Angelo doesn't need me in that way or in any other.

She stared at the pile of paperback copies of her husband's book, the book which had given them so much – and then taken so much away. The cover design showed distorted faces and bodies of children in clashing, angry colours. There was something alien and creepy about it. She'd never understood Expressionism and didn't want to. She watched a young man pick up a copy, flip it over to glance at the blurb, shrug his shoulders before turning it back to examine the front.

'Only ever judge a book by its cover.'

He was grinning at her with a relaxed cynicism that Imogen secretly admired. She would never be the sort of person who tossed off witty remarks to strangers. Wit always came to her from outside, a foreign language lost in the translation. He waved Angelo's book at her.

'Have you read the blurb and author puffs? Can *any* of these books be as life-changing as the marketing departments tell us?'

'Most of them are pap, crafted for the market, with a sugar-coated formula,' said Imogen, repeating what she'd heard Angelo say.

'Like all those books with a food or art history motif. Churned out to appeal to middle-aged women on diets or in search of some cosy culture. I can only agree. It's patronising to girls like you.'

Girls like me. I wonder who they are? An empty phrase, unconsciously intended to flatter, to console. He must guess I never say anything original or clever. I've just given myself away.

Why did she always do it? Why couldn't she *think*?

But then if he was trying to pick her up, this was how he wanted her to be. All looks and nothing between the ears. She hadn't an identity of her own at all.

'Actually,' Imogen said, 'I'm married to the author of the book you picked up just now.'

'*Priest and Victim* – Angelo Arzano – wow! That must be amazing!' The man looked at Imogen with admiration and a hint of disappointment. 'What luck I should meet you here. Do you – ' He broke off suddenly, as if remembering something. He looked down at the pile of books. 'He's an extraordinary writer,' he finished lamely.

There was a long moment of silence as Imogen stared into her own emptiness. Then she found herself smiling directly into the young man's face.

'Yes, he is. He's an extraordinary person too. But when I said I was married to him, I misled you.'

'Misled me?'

'I have been married to him. But not for much longer.'

The things you could say! Imogen felt a release of venom run through her, driving her on. She felt exhilarated, on the brink of discovery.

'I've only just decided. Just now, when you spoke to me. To get a divorce.'

What did it matter what she said! It was fun, saying these things to this young man whom she would never see again.

The man's eyes flickered away from her.

'You don't mean it?'

'Oh yes, I mean it,' she said, testing herself. But that wasn't true. How did you know if you meant things? It was as if she'd made up her mind only as she heard herself saying the words. How do I know what I think

174

until I hear what I say? Her mother was always quoting that with a laugh. Imogen couldn't see why. Her mother never had any doubts.

She knew exactly what Imogen ought to do about her children, about Angelo, about her whole life. She didn't have to say so; she *looked* her well-proven certainties, her limitless capability. She was an entirely perfect mother, and the thought of ever being without her made Imogen shiver. But other people telling her what a wonderful person her mother was – and they never stopped – made Imogen feel tired.

This man's ears are too long and thin. He'll probably pass them on to his children. Unfair on them, but it was only a small thing after all. She picked up a copy of Angelo's book and looked at the cover as if for the first time. It was only then it came to her that it was okay to dislike it. Why should *anyone* like it?

She'd said the word divorce, trying it out on a stranger. It was easy. Funny how once you did things you found you could. Like when she'd come first in the sack-race aged eight. Thinking about divorce was suddenly something she could actually consider, without breaking out into a cold sweat. The discovery gave her a tiny injection of self-respect, of daring.

'It's not a bad book,' she said, caring nothing for the alarm in his expression. 'Why don't you try it? But it doesn't do anything for me. I don't care either way.'

The man started backing away from her. No surprise there. What person in their right mind announced to a complete stranger in a bookshop that they were considering divorcing their husband? And he didn't even know the half of it.

She ought to feel sorry for him – she supposed

175

he was quite an inoffensive young man – but there wasn't any room to feel sorry for anyone else just now. Anyway, he hadn't believed her. He'd have told himself she was trying to catch his interest with her ridiculous story, having a go at picking him up.

She drove home in fading twilight. It was an incident somebody else might find amusing. Would she ever laugh at it herself?

# TWENTY-SIX

Jane walked up the little path after giving Jonah a piano lesson. It was late November now and dark early. The house where the Arzano family lived was shrouded in shadows and there were no lights on. They were still away in the New Forest.

She missed having fun messing around on the piano with Terzo. Sofia too.

'Please always come, promise you won't stop.'

It was the last session before the family had gone to stay with the grandparents. Terzo, picking out the notes of Pachelbel's Canon, was concentrating on the keys and didn't meet her eyes.

This was that breakthrough moment that came when you worked with damaged and frightened children. There might be weeks or months of music making, the slow, patient building up of trust and communication through sounds. Then a sometimes unexpected and joyful flash, as if the next step of the mountain had been climbed and a patch of mist cleared. At these times, Jane knew that the failures in the rest of her life were irrelevant.

'I wouldn't miss it for all the tea in China.'

She wouldn't say anything to Imogen today. She'd wait until the next time. Terzo's first words should be to his mother, not to her.

Now, a month later, Jane longed to know how Terzo was doing, pictured him staying with his grandparents, talking to them like a normal happy child … Perhaps Imogen would telephone soon but Jane doubted it. Imogen was someone with whom it was difficult to get any further. Her graceful manners removed all possibility of intimacy and produced a static and mutual politeness. For men it would be different. In their eyes she must hang like a desirable ornament forever and tantalisingly out of reach. *Men prize the thing ungained more than its true worth* – Shakespeare had said that or something like it.

Was Austen missing her? What could be more natural than that he should be more than half in love with Imogen, for she was a woman with whom men must always fall in love. Even though she was married and Austen a man of principle, he wouldn't be able to help himself. But Ellen couldn't have meant her when she'd said that Austen had a new girlfriend. There must be someone else in his life, someone whom Nora hadn't wanted to tell her about.

The dank chill in the air made Jane realise that a prickly soreness was starting up in her throat. She hoped she wasn't getting a cold or had already given one to Jonah. He'd been subdued this evening, playing with an undertone of anxiety. Kate too had been more than usually uptight, whisking around tidying and cleaning even though the house looked immaculate already. She wondered if Philip was one of those quiet domestic tyrants who demanded an impossible standard of order. He hadn't looked it the one time she'd met him, but then you never knew what went on in apparently harmonious homes.

Jonah's strained expression bothered her. She'd

spotted something like it in his elder brother's face on other occasions, some unexpressed trouble. She'd put it down to the inevitable moodiness of older teenagers. Now Jonah looked as if he was hiding something.

None of this was any of her business.

She turned into the road and nearly bumped into Ellen and her friend Clover hurrying the other way, but the two girls were giggling and didn't recognise her in the darkness. Or else, Jane told herself sadly, they'd deliberately ignored her. It wouldn't be the first time.

She woke the next morning with a splitting headache. Her body was hot and shivery all at the same time and every bit of her ached. There was no way she could teach at Wharton in this state or do her evening duty in the boarding house either. There was nothing for it but to stay in bed until she felt strong enough to face doing anything except wish her head would stop hurting so much.

She was ill for ten days. By lunchtime the following Saturday life was worth living after all – but not enough, she decided thankfully, to face going that evening to Stephen and Beth's party. Days of not wanting to eat or get out of bed had left her disagreeably weak and miserable, but did give her the perfect excuse. Instead, she would go and help the Sunday school teachers stick sweets into oranges for tomorrow's Christingle service.

She could ask Imogen if she'd like to bring the children to the service, or she could take them. Her mother had seen Imogen in Waitrose, so the family must have come back from the New Forest. She hesitated by the church doors and heard someone calling her name. Nora was coming round the corner with Ellen, both of them wearing unusually tidy clothes.

'We're on our way to the station,' explained Nora,

'we'll be having a look at the London shops and then it's off to the National Theatre for the Alan Bennett play. You're not telling me you're going to that party of yours after all?'

Jane took a sudden breath. So it was a family occasion Austen had planned, not just the two of them. She might not even have been his first choice for the spare ticket. She said slowly, 'No, a cold shouldn't leave you feeling rotten, but it does. It cheered me up a lot when you phoned to see how I was.'

'We were worrying about you. Your mother said it was proper flu, not just a cold.'

'Thank goodness she shows no signs of catching it. But Austen isn't ill or anything, is he – I mean, isn't he going with you to the play?'

'He'll be meeting us at the station, we're only hoping he'll remember. He'll be coming straight from morning school.'

'Of course,' said Jane, thankful that Austen wasn't there to see how awful she was looking. A glance in the mirror before she'd set out had told her that her face was grey and blotched, with hair dragging round it like a wrung-out dishcloth, but she was too exhausted to do anything about it.

'And Imogen is joining us at the theatre. She's back from Keyhaven and went up on an earlier train to see if – that is, we're not sure of her reasons exactly. Dear Teddy is babysitting. A fine thing for Imogen to have a break, though I'm not sure an Alan Bennett play is quite what she'd have chosen.'

'I don't see how anyone could fail to enjoy it.' Jane couldn't keep the niggle of resentment out of her voice. 'Is Angelo not around then?'

'It's in London he's been all this time, not Keyhaven at all. He'll be writing something and needing to be there.' Nora glanced at Ellen, sounding unusually reticent.

'So Imogen is on her own – '

'Did you know that Dad's going back to Dublin at the end of term?' Ellen interrupted.

'Going back to Dublin?'

Shock and the remains of flu made Jane stupid for a moment. Austen couldn't be leaving Wharton for good? Ellen shot her a challenging glance.

'It's the anniversary of when Mummy died. He always puts flowers on Mummy's grave.'

There was a silence during which Jane asked herself why Ellen was telling her this, before Nora said in her usual easy tone, 'He'll be doing that, but that's not the only reason for him going this time. He won't have told you, but he's to attend a reception at Trinity College to do with an academic book he wrote some years ago. It's won an award. But of course you won't be knowing that, Austen never tells anyone anything.'

'I did hear something about it, but not from him. You must be very proud. What a pity you couldn't both go with him.'

'Mummy was a brilliant scholar too. It was her who inspired him.'

'Ellen, I know we've got to catch that train but you don't need to keep – dear Jane, you look as if you could do with being tucked up in bed still.'

'Have a wonderful time at the theatre,' Jane burst out. She turned away. She wouldn't go and help with making the Christingle oranges after all. An hour of sitting with virtuous women exchanging platitudes: it was not to be endured. And Nora had almost certainly already arranged to go with Terzo and Sofia, if not Imogen as well, to the service tomorrow. They didn't want or need her.

Arriving home, Jane sat down at the piano she'd been too ill to touch during the past week. She ought to run through some scales to exercise her fingers. She banged the keys, her eyes on the silver-framed photograph of herself as a child, plain and anxious, her father and mother on either side in a classic family pose that hid their disappointment.

By now Austen would be at the station. This evening Imogen would be sitting next to him at the theatre. He hadn't cared enough to send her a message when she was ill and was probably glad to have Imogen's company instead of hers.

She reached for a particularly dog-eared book among the pile. She needed to play some Bach. That usually went some way to get rid of unkind thoughts and small-minded meanness.

Imogen, so intriguingly beautiful, rich and privileged, had lost a child. She was living with the probability that Terzo would never completely recover from his head injury. Angelo might be extraordinarily attractive as well as being a celebrated writer but he was hardly ideal husband or father material.

She snatched open the pages of music. First Beth and now Imogen. Jealousy was hateful. She was turning into a thoroughly unpleasant person.

# TWENTY-SEVEN

'She'll need to start pulling herself together and make some decisions.'

Judith handed Howard his cup of tea as she spoke, and watched him stir in the sugar. Was he going to exert himself and discuss the problem of Imogen or was he going to maintain the manner to which he so often retreated: closing off the conversation and edging out of the room?

'Perhaps going back to Wharton *was* a decision of sorts.' Howard balanced the teaspoon on his forefinger and considered it. 'Has she said how long Angelo is to be in London?'

'She hasn't said anything. Just that he'd gone there to work and she didn't know when he'd be back.'

'Or if he plans to come back at all.'

'Do you think he does?'

He gave her a look she was long familiar with; a male one that said, how is it possible to have a rational conversation if you won't stick to facts but insist on basing your premises on guesswork?

'As Angelo has not confided his intentions to us, or apparently to our daughter, nobody can possibly know. My bet is that Angelo doesn't either.'

'But you suspect it'll end up with him scarpering for good.'

'Hasn't it always been a matter of time for this particular partnership? Imogen isn't capable of dealing with a man like that. She brings out the worst in him.'

The detachment in Howard's voice was almost cruel, Judith thought. She drank her tea, resenting the callousness of men.

'There shouldn't *be* a worst. What you mean is, he's bored with her, and he thinks he can just walk away.'

'Angelo's too clever for her, always has been.'

'Imogen's got a perfectly good brain when she chooses to use it.' Judith said this defensively, partly with reference to herself; was Howard obliquely referring to his own marriage?

'Did she ever read anything except Barbara Cartland while she was growing up? Hardly the sort of thing to develop a realistic attitude to relationships.'

This couldn't be denied. Judith thought she remembered that Princess Diana had been similarly addicted to Barbara Cartland as a teenager, and possibly her choice of reading matter hadn't done her any good either.

'Even without losing their child, they would have been in trouble before long. That brought it to the surface. And no, Imogen isn't exactly dense, but she flounders in unfamiliar territory. Too easy a childhood perhaps — or it's just the way she is. Limited in her thinking.'

'You're being rather hard on her. I thought suffering was meant to ennoble people.' There was a faint trace of bitterness in Judith's tone. Did he have any real idea of what those years of running the house and bringing up the children largely single-handed had meant? Guilt was a woman's thing. That was what it boiled down to.

'Occasionally it may do. In most cases, I would have said it breaks people – their spirits, their marriages, their mental health. Tragedy doesn't always draw people together; it's more likely to tear them apart and usually does.' Howard took another sip of his tea. 'I don't think it's being hard on Imogen to see her as she is. That way we're more likely to be able to give her the help she needs – when she needs it.'

Had Angelo treated Imogen with this degree of objectivity? The dry decision of her husband's voice made her wonder if all men were prone to some measure of this *unconnectedness* with other people's feelings.

'You needn't look at me as if I was a particularly stupid animal at a zoo. Are you saying she just needs more time?'

'She didn't show much sign of wanting to think about anything constructive while she was here. In her own home she'll have to get on with it.'

'She certainly can't go on escaping here for the rest of her life … I suppose we could – or I could, if you didn't want to – you know, go and stay for a bit, to give her support with the children.'

'Not for the moment, if you want my advice.' Howard leant back into the old chesterfield sofa, his gaze wandering over the exaggerated waves in the seascape oil painting that hung over the fireplace. 'She's got friends, hasn't she? They were in Italy for less than a year. There must still be her old circle in London to rally round her.'

'I don't think she sees any of them now. She can't face it.'

'Well, hasn't she made a few friends at Wharton? The Irish woman next door and the piano teacher? No doubt they'll give her support in different ways.'

'The piano teacher, Jane somebody or other, is hardly a friend.'

'Terzo was saying how he loves her. Tells her things.'

'She's obviously good at her job. We have to give Imogen some credit for thinking of music therapy. Terzo's a different child.'

'My dear, I have always imagined it was you pulling the strings on that one.'

'Howard, that's nonsense. It was entirely Imogen's doing.' Judith sounded unconvincing even to herself. 'But Jane isn't a person I would have thought Imogen is likely to confide in, or who would be any help even if she did. What does an unmarried woman know about this kind of heartache and grief?'

'The point is, Imogen will do far better looking to the people around her than her family. It's a lucky thing Charlie's still away. Make her branch out, learn to exercise a bit of judgment. No good her always running to us.'

You weren't there very much for her to run to when she was a child, Judith wanted to say, but what would be the use? It was often better not to say things to men. Knowing when to keep quiet brought you a happier marriage in the end, even if it was at the expense of short-term satisfaction. Howard was here now, and he was being surprisingly helpful about Imogen. He might stand on the sidelines of family life, but maybe that gave him a better perspective from which to judge. And a man's viewpoint was so important!

She got up to pour him out another cup of tea and

added milk and sugar. The thing to remember about Imogen was that she was a pleaser at heart. She could always come for Christmas, if Angelo was going to stay in London.

Howard might say from the comfort of the sofa that Imogen should fight her battles for herself, but how could you abandon a daughter who crumpled at the prospect of living her own life?

# TWENTY-EIGHT

Today was the most miserable day of the year for the vast majority of the British public, Philip read, as he sat on the train to London. Lack of sunlight, failure to shift the Christmas weight-gain, and above all mounting debt as super-size credit bills arrived.

Well, there was some comfort to be told that he was not alone.

But the money they were getting through! Checking the bank statements at the weekend, Philip had been unable to believe what Kate had spent over the last few months. He'd stared at the columns of figures, staggered by the total at the bottom. Marks & Spencer, Waitrose, John Lewis, Boots he recognised and though the amount Kate had spent at these outlets seemed excessive, it must have been for ordinary household necessities.

But there were also the names of other shops that meant nothing to him. Eleven hundred and fifty pounds at one of them. What on earth was that?

Then he remembered. Jonah's new clarinet. Kate had said he needed a better one now he was becoming an advanced player. You could hardly begrudge him; Jonah was a good boy and had worked hard to pass an exam last term. Grade seven, had Kate said? Still a disloyal question remained in his mind. Did even undoubted talent need so much money thrown at it? Might it not be better for children *not* to have the best of everything?

And what was the best? Should children be the focus of such intensity of investment? Wasn't it piling it up too much on both sides? The whole business of the mixed messages coming from Wharton disquieted him. Achievement and success were the air the boys breathed, yet within this they were urged to be kind to each other. Was it possible in an environment where elbows were essentially out? If you were being taught to push your way to the top, he had reasoned to Kate, it must involve pushing other people out of the way.

He lost the argument – he always did – but he felt again he was being swept along a fast-flowing river in a raft he hadn't built or chosen himself, and which he suspected would prove to be full of holes. He knew he was being unfair; he *had* chosen the raft, or agreed to it. It had been a joint decision to send the boys to Wharton and to move to this more expensive house and way of life …

He was aggrieved at having to admit this. He'd allowed himself to be persuaded against his own instincts. Hadn't he felt back in the early part of last year that this was too big a bite at the cherry? They didn't *have* to send their sons to a private school. All three children had been doing well at their comprehensive and appeared to be happy. Why had they been dissatisfied with this, which was already more than many parents would settle for?

Because Kate always wanted more, there must never be any hesitation, never any half-measures; it was what he loved in her. But tensions had been inevitable in such a pairing: she so whole-hearted, at times prone to passionate misjudgment, he with his dull caution and slower mind.

The bank statements stared silently back at him. They couldn't go on like this. Ever since they'd moved to Wharton last July he'd intended to suggest some guidelines for their new life, but he'd kept putting it off. Commuting each day was a killer. He wondered how people endured it as they grew older. He was becoming aware that the energy which had been his during his twenties and thirties was dwindling. Now that he was in his mid-forties he felt his body protesting at the long working day. Train cancellations and delays filled him with despair. On those days his workload at the firm felt like a monstrous treadmill.

For months he hadn't been able to summon up the strength to have things out with Kate. As he thought of it like this, he was appalled. Was this really what he meant? That he must somehow combat his wife went against every precept with which he'd striven to live his married life. He was a man who held notions almost sacred about his own wife and his position as a husband. She was a thing on a pedestal, as above criticism as Caesar's wife; he must protect and provide for her.

But this in itself ran concurrent with some innate inadequacy in him. Had he subconsciously wanted to compensate for some lack of sufficiency elsewhere in their relations? The idea was distasteful to him. It suggested a smallness which he did not wish to identify as part of his character.

He'd failed her in a deeper sense; this was the

accusation that nagged at his conscience as he sat alone at the desk in the study. Yet the decisions he'd made during that never-to-be-forgotten year early in their marriage had been for her good as well as his own. He'd known that in some way she needed him, in spite of herself, even if she didn't know it.

For months she'd been detached from him, and he'd waited, with the dumb helplessness of a neglected dog, he thought despairingly and occasionally with self-contempt, for her to return to him. His patience, or perhaps his cowardice, was rewarded, for quite suddenly Kate went back to being the person he knew. Nothing was ever said, no explanation given.

The thought that he'd kept quiet for his own comfort rather than hers nagged at him. Had he refused to face what had happened, because he was afraid that if he confronted her, she wouldn't have stayed?

Afterwards he asked himself if anything *had* really happened. He wasn't sure even then, swinging in his imagination from a belief he'd imagined the whole, to a painful conviction that she had, during those months of distance, been seeing someone else. He strove to come to terms with the uncertainty, teaching himself to erase it from his mind. His fears might be like a grave which if unvisited long enough could be dug up and all substance found to have withered away.

If anyone had ever asked him if his marriage was happy, he'd have asserted – with a touch of inner self-congratulation – that it was. He'd been obliged to work very hard, for they'd begun their life together with no capital behind them, but he'd been proud of being the main breadwinner for the family. He remembered how in the early days in London she would watch him dress as she sat up in bed drinking her tea. 'Is this tie all right with this shirt?' he would ask, wanting her reassurance. She always had an opinion, knowing her sense of colour and style was superior to his. She'd been interested in his appearance then; she'd cared about what he looked like.

The polished mahogany of his desk was a mockery, symbolic of the efficient care Kate gave to the house. To him too, on one level. When they'd moved in, she'd insisted the little room off the downstairs hall should become a study for him. Their house in London had been too small for such luxuries; three bedrooms only, Teddy and Jonah having to share, spilling out onto the landing. Now he had this little sanctuary. It kept him from falling apart.

In his study he felt he could relax among objects that were familiar and undemanding, dating from the years before responsibility came to weigh him down. There on the shelves were his Agatha Christie paperbacks, their broken spines and yellowing curled pages testifying to the hours of pleasure they had given to him during his teenage years. On the wall he'd hung a photograph from his grammar school days. He was the only one in his year who had won a place at Cambridge; after that he'd gradually lost contact with his old school friends. Now the room was one that welcomed him as he was, the less-than-brilliant schoolboy who had done well at exams and university more by dint of plodding than flair.

It was the same story at the office. Philip had known he didn't have the rapier-sharp intellect of his friend Neil. It was why he'd chosen the softer option of family law in a small firm, rather than joining the high-fliers in the big partnerships. Their rewards might be vast, but Philip knew his own limits. To earn enough to support his family in reasonable comfort; that was his principle in life, and up until now he'd succeeded.

In the corner, under a standard lamp that lurched on its stem like a triffid, was an armchair that dated back to his bachelor days and which he had bought in a junk shop in Muswell Hill. Here he would sit and read, or pretend to himself that he was reading. It was covered in musty linen, and paper clips and coins slid under the cushioned seat, where they collected dirty fluff. From the chair he could see his old fishing rods and a cricket bat, the black-threaded handle unravelling at the top, the wood parched and dull.

He wondered if Kate's insistence that he had his own study was a ruse for keeping him out of her way. Or that it was a sop, thrown to keep him happy. As he stared at the row of law books he told himself it was so, and yet in his heart he knew he was being unfair. It had been thoughtful of her to provide for his need to be alone, to retreat into himself when the demands of his job exhausted his strength. She worked hard to keep the house running smoothly. His shirts were always ironed; the house was organised and clean; health-giving and carefully cooked meals appeared on the table every night.

But these were outward things. It was as if she wasn't *interested* in him, as if she'd deliberately detached herself from him to follow some secret and troubled path of her own. He pictured his wife's face, knowing her inner self eluded him. In his mind she'd become like someone in a Victorian photograph, veiled and enigmatic, staring at the camera and yet revealing nothing of the passions within. Was this the way it would be until the end? Never knowing, never being known. Living side by side, not acknowledging what was happening to them. Was this what marriage was like for everyone – for that Italian writer next door with his beautiful wife, for his own parents, for the man who examined his train ticket?

And yet he loved her! In all the confusion of this last year, he'd never for one moment doubted his feelings for the girl he'd chosen. He knew himself to be a man incapable of switching his love, as others did. He'd given it finally and completely to Kate, even if he should lose her entirely.

It was cold here alone in his study. He wanted the comfort of being with his family. But he felt too desolate, too lonely to face them. He might go and watch the remains of the television news and then creep off to bed. If Kate made him feel he was an irrelevance, a workhorse who paid the bills, he had only his own inconsistency to blame. The knowledge sharpened his sense of injustice, the desire to assert himself.

He opened the sitting room door and saw Kate push something she was writing into the leaves of a book.

'Teddy isn't happy.'

Philip wasn't sure why he'd started like this, he only knew the image of his son's face had worried him in recent weeks. At bottom this was what frightened him into anger; they were spending all this money and yet his son was troubled. He should wait until he felt calmer; half past ten at night was not a good time for a calm discussion. At the least he ought to have kept it until they went upstairs. But he hated bedroom rows.

Kate wheeled round on him.

'What do you mean, he isn't happy?'

'Just that. There's something wrong.'

'Of course he's happy,' said Kate sharply. 'He's at a top class school, isn't he? He had an excellent report at the end of last term. Lots of comments about how well he's settled in.'

Philip heard the certainty in her voice and marvelled at it. Clever people could make such disastrous errors of judgment, could be so blind to what was happening in front of them.

'A school isn't like buying a product,' he said slowly. 'You don't pay your money and get out a certain kind of child at the end of it. Happy child, Oxbridge child, whatever.'

'So you're saying Wharton isn't a good school?'

She could not, or would not, understand what he was saying. He tried again, wearily, knowing he was sounding pedantic.

'However good the school is – and in whatever way you define good – it doesn't do the whole lot. You can't expect it to provide everything a child may need or to solve all the problems a child may have. When I said I don't think Teddy is entirely happy at the moment I wasn't necessarily saying it's the school's fault. It might be nothing to do with school at all.'

'Something at home, then. Is that what you mean? You've been coming home very late recently. Perhaps he thinks you're having an affair.'

Her flippant tone stung him.

'Is that so impossible?'

'Not at all. Are you?'

Something menacing and unsaid lay heavy in the

air between them. Both were silent for a moment, selecting weapons for the next blow.

'I'm asking you about Teddy,' he said at last.

'So you've already told me.'

'Why do you always dismiss anything I say about the children? Why do you have to be so possessive of them, keeping me on the edge?'

'And I'm telling you Teddy's perfectly all right. But go on, you're going to say I might not have noticed anything.'

'No,' he said, unable to keep the bitterness out of his voice. 'You might not.'

'He is my son, remember.'

Don't say it, he told himself, just don't say it. He looked at her set face, her sharply angled dark hair. She wouldn't, of course. She never would. He was quite safe from that shaft of cruelty, if not from any other. He didn't need to stand here in this agony waiting for her to tell him what he'd refused to confront in seventeen years.

'We must spend less,' he heard himself say, his voice sounding sulky and petulant. 'That's something I do know about. Even if I don't know what I've done that you should treat me with such contempt.'

There was an expression in her face he couldn't understand, a mixture of obstinacy and hopelessness.

'You give in because you're afraid of the alternative.'

Now, as he sat on the train, he grappled with the unresolved scene from the weekend. What had she meant by those words, pronounced with a quiet desperation directed more to herself than to him?

He hadn't read a word of *The Guardian*. As the train drew into Charing Cross, he noticed the girl with the silky blonde hair was sitting opposite him again. She had that seat most days. He liked to see her there. She looked up at his gaze and smiled in his face. A warm smile, redolent of admiration and acceptance. Even of invitation.

And why not? He could ask her out to lunch, for a drink after work. Her expression was a guarantee of what her answer would be. In his head he heard the words and her demure acceptance. Each of them would be playing a game, knowing where it would end up. They were men and women of the modern world. For a moment he pictured that white gold hair spilling over the pillow, the green eyes cloudy with desire, soft flesh reaching out for him.

As they walked towards the ticket barrier he could feel her expectation and his own weakening. Why not give in? But even as he opened his mouth a feeling of revulsion with himself overtook him. He swerved away, shame burning through him. He could hear his own breathing as he slammed towards the barrier, randomly pushing into other commuters. What sort of man was he turning into, that he could consider picking up a girl like this on a station platform?

He hadn't set out in life to be one of those who accepted an accommodating morality; he'd begun early to determine that he would forge a higher code for himself. He would keep himself clean from the sordid affairs that soiled the marriages of so many of his contemporaries. During those Cambridge years he and Neil had discussed their ideals for life; they'd been through the high-flown undergraduate idealism and out the other side. Over endless coffee or cheap beer, they and other members of the college had debated the confusing contradictions of selfish desire and love within personal relationships. In his early years in

London he'd still believed he could live according to the standards he'd laid out for himself then. He had done so – in part.

If Neil hadn't drowned, how would his life have worked out? He'd died with his ideals untested. Would Neil, with his greater strength of character and purpose, have become caught up in the endless compromising and defeats of daily living? He'd never known the creeping self-indulgence of middle age which masqueraded as enlightened tolerance.

He'd shaken her off. She was lost among the crowd now.

But he told himself he was glad – or would be. And that he'd get a different train tomorrow – and go on getting a different one.

'Security check, sir.'

Police officers were stopping what looked like random passengers at the ticket barrier. They offered themselves up with the weary resignation of commuters who know it's useless to protest. Philip waved his season ticket angrily. It was intolerable to be subjected to such outrages.

'We need some personal details, sir.'

'Do I look like a terrorist?'

He wasn't usually rude to officials. He considered himself to be a mild-tempered man.

*You give in because you're afraid of the alternative.*

Was this why, when he felt a touch on his arm and breathed in a heavy perfume so different to Kate's, he made no protest?

Much later, lying in a hotel bed, sticky with sweat and satisfied desire, the question hung over him as if from the tarnished chandelier above his head.

# TWENTY-NINE

'Jesus is changing me day by day ...' a voice crooned as Jane turned a corner on the way home from school and saw a Bruegelish figure, drunk and filthy, zigzagging the pavement in front of her. It's to be hoped he is, she muttered crossly.

Christmas had come and gone. An unexciting day with her mother and Mary Silcox – and at the last moment in a fit of conscience, Grace and Mabel, who would otherwise have been alone in their flats. A card pushed through the door addressed to her and her mother, with love from the Kinsale family written in Nora's idiosyncratic handwriting.

Nothing from Austen. Not that she'd expected anything.

But there *had* been something. Not a card or present. She hugged it to her now, reliving the moment. It wasn't much, and it was growing smaller and dimmer because it was nearly six weeks since it happened. Sometimes she asked herself if she'd imagined it.

'Can we do that really noisy galloping one we played last time?'

It was a few days before Christmas and she was in the Arzano family sitting room, mixing up funny tunes on the piano with Terzo and Sofia.

'You mean *Wipe Out*. Yes, let's all do it together, if your mum doesn't mind being deafened! Sofia, you do the top bit first. Then we'll swap about and each of us have a go at the swooshing part.'

The children crashed the keys louder and louder, up and down the piano. She didn't hear the doorbell or even the sitting room door open. She turned round from the piano stool and saw that Imogen and Austen were standing in the doorway.

'Austen's just back from Dublin,' Imogen said, 'and he's brought something for you two. But not to be opened now.'

She looks more beautiful than ever, thought Jane. Like a heroine in a book, with those huge speaking eyes and white skin against her dark blue sweater. No wonder Austen has come round with the excuse of presents for the children the moment he arrives home.

'Why don't you say thank you to Austen and then go and put the presents in the box in my bedroom?' Imogen continued. She turned to Jane. 'I'm trying to persuade him to stay for a cup of tea. He might agree if you'd play us something.'

'I shouldn't be taking the credit for these.' Austen looked a little self-conscious as he too glanced at Jane. 'They're actually from my mother. I'm only the delivery man.'

'Make her play *O Holy Night*, but call to tell us first,' said Terzo, putting his head back round the door after he and Sofia had said thank you to Austen and escaped with the parcels.

'Yes, please do.' Imogen smiled at Jane. 'Terzo's come to love that, just as much as all those fun pieces you do with him.'

'It's certainly different from *Wipe Out*,' said Jane, laughing. 'Thank goodness neither of them has asked for a drum kit – *Wipe Out*'s quite deafening accompanied by drums. There's a lovely Schubert sonata I'm working on with Jonah. I'll play you that if you like.'

She sat down again at the piano while Imogen disappeared into the kitchen to fetch tea. All at once she felt strangely happy. Terzo was starting to sound like any other child, open to life. It was what she'd worked and hoped for during all these months of music-making with him. She played the first few notes, acknowledging quiet thankfulness as Austen leant against the mantelpiece at the other side of the room.

It wasn't until she'd finished playing and looked round that she realised he had moved nearer to get a better view of the movement of the piano keys. She could understand that; people always wanted to see a pianist's hands. Only he wasn't looking at her hands; he was staring at her face. She met his eyes and knew herself to be blushing, just as Imogen came into the room with the tea tray.

That was six weeks ago now. It wasn't much to live on.

January's short dark days had crept slowly past and soon it would be the beginning of Lent and the penitential season.

Specks of rain started to fall. Jane shrank away from the stench of unwashed human body and tried not to breathe in. She wanted to see Austen, and instead, like a bad joke, she was landed with this man who was leering at her with speculative eyes.

She quickened her pace. Then guilt set in as it always did. Wasn't she meant to love all God's creatures?

Something Mother Teresa of Calcutta had said about Jesus Christ appearing in distressing disguise came into her head. *She* wouldn't have minded about this man being so smelly or hurried away from him.

By the church, two Dalmatian dogs waited miserably at the kerb. Their owner was displaying her perfect control over her pets by making them sit before they crossed the road. Jane noticed that both dogs obeyed but with reluctance, crouching down while trying to keep their bottoms off the cold pavement. She stared indignantly at the owner, knowing it was pointless since a woman with a mouth like that would be impervious to anything outside her own conviction of always being in the right.

The rain was falling heavily now, in thick blinding sheets. A gang of boys on skateboards zoomed towards her, spanning the entire pavement. Jane jumped out into the road to avoid a collision, straight into a puddle. She looked down at her sodden feet and fought the desire to kick somebody.

'Jane – it's my lucky day – are you going back home? Why don't you share my umbrella?'

When the man you want to see isn't available, his mother may or may not be a happy substitute. Jane, turning round and seeing Nora waving an orange spotted umbrella at her, felt her heart lift. There was something so easy about Nora. She was always on your side.

'I've been hating people. Seven in ten minutes. Nora, do you ever have really vengeful thoughts?'

'Especially when I've had a disagreeable lunch. Will we walk home together and I'll tell you all my murderous longings?'

It was impossible not to smile but nor was it the first time that Jane found herself wondering if Nora was only partly joking when she came out with statements like this. Was there a certain ruthlessness in her character or did she say things which nobody else dared to confess?

'I'm thinking umbrellas might be a useful pick-up line.' Nora thrust hers over Jane, knocking off the hat of a man who was passing them.

Jane leaned her head in under dripping orange and made an apologetic face at the man as she dived to restore his hat.

'My favourite one of those was when a married choirmaster suggested to me various arrangements of a doubtful nature and asked me to contribute the food. I felt like Jemima Puddleduck being asked to bring along her sage and onions.' The incident, so embarrassing at the time, now reinvented itself as something to be laughed at.

'And would he be a foxy gentleman with sandy whiskers?' asked Nora, eyeing Jane with quizzical interest.

'Actually he did have reddish hair,' admitted Jane. 'I knew his wife, which made it even more sordid and ridiculous.'

'But aren't musicians expected to be what you might call bohemian in their private lives? All that creative energy needing release. They're to be excused their excesses or irregularities because they're living on a higher plane than the rest of us.'

'Another proof that I'm a very second-rate musician, not a real one at all. I actually sing rather badly and piano teachers aren't exactly the last word in glamour.'

'It's a harp you'll be needing for that. Don't you remember Jane Austen writing about the attractions of a young woman playing the harp in *Mansfield Park*? Not that you'd want to be like Mary Crawford?'

'I can't condemn her as much as Jane Austen obviously meant you to,' said Jane. 'She was the only person to be reasonable about Maria. Everyone else was inhumanly cruel in the way they banished her. Morality then was different, I know, but it was a frightful punishment. She never had the chance to meet any other men after that.'

'Better no man at all than living with the wrong one,' said Nora. 'Charlotte Collins, now, aren't you always feeling sorry for her? I'm thankful she had her head screwed on tight enough to fix it that she spent as little of the day as possible in Mr Collins' company. The nights must have been a trial for sure … now you're not thinking that I'm implying any comparison with your Stephen?'

'Oh, Stephen had plenty of what you're talking about! And he's certainly not a hypocritical creep like Mr Collins. He's a good man, even a noble one in his way. I can't imagine him thinking anything mean. He was always very disciplined about everything. When people asked him to pray for them, he didn't make promises and then forget like I once did, and then felt too ashamed to confess when they thanked me. I pretended to myself that I could live up to him – at the same time as I was pretending to him.'

'Don't you be putting yourself down now. You spoke a different religious language, and what's wrong with that? A fine thing it would be if we listened to rules made by those misguided people who think they're right and everyone else is wrong. There's no end to the trouble we give ourselves and others if we go round thinking there's only one way of talking about God – or to him, if it comes to that.'

'Mmm, but I *envied* that kind of conviction and certainty. At least, when it's in people like him who are undeniably wonderfully good and go around doing good! As to being my Stephen, he didn't think of it like that. It wasn't as if I was his official girlfriend. He was one of those sought-after Christian men who don't mean to be cruel, but that's the effect they have. Surrounding themselves with adoring girls, oblivious of the pain they might cause. They're waiting for God to tell them which one to marry.'

'And why didn't you ask him straight out, instead of hanging around hoping and screening out everything that might have told you it wasn't going to be you?'

'I was afraid of his answer … I couldn't have shut my ears to it. You see, he'd already given it to me in roundabout ways, I know that now, but I didn't then – like when he said I was born to be an aunt. I suppose he was trying to tell me as kindly as he could that I wasn't going to be the mother of his children. I don't honestly think he realised that I was in love with him. Sorry, I'm being boring.'

'I'll be as saintly as Stephen and forgive you. Look, the rain's stopping. Aren't we all of us wanting someone to love?' Nora ignored her apology. 'It's the human condition for all ages, we'll be going to our graves with the same wish. You'll be needing to – '

'Have you heard the news?' Winnie Pumfret appeared in front of Jane and Nora as they turned off the High Street. 'Mabel had a stroke last night and was taken off to hospital in an ambulance. Grace phoned me this morning in a right old tizzy, and who's to blame her? *She's* the one you could knock down with a feather.'

'Is she expected to live?' interrupted Nora. 'I'm thinking it'd be no bad thing if it carried her off.'

'Oh dear, yes. She wouldn't enjoy lingering on if she was left incapacitated. Mabel's always been the active one, buzzing about all over.'

'I suppose not,' said Jane, unable to think what Mabel had enjoyed apart from preying on other people. She made an effort to repress a picture of a venomous insect wasting away in a bed.

'Life goes on, so sing as well,' quoted Winnie in the cosy tone of people who are able to receive comfort from sayings on tea towels and fridge magnets.

'Grace could do something surprising, even if she does miss her tormentor. It's never too late, we oldies are told that often enough.' Nora shook the drops off the umbrella, as Winnie twinkled off in search of someone else to whom she could spread the news. 'What a relief to be folding this up. I bought one in the most garish colour I could find in the hope I'd be less likely to lose it, but Ellen says it's the most shocking embarrassment. You can never win with umbrellas. But you do in the end with confused eleven-year-olds. *Ride on, ride on in majesty* as the hymn tells us – and isn't it infuriating when people say that to you?'

'Taken out of context it does grate,' agreed Jane, wondering who apart from Nora might do so, whilst storing away for future examination Nora's casual reference to Ellen. 'I suppose we only sing that hymn at the service for Palm Sunday.'

'It's *Lift High the Cross* I'm always wanting. All those

verses now, I'll be asking the vicar not to be missing any of them out.'

When Jane arrived home, her mother was sitting in her favourite Parker Knoll armchair chatting to her friend Mary Silcox. Both of them had their feet resting comfortably on footstools; cups of tea and a plate of best shortbread biscuits filled the table between them. Jane guessed that the drama of Mabel's stroke had kept them happy all afternoon.

'I wonder how well the funeral service will be attended,' mused Mary. 'She is such a tricky woman, and not on speaking terms with her son. There was a quarrel when her husband died, doubtless something to do with the daughter-in-law and money.'

'Mabel has often said his marriage isn't a success,' said Dorothy. 'He's probably too like his father.'

'Very true, that was a difficult marriage as well.' Mary fell silent as if remembering with relief that in heaven there was apparently no marriage or giving in marriage. She at least had chosen the better path here on earth.

'He will be here for the funeral, which would surely be held here, in her own church,' said Dorothy. 'I believe the son lives somewhere in Buckinghamshire and he will inherit her flat.'

'She might not die at all,' Jane protested, imagining the giant insect raising a protesting claw.

'It's only a few months since she was telling me about the new carpet in her bedroom,' pursued Dorothy, ignoring Jane. 'I want one that will really *last*, she said. I particularly noticed her insisting on it. I hardly liked to point out that this was not precisely a priority at eighty-six.'

'So what did she choose?' asked Jane, momentarily diverted.

'Sea-green wool, heavy duty. It cost a pretty penny.'

'She will see her husband again in heaven,' said Mary, a sceptical note creeping into her voice.

'She might not want to. Really, Mary, it's a little hard if she cannot escape from him even there. That is hardly an outcome to be wished for.'

'We are all called to be jewels in the Lord's crown,' sighed Mary.

'Then I can only hope my jewel isn't next to Mabel's,' Dorothy said, offering her some more shortbread.

# THIRTY

When Angelo came home just before Christmas, he'd walked in the front door as if he'd only left the house hours earlier.

Imogen saw he was carrying nothing except two carrier bags, and tried to ignore the panic that was hitting her stomach. She shot him a quick glance, already afraid. There was a distance about him that warned her not to ask any questions. He sat down at the kitchen table, and then immediately got up again and walked over to the window.

'The children are next door with Nora and Ellen,' she said. 'They're making Christmas decorations.'

'Then I can say all that's necessary now.' He turned away from the window to look at her. 'Imogen, we have to stop.'

She fetched coffee cups with trembling hands. This is the man I loved, she thought. He is the father of my children, and here I am, afraid of him. She felt a moment of such total self-scorn she knew she must sit down. Her limbs felt heavy and weak, her brain incapable of adult reasoning. She made the strong Italian coffee he liked, as she always did, in the machine they'd bought all those years ago when they first married. It was easier to fuss over the coffee than to look into her husband's face.

'I can't stay,' he said, taking his coffee cup and holding it as if it hurt him. He jerked his head towards the carrier bags. 'Presents for the children – and something for you.'

'Aren't you going to be here with us? My parents aren't coming. I asked them not to because of you.'

There was a long silence, and then Angelo came over to her and stood quite still before her.

'It's all over,' he said. 'We can't go on like this. I have to tell you about Italy. To tell you what – '

She put her hands over her ears, pain shooting down her face into her jawbone and the sides of her head.

'Don't say things, don't tell me things. I won't hear them.'

'For God's sake, Imogen, you can't live the rest of your life like a child running away.'

'Haven't you run away?'

'I've run away too long – in another sense.'

'Can't you do this one thing for me? Leave it all unsaid?'

He stared at her wordlessly for a long moment and let out a slow breath. His eyes went opaque, shuttered against expression.

'A divorce then,' he said. 'We can speak about that, can't we? I've written to your parents. They'll look after you. They know you'll be shot of a bad bargain.'

'Please stay for Christmas.'

She looked at him, the tears streaming down her face.

'It was you who wanted children,' he said. 'You who got yourself pregnant. Twice. Don't bother to keep up that old pretence of mistakes – do you really think I

210

ever believed you? Can't we be honest with each other on this matter if nothing else?'

'Angelo ... I only wanted – don't blame me.'

'Blame you? My God, where does blame come into it? That's a child's game. Imogen, you were made for something different. For a happier life. It won't happen with me. You'll find it all right in the end.'

'For Christmas, Angelo. Only that – no more.'

So he stayed. They went through the motions of a family Christmas, each one of them following the arrangement like sleepwalkers in a nightmare. The children decorated the tree; they opened their presents; they ate a roasted goose which Imogen bought from the farmers' market. He gave her a diamond and sapphire studded bracelet from an exclusive Regent Street jeweller.

'It's in the traditional English style,' he said. 'Nothing Italian about it.'

Two days later he was gone.

Imogen packed up the car and drove to her parents' home in Keyhaven. Angelo had finally left her and was never coming back. Her parents told her that their solicitors Flimwell and Farr would arrange the divorce, without her having to worry about any of the details. They would take it out of her hands and she wouldn't have to do anything except wait for it to be completed on her behalf.

For one ghastly moment she'd wondered if Rupert, her brother Charlie's old friend, would be handling it. But her parents would never have made such a false step. She'd been put into the hands of a silver-haired elder statesman, one of the partners experienced in managing young women who mismanaged their lives. Not her parents' own solicitor who was a longstanding personal friend of theirs, but one of his senior colleagues. After a couple of meetings in Flimwell and Farr's office in Lymington, she'd given up understanding the money side and agreed to whatever was suggested by her lawyer.

Now it was late February, the long hopeless winter almost over, and she was arriving home after another short break in Keyhaven. Coming back to an empty house was getting easier. Spring was more than a distant hope; the beginnings of catkins were appearing and a faint fuzz of greeny-pink covered the shrubs in the drive.

She opened the car doors. She belonged here now. Nora, her face lit up in welcome, was waving at the children, before hurrying across the drive with an untied apron slopped over her and a cloth, looking suspiciously like an old vest, scrunched in her hand.

'Imogen, my dear, it's grand to see you back. Goodness me, Terzo and Sofia, Mousie's bigger than ever. That'll be the sea air. There's no knowing what Semolina will say.'

Sofia scrambled out of the car.

'Can we bring Mousie over to see Semolina now before tea?'

'Why don't you help Mummy unpack the car and then all come and have tea with us? We could have pancakes – get in a bit of practice at tossing for Shrove Tuesday – it's this week.'

Imogen looked at Nora.

'Are you sure you want to be invaded?'

Nora crumpled up the vest.

'It'll be my reward for cleaning the front door. I

hardly ever do it. Virtue is supposed to be its own reward, but it doesn't always feel like that, does it?'

'I don't know,' said Imogen, who had never thought about it.

'I've been looking forward to you coming back, that's the truth of it. Terzo and Sofia can rescue the pancake mixture from going into lumps, such a help. Ellen's never forgotten the time I made lumpy custard. To think of all those times when I get it perfectly smooth!'

'Granny never makes lumpy custard,' said Sofia reflectively.

'Mummy buys it ready-made,' said Terzo, clearly wanting to be helpful.

'That sounds an excellent idea. I'll be trying it sometime.' Nora crinkled her nose at Imogen. 'Come on over when you want, or send the children on ahead, if that's easier. I've got Jane coming to supper, but that's not for hours and I've already made the lasagne. No lumps in the sauce for that, I should hope. Not that she'd notice and Austen certainly wouldn't.'

She sighed, as if Austen's inability to notice things was somehow irksome.

Later that evening, after the children were in bed, Imogen sat wondering about Nora and Jane and the different ways people went about their lives. She'd never come across anyone like either of them before, or hadn't noticed if she had.

For years she'd led one sort of life without ever thinking much about it. There had been the fun of those early months in London doing her first job, then meeting Angelo and falling in love. After that the days had followed hectically, like balloons on a bright windy day, hurtling off one after another into a dazzling sky. She'd never been able to grasp her time, pin it down, to think, this is happening now, this is what I understand about myself in relation to the world.

Then had come that day which had sliced their lives into a before and an after. Nothing could ever be the same for any of them; such devastating grief would go on for ever. Toby's death and all it had led to would spread its sharp stain through her family for all the endless uncharted years ahead.

As she sat huddled on the sofa, her mug of coffee warming her hands, she thought how when she'd lost Toby she'd also lost Angelo. It should have brought them closer together; they should have clung to each other in their brokenness. But he hadn't been able to speak to her about his feelings; he'd turned in on himself, shutting her out from his own private darkness. In his agony he'd left her to flounder amidst the shipwreck of their family life.

Since Angelo had walked alone to the station that evening last October, feelings of bitterness at his cruelty had seized her. He'd abandoned her to face the full weight of her sorrow alone; the husband who should have stood by her side had crept away licking his own wounds, caring nothing for hers.

But now as she sat there turning it all over in her mind, she told herself that Angelo had withdrawn from her long before. The day when Paola first came to their flat marked the first uneasy whisperings of a chill wind.

She was a tall girl, with brilliant dark-fringed eyes and a crooked nose which shouldn't have been so seductive. A researcher. She was helping Angelo with a script for television, she said. She looked clever, much, much cleverer than Imogen.

Imogen was wiping sick off her shirt with one hand, and keeping Sofia balanced on her hip with the other. She took in the slow, secretive smile, the dipped-in-toffee smooth skin, the tight skirt.

'You speak no Italian?' The girl looked at her as if amazed, and threw a few words over her shoulder to Angelo, who was standing in the doorway, watching them both.

He answered rapidly in Italian, and then said in English, 'Why should she? Doesn't everyone understand English if you speak it loudly enough?'

Paola laughed and so Imogen laughed as well – to be polite and because she felt too outclassed to do anything else.

'What does Paola do the rest of the time?' she asked Angelo when Paola had left, bequeathing to the space she'd occupied a lingering aura of sensuality and mockery. She wanted to say, but didn't dare, that she didn't like the way Paola looked at her.

'She's a journalist. A very successful one.'

'She looks like she would be.'

'She's got contacts in the right places. She's useful.'

Useful. Was that all she was?

'I need to chase up a few leads in Naples. I won't be away for long. You'll be all right for a few days?' This came a month later and of course she agreed. She always agreed to anything Angelo asked of her.

In Italy she'd been too alone, too afraid to see things. She hadn't made enough effort to learn the language. Here in England she had friends she could have turned to; young mothers and single friends from her years in London, and old friends from childhood and boarding school. But she hadn't done so, unable to reconcile herself to the shame. It was impossible to relate to them now. Everything had been given to her first by her mother and then by Angelo. She'd always been the spoilt one who'd never had to struggle, whose path had been so enviably smooth. Hadn't she always been smug Miss Lucky?

Now she was going to be divorced – Imogen forced herself to say the word aloud in the empty room – she could ring someone up and confide in them, have one of those conversations about men and relationships that other women had with their friends. She could wallow in Angelo's perfidy, his selfishness, and her confidante would gasp and murmur, all the time feeling a delicious sense of excitement that all this was happening to someone else. Above all, happening to Imogen, whose looks and background had appeared to insure her against suffering of any kind, whose life was so entirely advertisement perfect.

You poor, poor thing, she could hear the voice full of sympathy saying, how *awful* for you. You must come and have kitchen sups sometime soon, with all the old crowd. I'll ring you when my husband's next away and we can have a really good natter.

Imogen didn't want to have an all-men-are-shits conversation. She felt simultaneously too young and too old for such talk. Too young for humour and a long view; too old for optimism and the energy needed to face change. Too old? She wasn't even thirty.

Many of her contemporaries hadn't got married yet; they were living experimental lives, discovering jobs, careers, men, friendships. They travelled, they pursued creative interests, they learnt languages. They were developing themselves and expanding their abilities. Imogen had done nothing. She was somehow stunted, as if she'd failed to grow in ways that people needed to grow.

'He only loved me for my face.'

Nora hadn't looked surprised when she'd come out with this. They'd been sitting in the kitchen after the pancakes had all been eaten, watching the children playing with Mousie in the garden. It was as though Nora understood everything about her and Angelo already.

'If he did, that was his mistake, not yours. And all that anger … it'll have been about him, not you.'

'I don't know … it *was* all I lived for. My appearance, clothes, make-up, men finding me desirable. It was what attracted people, why they loved me.'

'You were just young – '

'Ever since I was a child people have told me that I'm beautiful. After a time you start believing that it's *all* you are. Just a surface, with nothing underneath.'

'You'll have been making a mistake as well then.'

'Not altogether, because it was true. There wasn't much else. But I don't want to be that sort of person any more.'

'I'm thinking you've already stopped being that person.'

Now, as she remembered this conversation, she asked herself if Nora had been right. She was beginning to see that the narrow horizons by which she had once lived were altering, revealing possibilities beyond them. Was she fit for this wider world where people got up and helped themselves?

A job while the children were at school … her Cordon Bleu training; she had that. She could put it to use, please her mother at last. She pictured Angelo's ironic expression.

There were other people as well as Nora to whom she could turn. Not Kate, who had an intimidating way of looking as though she was rushing somewhere, and who probably didn't even know that Angelo had left, but Jane, who plodded along apparently happy without a man around, and who had somehow become part of the family.

'Mummy?'

Terzo stood in the doorway of the sitting room, grave-eyed, his face pale against his scarlet dressing gown.

'You should be in bed asleep – '

'I didn't feel tired – '

She patted the cushion of the sofa beside her.

'Come and sit with me. It was fun making pancakes, wasn't it? Shall we do some of our own next week?'

'Mummy? Is Daddy going to come back ever? I thought he would stay when he came for Christmas.'

'No darling, that was just for Christmas. He wanted to spend it with you.'

'Not with you?'

'Terzo – '

He ran his finger along the piped edge of the sofa cushion. He said, not looking at her, 'Are you and Daddy going to get divorced?'

She took a deep breath.

'Yes. I'm sorry.'

'Because of me? Because I can't remember things?'

She looked down at the dusky hair shrouding his

face, a painful lump settling through her neck and head. She pulled him close to her and kissed him, her eyes prickling, willing her voice not to tremble.

'Nothing on earth to do with you. It's just one of those things that happen sometimes, however much we wish they didn't.'

'I asked Ellen.' Terzo kept his eyes fixed on the cushion. 'She said it wasn't my fault either.'

'Ellen's telling the truth.'

'Daddy's still alive. Ellen's mummy's in heaven.'

She thought of Toby then, and a sharp twist of agony went through her.

'Let's tuck you up in bed,' she said. 'I'm coming up too now. Everything will be all right in the morning.'

'The boy in my picture,' Terzo said, putting out his hand to touch her face. 'I *know* him. Mummy, who is Toby?'

Soon she would be able to lie down on her bed and cry and cry. Just now, though, she must find the right words for her son.

She kept her voice quite steady and calm. How very like her mother she sounded! The thought of it was absurd. She would *never* resemble her mother. Of that she was quite certain.

# THIRTY-ONE

Ellen woke up with an agonised start to find she was screaming. She lay in bed, taking in sharp painful breaths, her brain dazedly registering that she was safe from the terror engulfing her. I'm not *dead*, she told herself, her heart beating rough and hard. I'm alive – it wasn't *real*.

Her bedroom door opened and she could see her grandmother in her brushed cotton pyjamas framed against the light on the landing.

'Was it a bad dream? Here, let's put your lamp on.'

Ellen shuddered.

'Yes. I'm sorry, were you in bed? Did I wake you up?'

'It doesn't matter. Nightmares are beastly.' Her grandmother sat down on the bed and kissed the top of Ellen's head. 'I can still remember one I had when I was about six, after reading *The Tale of Samuel Whiskers*. There was a picture in it of Tom Kitten being rolled up in pastry by some rats. It gave me the most frightening dream imaginable.'

'Granny! It didn't! Can I see the picture?'

'I made quite sure we never had that particular Beatrix Potter book in the house, so no, you can't. Though I was most likely very silly about it. You might not have found it sinister at all, but just laughed and been unable to imagine how I could have ever been haunted by it. You can never know what frightens different people.'

'I had a nightmare once after reading *Marianne Dreams*. Do you remember the drawings of the stones, and how scary they were?'

'Were they those sinister boulders with a single eye that watched the house? Those old Puffin books always had wonderful illustrations by artists who could really draw. Didn't Marianne keep going back to what she'd drawn in a parallel world of her dreams? That might have been one reason why you found the stones disturbing. Being afraid to go to sleep because of the possibility of the same nightmares coming back is not a lot of fun.'

'Can you stop them coming?'

'They're not usually in the way of repeating themselves – and the nice ones don't come back either. It's a strange thing how often I wake up when I'm about to eat a delicious piece of cake. But what was the trouble tonight – you weren't watching anything violent on the telly?'

'No – at least – not exactly.' Ellen twisted the corner of her duvet cover, knowing her voice was going to wobble off course. Desperation drove her on.

'Granny, when people are killed, or murdered I mean, does God – does he just allow it to happen? I know that Mummy … you explained … and it's all right remembering her, but I can't bear to think about it happening to anyone now – ' Ellen burst into tears and threw herself face down on her pillow.

'Were you thinking about the little girl on the television news?'

221

'Me and Clover read the headlines in the newsagents on the way home from school. It said the man they are looking for comes from the Dublin area. I thought – I thought that – '

Nora put her arms round Ellen and stroked her hair.

'Yes, my lamb, what did you think?'

'That the man might be Glen Tollerton!' Ellen let out the name in a stifled sob and clutched at Nora's shoulder.

'Glen Tollerton!'

'He used to be with his gang down at the recreation ground near us in Dublin. He was in my dream, and he was – ' Ellen broke off, the nightmare image of the man's white face and strangling hands reaching out vivid in her mind.

'I certainly remember Glen Tollerton, because I knew his mother. She was the lollipop lady at your primary school when you first went there, the woman who wore that funny coat with bobbles on it, and gave all the children little chocolate eggs at Easter. She went to work in that nice baker's shop afterwards, where they sold those sticky buns, so I saw her every now and then. She was always tearing her hair out over Glen. He was one of those lads who lose their way and make a nuisance of themselves for a time until they find something that interests them again. He settled down when he grew up, and joined the police. I believe he's done very well.'

'So now he's really a policeman?'

'Yes, isn't it odd? The last I heard of him is that he's a proud dad of a little Glen – his mum did tell me the name but I'm forgetting what it was. Not Glen I hope.

I wouldn't be choosing that, would you?'

'He once made me kiss him.'

'How horrid. He'll have done it for a dare. Most likely he was being teased by one of those silly friends he went around with. Boys of that age all lead each other on to do things they'd never do off their own bat.'

'I felt *smirched.*' Ellen brought the word out with an effort.

'I'm not surprised. But be thinking of it as like nits – a wretched nuisance but harmless in the long run, and something that happens to almost anyone. Most people's first kiss is a disappointing experience with a spotty teenager, and afterwards you're looking at him and wondering how you *could*. I wouldn't be giving it another thought.'

'Are you sure he couldn't be, you know, someone who murders children? When I saw the newspaper article saying the police were looking for a man who lived in Dublin, I told Clover what Glen did to me, and Clover said he might have gone on to be a child killer.'

'You don't think she was leaping to unlikely conclusions?'

'Yes – no. Because if it was Glen, it would have been my fault because I didn't say about that time when he kissed me.'

'But it wasn't, and you've allowed Clover to feed your mind with all sorts of wild imaginings. You need to be wary about listening to a friend with a craving for excitement and drama.'

'I do like her.'

'So do I. But don't you be forgetting your own common sense. Glen was a silly boy who probably wanted to boast to his mates that he'd kissed a girl. There are hundreds like him. Terrible things like you and Clover read about in the paper are done by people who are mentally ill. Such things are impossible for us to understand, but mercifully they are very rare. Can you see the difference now?'

'So it absolutely wasn't Glen Tollerton who abducted that girl?'

'Quite, quite certain. And I'll tell you something else that was on the late news. A man has been called in for questioning. He isn't Glen.'

'I dreamt he was strangling me, or it was someone like him.'

'My dearest one, you must try filling your mind with something beautiful and good. Then there won't be room for anything else. Do you remember the book of Rembrandt paintings Dad gave me last Christmas? The one in the sitting room? I want to show you something in it that always helps me and does *not* give me bad dreams.'

Nora padded off downstairs and reappeared in Ellen's bedroom with the heavy book in her arms.

'Am I squashing your feet now? Here's the painting I was looking for, and look, here opposite, there's a pen and brush drawing of the same subject. Can you see what it is?'

Ellen peered at the pages.

'The Return of the Prodigal Son.'

'It's from the parable – the one when the son goes off and wastes all his money and then gets abandoned by his so-called friends.'

'And ends up wanting to eat the pigs' food,' finished Ellen.

'Then he runs home to his father and asks to be

taken back – but he doesn't even need to ask because the father is already looking for him. I love the way Rembrandt shows the son on his knees because of how sorry he is, and how the father wraps his arms round him because he loves him so much. When I look at those hands, so tender and protective, I think of God's hands.'

Ellen stared at the painting.

'The son's very ugly,' she said at last.

'He is that, and he could do with a good scrub. But maybe that's part of it. You don't have to be all nice and clean when you meet God. You can just run into his arms.'

'Anybody at all?'

'Anybody. Sometimes pictures can remind us of important things like this. It's worth looking carefully at the ones that do.'

'Are you saying it's like that for people who are being killed?'

'There must be moments of pain and terror, but then it must be like stumbling into God's outstretched arms, as his precious beloved child.'

'So it might be like waking up from a nightmare, only one that was real life?'

'Waking up in heaven – yes, we can be quite sure it'll be like that.'

'So that little girl is safe in God's arms this minute?'

'Yes, my dearest one. Let's remember her and her family when we're saying our prayers.'

There was a long silence as Ellen digested this.

'Granny?'

'Yes?'

'Can I ask you about something else?'

'Something else that's been worrying you?'

'Mmm. Jane's really your friend, isn't she?'

'And yours.'

'Not Dad's as well?'

'It would be grand if she was, don't you think?'

Ellen searched her face.

'Dad never goes out drinking, but he did take her. And Clover said – '

'Is that why you've been giving Jane the cold shoulder lately? I had noticed. I think she might have done too.'

'Sorry. I do like her a lot, but – well, Dad isn't a girlfriend person, is he? He's always serious about everything. He doesn't want anyone else.'

'He hasn't – not until now.'

'You mean he's changed. I wish he hadn't. I want everything to stay the way it is.'

'Would it help to think what Mummy would have wanted if she was looking down from heaven?'

'You mean she'd have wanted him to be happy with someone else?'

'She was the most generous person imaginable, so I'm thinking she would.'

'Would she?'

'You're very like her, you know.'

There was another silence.

'Granny? Shall we have some hot chocolate now we're both thoroughly awake?'

Nora got up from Ellen's bed.

'Did I ever tell you that Jane hates liver and beetroot, the same as us? We'd better put on our dressing gowns and slippers. I wonder if Semolina is having a dream about Samuel Whiskers?'

# THIRTY-TWO

Judith disliked being away from home. There was nothing to *do* in other people's houses and Howard was under her feet all the time. At Keyhaven he took himself off on his own little ploys, be it golf or gardening centres. This was how retired couples ought to operate.

During the years of separation, when he'd been working in Hong Kong, she'd learnt to create a life of her own and to enjoy her own capacity for doing so. However much you loved your husband – and Judith assured herself she loved Howard a great deal – you didn't want to be with him all the time. People needed space, and even more of it as they got older.

She and Howard had come to spend half-term in Wharton and she was worn out with trying to instil some of her own energy into her daughter. It was as if she considered her life to be over, when it was likely she had years ahead of her, years that might contain recovery and happiness if only she'd look about her a bit more.

Judith knew her own strength wasn't what it used to be. She'd lost a grandchild and not a day went by without moments of grief so fierce she felt winded, unable to steady herself. Only the determination to be strong for her daughter's sake enabled her to get a grip.

There had been moments last year when she'd been afraid she would lose it and disgrace herself. The first terrible telephone call, an immediate flight to Italy, fraught days looking after Sofia, one appalling visit to the hospital where Terzo lay inert and mute. Finally they had all come home to Keyhaven, for the heartbreaking little ceremony where Toby had been laid to rest. Through it all, she and Howard had seen their daughter stricken into white-faced, silent agony. They had lost their grandchild, but Imogen had lost her son. Judith knew that a mother's love was the strongest love of all.

No mother could recover from the death of a child; Judith understood that Imogen would never entirely lose the stunned look of loss lying at the back of her eyes. But she still had two children to love and nurture. Most of her life lay before her. Yet, nearly a year on, she was like a doll with no insides, inert and apparently without any kind of hope or realistic plans for the future.

Looking at her, it was incomprehensible how she managed to look after the children by herself; she seemed so incapable of effort. Yet she evidently did. It occurred to Judith for the first time that Imogen *was* managing. Howard might well be right when he grunted – Howard was given to grunts – that Imogen was better left to get on with it.

Nor did Howard like the South-East.

'Nothing but bloody Chelsea Tractors in traffic jams,' he'd grumbled on the M25.

'It's no worse than all the day tripper traffic queues we get in the New Forest,' said Judith. But she knew these wifely pacifying comments were futile. She wished she'd elected to drive. Not that Howard would have agreed. He liked to do the driving himself so that when he arrived anywhere he was entitled to be tired and allowed to be taciturn.

Now, after several days in Wharton, he'd woken too early as he always did when sleeping in an unfamiliar bed, and was complaining about what he called tasteless affluence.

'Towns like Wharton were pleasant market towns once. But not any more. They're getting swallowed up into the commuter belt, and stinking of materialism and endless vulgar consumption.'

'There's plenty of wealth all around us in Hampshire,' objected Judith.

'Wealth, yes. But people have got it already, they aren't all rushing about making it. That's what's objectionable about commuter towns.'

'Imogen doesn't have to stay here now Angelo has finally left,' said Judith, though she couldn't see any appreciable moral difference between having inherited money stashed away in possessions and houses, and going about the business of earning it. She didn't argue the point, knowing it was better to indulge Howard's small prejudices and save her big guns for something more important.

'After all, they came here because it was convenient for London. But that doesn't affect Imogen now.'

Howard began to hum. It was a familiar signal to show he guessed what was coming next. Judith ignored it.

'She could move somewhere in our direction,' she pursued, the thought of Charlie's friend Rupert hovering at the back of her mind. Imogen was two years older than he was, but then she was young for her age, and still looked such a child. Rupert could be made for her; the right background, not too clever and yet utterly reliable.

Above all, she was confident he hadn't recovered from the schoolboy worship he'd shown for Imogen when they'd been teenagers. He hadn't married anyone else, had he? Something his mother had said to her when they'd met up at a charity lunch recently suggested that Rupert might be still waiting in the wings. Judith suspected she was trying to find out if Imogen was free of entanglements. She would be a dependable mother-in-law to Imogen, and it would be such a relief to know one's fellow in-laws. That had been impossible with Angelo since his mother as far as she could make out was thoroughly unsavoury and his father didn't appear to exist.

Rupert's family in contrast was reassuringly predictable and familiar. It might sound snobbish – and she told herself she wasn't, not at all – but it did make life easier! Marriage was hazardous enough without contending with different backgrounds and cultures. Particularly for Imogen, who was somehow (Judith struggled for the right word but couldn't find one) *limited*. She wasn't made for the deeper, more confusing, complexities of relationships.

Rupert was a dear; if only Imogen hadn't been perverse and fallen for Angelo, whom anyone could have told her had danger written all over him. Rupert would be an excellent stepfather too, so besotted with Imogen he'd be glad to take on two stepchildren. He'd say he was thankful for two more beings as perfect as her.

It would be a good thing if Imogen could put herself in the way of learning to appreciate Rupert's possibilities as a future husband. It wasn't likely she was going to do this by herself. She'd need to be manoeuvred into it. At least she'd promised to start the children off at their school next term. That was something achieved. Judith felt the familiar sense of love and frustration when she thought of her daughter and found herself sighing.

'She's begun to put down roots here,' she continued, thinking aloud. 'And I suppose when the children start school she'll meet other parents. At the moment she only really knows the immediate neighbours. There's that man Austen Kinsale, of course. He's a widower, with a child of his own.'

'He's also head of classics at one of the most academic schools in the country. I hardly think they have much in common.'

Howard spoke with decision, for he'd met all the neighbours several times and last night there had been a supper party at the Kinsales' house. Nora had produced a flamboyant array of Indian dishes, and he was beginning to feel the effects of having eaten too much. Had Judith remembered to bring the Andrews Liver Salts?

'He might see her as his Helen of Troy,' said Judith lightly, more to provoke him than anything else. She too knew that Austen would never be attracted by Imogen.

'In the first place, they might have difficulty conversing.'

'Clever men are often attracted to less-than-clever girls,' said Judith defensively, feeling she'd had this conversation with Howard before.

'Any fool can see he'll marry that piano teacher.

Might need a bit of push first.' Howard paused. 'Nice man. She too. In their way.'

Judith reflected that this wasn't his way, but as he'd taught himself to be as tolerant towards others as he was towards himself, she gave up and switched tack.

'Jane? She's a complete oddity. Do you suppose she has any experience with men? She looks what you might call untouched. You must admit that's fairly strange these days.'

'Unique, I should imagine,' said Howard dryly.

'I don't know how you can be so certain Austen's going to marry her. It would be like marrying a younger version of his mother.'

'Many men have done the same – and it may suit some of them very well.'

'The pair of them talk as though characters in novels were real people,' continued Judith, ignoring the provocation. If there was one. You could never be sure with Howard. 'The way they encourage the granddaughter is almost as bad. It's very irritating to other people.'

She stopped herself saying pretentious, though the word hovered. But she admitted you couldn't use it in connection with Nora, whom Judith in her honesty recognised as being essentially unselfconscious. Nora's idiosyncrasy of identifying too closely with fiction of all kinds might be annoying but it was neither contrived nor condescending.

'Isn't literature meant to teach the truths of life?'

Since Howard rarely read anything except newspapers and the occasional biography, this struck her as a trifle inconsistent.

'But it's *not* real life, it's escaping from it.' Judith

sighed. 'Though I'll allow that people in literature are more easily understood and managed, and that's certainly an attraction.' She spoke rather sadly; trying to make people behave in the way they should was a labour which too often went unrewarded.

'You're probably right,' she said, her mind going back to Austen and Jane. 'It would be a very suitable thing for her as well as him. Some men *need* to marry their mothers. Or they like to. But do you think he'll ever ask her?'

'Is that necessary? They'll have to just fall into it, in the way people do.'

'Or she could ask him, which isn't ideal. A proposal of marriage, whether you mean to accept it or not, is still welcome. Women do like to have this experience in their lives.'

'I'm gratified to learn I've given you that, if nothing else,' Howard murmured ironically.

Judith flashed him a look.

'Well, it'll have to be Rupert then.'

'Rupert?'

'Howard, don't be tiresome, you know what I mean.'

'Rupert's a grown man, my dear. He's quite capable of asking Imogen himself. If he's remained faithful to the memory of her all these years – an unlikely scenario, for I've always thought him perfectly sensible – he certainly won't give up now.'

'No,' said Judith, in a disappointed tone. One did so like to make sure of things!

'I don't know why you think the answer for our daughter has to be a man. Aren't you being rather old-fashioned? There are other routes to salvation, you know, for women these days. Imogen could get herself a part-time job once the children are at school, start up a cookery business, get involved in some women's group.'

Judith failed to imagine Imogen doing any of these things.

'Initiative isn't her strong point.'

'It might be if you stood back more.'

There was nothing to be gained in making any retort to this because it was probably true.

'Yes, well. I still think we should do something. There are some women who don't thrive without a man beside them and Imogen's one of them. It's the way she's made, there's no getting away from it. And after all we've been through with Angelo, don't you think we should do something about Rupert?'

'Do something?'

'Encourage him to approach Imogen again.'

'I've no intention of doing anything at all,' said Howard irritably, 'except to go back home tomorrow and sleep in my own bed. There comes a time in life when staying with other people, even your own family, ceases to be a pleasure after a very few days, and we've been here nearly a week. Better save your plotting – I can see there's no stopping you – for when Imogen next comes to stay. But leave me out of it.'

Men always did want to be left out of anything troublesome, thought Judith resignedly, but they nevertheless enjoyed any benefits that might accrue. It was no good moaning or being surprised at such vexatious behaviour; better to tell oneself it was – in its own way – endearing, and save one's complaints for cosy women's lunches while Howard was on the golf course. A good mutual grumble and every woman would go home with the revitalised sense of humour without which marriage could be a lonely or even wearisome business.

'She could mature,' she offered, wanting to be convinced.

'Do people change that much? Are they capable of it? Certainly not if they lack the will to alter anything except their circumstances.'

Judith was silent, her thoughts shifting to Howard. Had he changed when he came back from Hong Kong? Not in essentials. She had merely learnt to accommodate him, to accept him with all his limitations. As he had learnt to accept hers. These may not have been conscious decisions, but she supposed they represented change of a sort.

When they went home – and Judith was beginning to long for this herself – it would be time to make some plans. Their son Charlie would be back from New York this summer and then based in London. He would help. Rupert was still his close friend. Really, between them all, darling Imogen would have no escape.

# THIRTY-THREE

Going to a funeral is not the most entertaining way of spending a free afternoon, but Jane pummelled herself into making the effort, if only to atone for the lack of it during Mabel's life.

Nora, with her occasionally unnerving habit of divining the way other people's thoughts were running, had asked her to come and have what she called a strengthening lunch with her first, so they could walk down to the church together.

'I hardly got to know Mabel, but I might as well swell the numbers at the service,' said Nora. 'Not that I'll be contributing to the singing, which can be so embarrassingly dreary at funerals.'

'I wish you'd let me come too,' said Ellen, appearing in the kitchen. 'D'you think Mabel's relations will look like beetles?'

'You can hardly go to a funeral when you're meant to be off school with a cold,' protested Nora.

'I thought you'd say you shouldn't anyway when it's a person you aren't sad about.'

'But is it for the sake of the person who's died or is it for your own sake?' Jane asked doubtfully.

'*The darkness falls at thy behest*,' said Nora. 'A ceremony is said to help us with our grief, or provide a focus for mourning, and that's not something to miss out on.'

Jane didn't pursue the matter, as she felt no particular grief for Mabel. Going to her funeral might be a way of drumming it up and that must be a good thing.

'Are you coming back with Granny afterwards? I want to hear who gets all her money and what the son she quarrelled with is like. It might be useful material for our church soap opera – you know, wicked old Bianco da Siena.'

'We'll do our best to find out everything,' promised Jane, feeling so happy that Ellen had reverted to her old friendly manner that she didn't like to point out that this might be difficult.

'You don't think we should be feeling a little guilty we've made the man who wrote *Come down, O love divine* into a villain when he must have been a saint in real life?'

'Granny, you're only saying that because you're imagining him sitting up in heaven and hearing everything. You know he can't. And actually, if he was as holy as all that, he'd probably find it quite funny. Good people ought to have a proper sense of humour and not be all disapproving.'

'You live in other people's lives too much,' Nora said, when Ellen had disappeared back to the sitting room and the television. 'I wonder if it's because of what happened with Stephen, or whether you were always like this?'

'It's an escape sometimes,' admitted Jane, 'or a defence against men finding me wanting in some way. Just as he did.'

'You might have found *him* wanting if you'd ever slept with him. But from what you've told me about

Stephen, he would have expected his wife to be a model of purity.'

'Oh yes, I passed that test, if not any other. The truth is, I'm jealous, because Beth is sweet, good and pretty. All the things I'm not.'

'What a lucky escape. Don't forget that Fanny Price is Jane Austen's most hated heroine. You're not wanting to be like her, are you?'

'At first I did, when Stephen told me he was getting married ... Stephen's rejection reinforced a sneaking feeling that I was an impostor at church, going along but not having the same spiritual experience that everyone else – especially Beth – was obviously having.'

'I'm thinking you'd be surprised if you could see inside their heads. I doubt if anyone is quite as holy as you seem to imagine. But God will be understanding all that.'

'It's more that I felt left out ... jealous really. Especially when people talked about the blessings God had sent them.'

'Yes, why does it often sound like boasting? But you know some people need to talk while others are more private – and who's to say the one is better than the other? It's a grand job you're doing here in Wharton, even if you don't see it that way yourself. *If our love were but more simple* – it's in a hymn somewhere ...'

'I've been re-reading what St Paul wrote to the Corinthians about how we all belong together, and are responsible for each other,' admitted Jane. She made a wry face at Nora and began to smile. 'I wonder if I ought to learn it by heart and repeat it three times a day?'

'I'd say you've got the idea already ...'

Nora looked down the garden to the willow tree where the children had made their den for Mousie and Semolina, her face clouding over with some unexplained thought.

'Some men are more unpredictable than others.'

'Poor Imogen,' said Jane, following Nora's gaze.

'Imogen? You're right about that, poor Imogen. She's like an out-of-season hothouse rose in fluted crystal. At any moment the rose will droop and the glass will shatter. Angelo is a mystery to her, and will always remain one.'

Both women were silent for a moment. Then Nora crinkled up her nose with the smile Jane was beginning to know.

'He may never ask, you know.'

Jane kept her eyes fixed on the kitchen window. Daffodil bulbs were poking up across the stretch of muddied winter grass.

'You might have to instead.'

'Nora, it's Verity – he never speaks of her, never says her name – '

'Words are coming out of silence with people all the time, aren't they? Austen will always have a deep area of reserve and I don't think anyone will ever change that. But any woman to whom he gives his love can be quite sure of keeping it.'

'You don't need to tell me that. I know. But – '

'There's only one thing you'll regret – missing the passing of your lives together. Would that be in a hymn too? No, I've an idea it's in *Daniel Deronda*. Have you read that lately? Goodness gracious, we ought to be setting off, and you'll need all your patience to endure me singing like that crow in the garden. I'm hoping for your sake the funeral hymns don't have too many high notes.'

The day had all the sharp cruelty of early spring, and the church when they arrived felt cold despite the best efforts of the boiler. In the pews people were exchanging greetings in the hearty manner peculiar to funerals, relieved that their own end has not yet come.

'I'm thinking we could do with some Celtic hymns,' Nora said as she put her gloves back on again.

'With their emphasis on the goodness of nature and the rhythms of life and death,' agreed Jane. She imagined the congregation standing on a rocky headland in the Outer Hebrides, feeling God in the wind and rain. Would this resonate more with the human spirit than shuffling like uncertain sheep into a gloomy building? Perhaps it was only very saintly people who could feel holy with numbed feet and the trickle of rain going down their collar. She wasn't one of them.

She looked around to see who else had come. Her mother had announced that she would bring Grace in case she was feeling in need of support, and Jane could see them now among a knot of women near the largest radiator. Rowena Royce was gazing at the vases of winter chrysanthemums with the untiring admiration people bestow on their own creative efforts. The churchwardens Brian Goodacre and Mary Silcox were standing by the door handing people their service sheets. In their usual pew in the middle of the nave, Jane spotted the shining head of Harry Pumfret, and Winnie in a felt hat turning round to chat with the strangers behind her, probably in the hope that they might tell her something about Mabel she didn't already know.

'That must be the son in the front pew,' whispered

Nora. 'I wouldn't want to meet his wife on a dark night. In that magnificent coat she looks as if she's about to swallow him up in one mouthful.'

Two little girls of around eight and ten whispered together, self-conscious and awkward in ill-fitting black jackets which might have been borrowed from a second-hand boys' school uniform shop. They must be Mabel's grand-daughters, but Jane couldn't remember Mabel ever speaking of them. Their mother turned round briefly to inspect the unfamiliar congregation of her mother-in-law's church friends. She was a woman whom an earlier century would have called handsome, with a small chin, prominent ice-blue eyes and a long, important nose.

Hadn't the family quarrel involved her and a dispute over money? Jane began to picture the scene, with its trivial beginnings which had then exploded ... a present perhaps given by Mabel, and then spurned by her daughter-in-law. She doesn't know the *meaning* of the word gratitude, she heard Mabel saying; it is *nothing* to her. Mabel's small, beady eyes darting around the rooms of her son's home and the calculating triumph of the daughter-in-law, married to a much older man, knowing time was on her side.

*I am the resurrection and the life.* Jane bowed her head as the coffin was brought in. It looked so small, almost grotesque. There were olive trees in the Garden of Gethsemane, she thought confusedly, they too were stunted and misshapen with age. People must grow and change in heaven. Olive would become all she might have been.

Then there was purgatory, but perhaps that was only for Roman Catholics. She must ask Nora, who'd been brought up as a Roman Catholic even if she'd gone to services in the Church of Ireland when she'd lived in Dublin, and now seemed to be entirely at home in the Church of England. She might almost be held up as an example of ecumenism. Really, it was a pity more people weren't like her. The image of Mabel as a giant insect hovered for the last time.

'It might be that dispiriting line *foul, I to the fountain fly*, but funerals always remind me that it's the good things we have *not* done, rather than the bad things we *have* done that matter most,' she whispered to Nora, as they sat down after singing *Rock of ages, cleft for me, let me hide myself in thee.*

'The small failures, the letter we never bothered to write, the boring person we didn't take the trouble to get to know, thinking our life was busier and more important than theirs,' agreed Nora, not whispering at all. 'Then something happens or someone dies and the chance has gone forever.'

Jane began to picture Verity's funeral; the packed church, weeping people squashed into pews clutching handkerchiefs to wipe away tears. Austen at the front, his shoulders slumped, his face full of bewildered grief; Ellen, frail from the attack, sitting on Nora's knee. Did Ellen recollect any of this, or was her mother only an idealised memory, like so many of the dead mothers in Victorian fiction?

The coffin would have been adorned with freesias and tiny, unostentatious roses. Not lilies; they were too grand, too richly perfumed for the person she imagined Verity to have been. She was about my age when she died, Jane thought, remembering that Nora had told her that Verity was a few years older than Austen. There wasn't a photograph of her downstairs in the lodge. It would be by Austen's bedside, showing a face that would always be beautiful and good.

People are often saying *I* must be a good person because of all those years helping children who have special needs. But I'm *not*. If they only knew how I seethed with frustration and felt like giving up when it seemed I was getting nowhere. Beth would never have thoughts like mine. She was given goodness as a birthright.

And now Nora is telling me I should ask Austen to marry me! She pictured his horrified face and almost wanted to laugh.

Nora is muddling up her beloved George Eliot novels with real life. Austen is far from being a romantic hero and I'm not a splendid heroine like Catherine Arrowpoint ...

Men don't see me as the sort of woman they might marry. He'll be attracted to one of the highly academic teachers at Wharton, or else someone at a classics conference, and they will be able to exchange Latin quips or discuss the latest translation of obscure Greek texts. She'll be one of those competent women like Kate who sweep through life and people, always managing to get what they want.

'Dying can be welcomed as the greatest adventure of all,' the vicar concluded, surveying the sea of faces in front of him, his voice becoming a little doubtful, and possibly realising that adventure wasn't at all what his listeners wanted. Jane felt the relief of the congregation as he hurried on to announce that the family would be pleased if everyone would join them for tea at the White Rose Hotel, following the private ceremony at the crematorium.

Jane shut her eyes and said a prayer for Mabel, and for her mother, and then for herself. What was she asking of God in that last prayer? That God would give her more gumption, make her less horrid, help her to accept whatever he asked of her? She hardly knew. Perhaps it was enough just to have tried to pray at all.

The congregation stood up to sing *God be in my head*, and she saw the family prepare to walk down the nave aisle, Mabel's son appearing from behind his wife's coat like a woodlouse emerging from under a stone. The funeral was a duty that must be done, and the day got through. Then they could all go home to Buckinghamshire where their lives would go on as they had before, except that there would be extra money for holidays if the flat fetched a good price.

*God be at mine end, and at my departing.* Jane watched the girls filing out, fidgety and bored with proceedings which promised nothing but grown-up ideas that didn't concern them. They had seen too little of their grandmother to learn to love her; her death meant nothing more than this long, dull day in uncomfortable clothes.

# THIRTY-FOUR

Was he gay? How could you be certain?

He'd read stuff, too much of it, about teenagers going through periods of confusion about their sexual identity. Teddy still didn't know where it left him.

Was it normal to feel strange longings for something one moment and something quite different the next? What did that really tell you about yourself; was sexual identity something which floated about until it got caught by someone or something, and after that it was fixed? And how could you be sure it *was* fixed? People sometimes came out when they were years older than he was. Maybe they'd repressed their real selves or decided they were bisexual.

He'd heard of people saying they'd known they were gay when they were still at primary school. They were the lucky ones. He was nearly seventeen and he was in a mess. You were meant to know about it long before this. He'd overheard Mum saying to Dad he was young for his age. That didn't make things any better. Basically, it made them worse.

When he was with his friend Ollie Benson he felt more alive in some new and unexplained manner, even strangely happy. But what did that mean? He didn't want to put his arm round him or anything. Or did he?

Ollie was someone who broke in on your thoughts, who did something you wanted them to do before you knew you wanted it, who guessed what you were thinking, who made you laugh.

His thoughts turned to Ellen. He liked being with her too, but in a different way. He and Ollie were equals, but when he was with Ellen he wanted to protect her, to make up to her for the lousy deal she'd had in life with no mother. He liked the way she trusted him and relied on him; it made him feel good about himself.

Something told him Ollie wouldn't altogether understand about Ellen, and it was this, together with what he sensed the other boys might be thinking about him, that made him uneasy. Maybe Ollie and the other boys knew more than he did. If they'd picked him out as gay then perhaps he was.

Ollie was gay. That was a dead cert. If the other boys saw him and Ollie going around together as close mates they would come to the obvious conclusion. Teddy didn't want to have decisions like this made for him; to be told by other people what he was or wasn't. Not when he didn't know himself.

But this wasn't the only thing swirling about in Teddy's mind, making him feel that his world, hitherto a fairly predictable one, was becoming too complicated for him to deal with on his own. He'd known ever since he'd been able to see his parents as people, rather than just as providers of basic comfort, that his dad worried about things. Dad worried about Mum, that she was overdoing it or bored; he worried about seeing so little of him, Phoebe, and Jonah because of his long office hours; he worried about whether he was really up to his job. But now there seemed to be other things worrying him that Teddy couldn't have exactly pinpointed, but which he felt threatened them all in some vague, shadowy form.

That night back in January, when he'd heard his parents arguing, the shadows had stepped forward and become shapes, and once they'd done this it was impossible to drive them back. He'd been on his way to bed and the sound of his name made him stop suddenly outside the sitting room door. He'd stood there knowing he shouldn't listen, but doing so all the same. Their voices were too low for him to hear anything more for a minute or two, and then he heard his mother say in a hard, light tone, 'Perhaps he thinks you're having an affair.' His dad's voice was quieter and he couldn't hear anything more until his mother's voice said angrily, 'He is my son, remember.'

*My son.* Why had Mum said it like that? Had they been talking about the possibility he was gay? Was that why Mum said *my son* in that strange voice as if she meant more than what she was saying? Had Dad flipped? Was he going to refuse to accept that his son was gay, would Dad stop loving him?

Thinking about this made Teddy feel so desolate he found tears coming into his eyes. He knew he was special to Dad in a way the others weren't. Probably it was because he was the eldest. Or maybe it was because he and Dad were kind of alike, whereas Phoebe and Jonah took more after Mum. Dad had once said to him he'd always had to work hard because he wasn't, underneath, especially clever or good at anything. Teddy thought he was like that too.

*Perhaps he thinks you're having an affair.* Did other parents make accusations like this, whether they believed it or not? Could his own parents be planning to split up because of – he slammed down the brakes on the way his thoughts were going.

His father had always been a quietly consistent presence in Teddy's life; in the background, but always there as an anchor. Teddy saw that his mother could be difficult to live with, but he thought Dad must love the way she was, everything so ordered and arranged as if something was driving her on. Sure, his father retreated into his job, which gave the impression his work was more important to him than anything else, but Teddy knew that when it came to the crunch it wasn't. It was always Mum and his three children. It was just that he wasn't very good at allowing this to show on the surface.

'Here's my dad in the First Fifteen. Things haven't changed much, have they?'

Teddy and Ollie were sitting in the school archive room, ostensibly to gather together material for an article for the school magazine. Ollie, who had a sharp eye, had been asked by the head of the English department to write a piece on the school's celebrity old boys spanning the last four decades, illustrated by old photographs. Teddy, despite his lack of any of that sort of cleverness, had offered to help – which meant keeping him company.

It was Saturday afternoon and most of the other boys were playing sport in various teams both home and away. Teddy, being incompetent at both hockey and rugby, was not in a team. Ollie had from the moment of his arrival at the school refused to be considered for one. He said he had more interesting things to do than move a dog-turded ball around a muddy field.

Ollie pushed a photograph across the table to Teddy, who picked it up feeling faintly curious. He'd wondered sometimes about Ollie's dad, what he was like. Ollie never mentioned his parents. Usually mates didn't more than necessary, and when they did it was usually with complicit despairing rolling of eyes. But Ollie's silence was the more noticeable because he had plenty to say about practically everyone else.

The photograph was mounted on thick cream card and showed boys dressed in the school's rugby kit. They sat with their hands over their knees, long striped socks over legs spread out to link with those of their neighbours. In the rows behind, boys stood with arms folded across chests; in the background there were shields hanging against a stone wall. Teddy examined the expressions on the faces and decided Ollie was right. They did all look exactly like those in the photographs of the current school teams which adorned the passageway at the entrance to the dining hall.

'No prizes for telling which is him. Does he have a go at you for not being in the team like he was?'

Ollie shrugged.

'I wouldn't care if he did. It's not as if – anyway, why should people have to be a replica of their father?'

Teddy was silent for a moment, digesting this.

'Are you closer to your mother then?'

Ollie didn't answer. He had picked up another photograph and was examining it with interest.

'Your dad didn't go to Wharton, did he? Or one of your uncles?'

'As if. Dad's parents weren't into private education.'

'This guy looks just like you.'

'Bullshit. For one thing, I haven't got hair like that.'

'Hair's a detail. His eyes are shaped like yours. That's why he's like you. Don't you see?'

Teddy grabbed the photograph. It was a close-up of a fine-featured face, with dark, expressive eyes that looked intently at something beyond the camera. He dropped it in disgust.

'He looks like he's wearing make up,' he said, half-offended. 'As well as weird clothes.'

'It's obviously taken at a school play, you idiot. Can't you see he's in costume? Of course he'd have stage make-up on. Here, let's see if there's a name on the back.'

They deciphered the faded ink scrawl on the reverse of the photograph. *Laurent Zinchenko, The Alchemist.*

'No date,' said Ollie, disappointed. 'Though as it's with all these other ones from the eighties it must be around then. He's edible, all right. He could almost be your dad – you don't reckon your mum was playing around?'

'Don't be so effing stupid.'

'Keep your hair on, that was a joke. Maybe he was a Russian prince. Come on, let's pack up. I'm getting pissed off.'

Teddy put the photograph back on the pile. For some reason he wished he hadn't seen it, but at the same time he wanted to keep hold of it and look at it again, away from anyone else. There *was* something about those eyes.

'I'll stash all these back into their box,' he said. 'We've got all we want.' He stole a sideways glance at Ollie and slid the Laurent Zinchenko photograph under his arm inside his jacket. Why shouldn't he borrow it?

He could always put it back later and nobody would know.

'Teddy – '

'Yeah?'

'Have you any idea what I'm thinking?'

Something new in Ollie's voice alerted Teddy, but before he had time to work out what it meant, Ollie had leant over and very gently slid a hand around his face and kissed him on the mouth.

For an instant Teddy watched himself accept the embrace, unsure of his own reactions, of anything at all. He sensed Ollie understood this, for silently he drew back and smiled quite easily at him as though nothing had happened.

'I need to be back at the house,' Ollie said as they left the archive room, and his voice sounded like it always did, casual and assured. 'See you Monday, right?'

It was not until much later that Teddy was able to begin to think properly about what he was feeling or what he'd felt at the time – and already the gap was widening. His head and his body stopped being joined up; they were going off in different and contradictory directions. Some part of him was intrigued, even excited, but at the same time afraid. And now there was the photo of Laurent Zinchenko which made everything more mixed up than ever.

After supper (which he didn't feel like eating but for once Mum didn't notice) he went up to his bedroom to do his history prep. The thought of wading through eye-witness accounts and sifting through conflicting evidence made him resentful. History was so bloody boring when it meant endless nitpicking over documents. Tonight there was Richard III; was he the villain who murdered the princes in the tower or was he much maligned by historians? Teddy didn't care one way or the other. How could he be expected to write essays after what had happened to him in the archive room? He could still feel the touch of Ollie's lips on his own, his hand around his face.

He did a hatchet job on Richard – Shakespeare had clocked him as a scoundrel which must count for something – then stuffed his books back into his bag. He placed the photo on the desk and sat looking at it. It was nothing like him. What a dick he'd been to sneak it from the archive room. He looked more like Ollie than this Laurent Zinchenko; Ollie had fair hair like his own.

He put out a hand to cover Laurent Zinchenko's forehead. Still he couldn't see what Ollie had meant. Why, he didn't have that straight nose and softly rounded chin! The boy in the photograph had classical features, the girlish beauty of Greek statues. *He* looked gay, all right. His own were rougher, more irregular, nothing like this. He put out his other hand and covered up the lower half of the boy's face. All at once, the eyes grew larger, looking at him, and with a shock Teddy saw they *were* his. He might have been looking in a mirror. He stared at them. Were they telling him something?

He'd have known if there was a relative who'd been at Wharton. Mum and Dad would have mentioned it; it would have been part of the whole business of him and Jonah coming here. Going back to the old family tradition, flying the flag for the old school, all that rubbish. But his family wasn't like that at all; they weren't those sort of people. Mum and Dad came from ordinary families. Wharton was a million miles away from their backgrounds.

The photo had come from the box labelled 1980s. That could mean someone his father's age.

He longed to tell someone, but there was nobody. Not his family. How could he possibly ask any of them when these freaky images were flitting in and out of his brain? He made a desperate effort to snatch at his thoughts and thrust them away. He was being a right prat, having these headcase ideas just because he'd seen some random photo that looked like him. Of course it wasn't his father. He'd heard somewhere that everybody was sixth cousins or even closer. Was Ollie really trying to tell him something else – for his own reasons? He ran a fingertip across his lips. The demon thoughts wriggled out of his grasp and regrouped.

He shifted restlessly in his chair. How else could he find out about Laurent Zinchenko? Reaching over to his laptop, he typed in the name but nothing came up. There would be lists of boys in the archive room, but that wouldn't be enough. He needed details.

What was the use of parents you couldn't talk to about things that mattered? Teddy's face hardened. Who could you ever trust with anything? He shoved the photo into a drawer, pulled some sweatshirts on top of it, and went downstairs. In the sitting room he found Phoebe and Jonah watching a police thriller. Standing in the doorway watching the screen for a moment, he wanted to hurt someone. He looked at Phoebe, sitting sideways on an armchair, her jeans-clad legs spilling over the armrest.

'Not like you to come back so early on a Saturday night. Mates all dumped you?'

Phoebe shrugged.

'I don't have to stay out to please you, do I? Just

because you haven't got a life. That can't be because you can't afford one, seeing as you never buy anything. God knows what you spend your allowance on.'

'It's none of your bloody business.'

'Since you ask, I don't have any cash, so I can't go anywhere. If Mum and Dad didn't live on another planet they'd know that everyone else gets more than I do.'

'I suppose you've put on two ounces and that's why you're in such a grump,' said Teddy as nastily as he could. 'Why aren't Mum and Dad here?'

Phoebe ignored him. Without lifting his eyes from the screen, Jonah said, 'They're arguing in the study.'

Teddy hovered. On the screen, a couple of police officers were hammering a black suspect. They looked out-and-out bastards.

'I suppose I've missed the actual killing.'

Phoebe glanced up at him impatiently.

'Can't you either come in or go out?'

'What's it about, d'you know?'

'For fuck's sake. You've missed too much to fill you in now – '

'Mum and Dad, I mean. What are they on about?'

'The usual – what else. Shut up, can't you?'

He could hear his mother shout, and then his father's angry voice. A door slammed. Then heavy steps up the stairs.

'Teddy, what's the matter with them?' Jonah wiped his nose with his sleeve and Teddy realised he was crying. Jonah, his jammy younger brother, who never cried.

'I don't know,' he said, shutting the door and going to sit next to him on the sofa. 'How should I?'

Another slam. Phoebe picked up the remote control and raised the volume. The three of them sat and watched television together, saying nothing. Murder, rape, intimidation; it was easier to lose yourself in these things.

# THIRTY-FIVE

The telephone was ringing when Jane arrived home from her Saturday afternoon of crisscrossing the town to the homes of different pupils. She picked up the receiver, trying not to hope. Ten to one it would be the head of music announcing a change to her teaching timetable at Wharton or the housemaster asking her to do an extra duty evening in the boarding house.

'Will you come out to dinner with me?'

Jane dropped her bag. It was Austen, sounding less hesitant than usual. Music books and a pack of frozen plaice fillets spilled onto the hall carpet.

'I'd like to very much,' she said. 'When were you thinking of?'

'Tonight?'

Jane smiled into the telephone, lifted in an instant to singing happiness. *I ought to be one of those women who tantalise men by not leaping at invitations, but surely such pretences are not for someone like Austen who has probably never learnt the rules of the game. Nor have I. It's stupid to play hard to get when every fibre of me longs to be with him.*

'Tonight would be perfect.'

'Then I'll pick you up around seven. Shall we go

out into the country? There's a place I've heard of – run by a French family – that I hope you'll like. I've booked a table but we don't have to go there if you'd prefer somewhere else.'

Jane put down the receiver. Everything was going to come right. She went into the sitting room, where her mother was watching the snooker with Grace.

'That was Austen,' she said casually, unable to keep the satisfaction out of her voice and knowing her mother wouldn't be deceived. 'You'll have to eat the fish yourself, as we're going out to dinner.'

'I thought it might be him,' purred Dorothy, with a significant smile at Grace. 'He called earlier and I suggested he try again around now. Make sure you wear something nice – not that terrible skirt you've got on now – and perhaps I can persuade Grace to stay for supper with me.'

\*

'A benefit of going out on the spur of the moment is that you don't have time to worry about what to wear,' Jane said, laughing. 'But you've got that nice jacket on, the one I imagined you wearing when I first saw you – and had on when I came to tea and met you properly. You probably don't remember these things.' She felt herself blush. She must sound like she was asking for a compliment.

'I remember *everything* about you from that time on the train.'

'Even the book I was reading?' teased Jane. 'I noticed yours. I thought how good it was to see a man reading Elizabeth Gaskell – people often dismiss her as one of those crusading Victorian authors who are so out of date they've become irrelevant to modern life.'

'I'd never read *Wives and Daughters* before.' Austen hesitated for a moment. 'Verity was a great admirer of Elizabeth Gaskell, and I wanted – '

'To love what she loved.' It was the first time Jane had heard him say his wife's name. 'It must help you feel still close to her.'

'She'd have liked you … Jane, you must never think that – '

'I wasn't and I know what you mean – '

'You always do. When you got out of the train and hurried away from me – ' He broke off, his face twitching slightly.

'I couldn't have hurried that much,' she protested. 'I could hardly walk in my horrid new shoes. I got rid of the hateful things the next day.'

'It was reading novels that kept me from going over the edge altogether.' His expression told her that he knew she would understand. 'They tell us we aren't alone, help bring together the pieces that are all over the place.'

'It always amazes me when people *don't* turn to fiction for comfort. You've had so much suffering, and I've had so little, but when I was a child I used to escape into books – especially ones about difficult children.'

'But you weren't ever a difficult child yourself.'

'Not exactly, but I was always the child at the back of the queue … I only worked so determinedly at the piano to give myself an identity at school. It was easier if you were good at something. I'm not one of those naturally gifted musicians. And it was a way of winning approval from my parents.'

'Were they so hard to please?'

'It felt like it at the time, but children have a way of hearing things in the wrong way – and get stuck in a pattern of responses. It's a habit that can stay with you.'

'I can't imagine your parents thinking you anything but wonderful. Your mother certainly does now, anyway.'

'I'm afraid she's a little overpowering when you first meet her. She misses my father more than she'd like anyone to see. She ruled him with a rod of iron, but they had a very happy marriage.'

Jane leant her elbows on the white tablecloth, running a lingering finger around the gold rim of her coffee cup. The tiny dining room was lit with candles and rich French tapestries glowed on the walls. They'd eaten and talked and laughed, every moment shot through with a sense of unquestioned togetherness, of coming home. Now, late in the evening, the other customers had left, and they were alone in the quiet room, enamelled cups of pungent coffee steaming in front of them.

'There's something I'd like to ask you.'

He lifted his hands across the table as if to cradle his coffee, almost reaching her fingers. His hands looked like all of him: clumsy, gentle, unassuming. She wanted to touch them. The extraordinary thought that he might be going to ask her to marry him burst into her head. In her confusion she jerked her hands away from his and into her lap.

'I wanted to find out – that is, I'm planning to take a group of boys on a classics trip to Greece immediately after the end of the summer term,' she heard him saying. 'I know it's a lot to ask, but it would be terrific for me if you'd come too.'

The tablecloth, so beautifully starched and pressed, swam in front of her. A stray crumb lay near her cup. Jane stared at it until it lost focus.

'I don't know anything about the archaeological sites.'

Austen didn't respond. She shot him a quick glance. The glow in his eyes had gone.

'I know you do a marvellous job on your evenings with the boarders. It would only be a case of helping with the boys ... being around.'

Being around. So that was it. She was always around – and usually in the way, except when she could be useful. Things hadn't changed.

'An unofficial matron, do you mean?' Disappointment made her voice take on a mocking quality. But she couldn't help it. After all this, was he going to turn out to be another Stephen?

'Well, not exactly, but ... we need a few extra adults – there would be several of us going, to help keep an eye on the boys.'

'You would be better asking someone else.' She knew she sounded like a sulky child. 'I wouldn't be any good as a sheepdog.'

'It's not that. Jane, it's not that at all. It's more that I – '

'More coffee, Madam?'

A French waiter was meant to know by instinct when not to interrupt. Being English, they managed polite smiles and said yes please, so he refilled the cups and retired with the air of one who knows he has erred. But the moment was lost.

'I expect you'd like time to think it over,' Austen said, showing by his face that he too wished to retreat.

'Maybe that would be best.' She gulped down the coffee she no longer wanted and which now tasted bitter. She forced her hands flat against the sheen of the napkin on her lap, bewildered by the wrong turning he – or was it she? – had taken.

I have let myself fall in love with you, she cried inwardly. I don't believe you only invited me out tonight because you want someone to help out with stopping over-excited teenagers drink too much red wine in Delphi. I *won't* believe it.

She remembered the expression in his eyes when he'd watched her playing the piano in Imogen's house just before Christmas. She couldn't have mistaken that look.

He'd already booked the table when he rang her. Had he been going to take somebody else and they'd backed out at the last minute?

# THIRTY-SIX

'Can I come in?' the girl said.

It was Monday morning and Kate needed to get through her rituals of cleaning and straightening. If they sorted her head enough, she'd get round to working out how she could earn some money.

She kept the door just open enough and switched on the hostile lack of interest she always awarded to street sellers and cold callers. Not a Jehovah's Witness this time. They usually came in respectable well-scrubbed pairs on a Saturday morning, when there was a better chance of catching people at home.

Another row over the weekend sparked off by their financial situation had – though she didn't exactly admit this to herself – frightened her. It had been the worst of a series of arguments between them, interspersed by speaking silences. It couldn't go on like this. She must take some kind of action.

Not that Philip had told her to go and earn money. He'd never done that. But something of bitterness had crept into his anxiety at their rate of expenditure. He'd made short, angry remarks about small things, seizing on them as objects for attack. Some instinct told her the real cause for his anger was not the thing near to hand. It was the move to Wharton.

He'd always been over-cautious, unwilling to take risks.

She'd told herself when they bought the house that once they were settled she'd go out to work, and now the time had come. French classes for under-fives was one idea. Or older children. She was pretty well fluent and she'd coached Jonah all right. There ought to be bags of opportunities among pushy Wharton mothers.

'What is it?'

The girl was looking her up and down as though she was judging what reaction she was getting before deciding on her next move.

'There's something I need to ask you.'

Kate closed the door a fraction.

'Yes?'

'Can I come in for a moment? I need to talk to you. About your husband.'

Kate froze.

'What did you say?'

'Your husband. There's something you should know about him. And about me. You'd do well to allow me to come in.'

Nora was walking up the drive towards the Arzanos' house carrying a bunch of pussy willow twigs. She bloody would be. The girl would have to be let into the house now.

'I haven't got much time. No more than five minutes.'

In complete silence Kate led her into the kitchen, furious at the triumphant I-knew-you'd-give-in smile. She pointed towards a chair, and sat down herself, trying for an indifferent face. This is what happens in sitcoms. Tart comes round announcing to Complacent Wife that she's got her talons into Unfaithful Husband

and they start screaming at each other. Surely it isn't what this girl is going to say; it couldn't be. She felt a hysterical desire to laugh.

'Your husband loves me.'

The girl didn't take her eyes off Kate. They were green, an unnatural viridian, like a model wearing coloured lenses. What a creamy complexion she had. And that hair! It was almost as pale as her skin.

'Has he told you so?'

How strange it was that she could say this, as if she were actually acting in one of those soaps she'd failed to stop the children watching. The script was written out and she had merely to play the part allotted to her.

'Yes,' said the girl. 'He loves me, and I love him. He wants to leave you and live with me. He's afraid of hurting you and the children. But he doesn't love you any longer. He feels his marriage to you is finished.'

'He said that too, did he? What a conversation you've been having. Pity it's all in your imagination.'

'He has to move on if he's to be happy. He loves me – and he wants to be with me all the time.'

She pronounced the words with emphasis, as if learnt for the occasion and practised many times for effect. Again, they struck Kate as if they were lines written by a scriptwriter.

'Then why isn't he? You take a lot upon yourself, coming here and spouting a whole load of rubbish which I don't believe for one moment.'

'Don't you?'

One up to you. Kate registered her mistake in allowing this creature into her house.

'No. I can recognise a tall story when I hear one. You wouldn't be here to plead for him.'

The girl's expression didn't change, but Kate caught a ripple of uncertainty.

'I told you. He's afraid. Afraid of telling you what he thinks must make you unhappy.'

'Yes, he might well be afraid to do that.'

'But you can't want him,' insisted the girl, ignoring the sarcasm and fixing her gaze on Kate. 'His marriage to you is over, a thing of the past. You know it is, for all your cold and disdainful looks. You can't want to cling on to a man who'd rather be elsewhere, who stays with you out of pity.'

She's mad, thought Kate suddenly. Using her creepy car headlight eyes to try and mesmerise me like a scared rabbit. She's one of those lunatics with some psychotic syndrome which makes her go around telling complete strangers that she's having an affair with their husbands. She's suffering from an obsession, a delusion that people are in love with her. I'll probably find out she's been to half the women in the neighbourhood with the same crazy tale.

She stared at her, realising she'd seen this girl before, in the road several times, and in the train last year. That green jacket – Kate remembered it now, how subtly it went with the girl's magnolia face and white-blonde hair. As the images came back to her, shreds of a teatime conversation came with it. She could hear in her head Jonah saying in dismissive tones, 'that yucky green she was wearing, it makes me think of slime,' and then Phoebe's voice, 'you don't know anything, it looks cool.'

That had been weeks ago. But why had they been talking about this girl? Had the children met her? What had been the rest of the conversation? She couldn't remember.

Sap-green. A young, cruel colour.

'Think about it,' said the girl, leaning over towards Kate. 'Wouldn't you be ashamed to hang on to a man who doesn't love you?'

She isn't mad, thought Kate, her mind swinging wildly. She's a scheming bitch who thinks she's seen something she wants and will ride roughshod over anybody to get it. Go out and grab it, take a lover, make him jealous, spice up your life. Wasn't that what the younger generation of women believed? Have it all, and have it now. She felt old and alienated all at once, past it, sick of the whole business of women driven by biology competing for men, cutting each other up.

'It's dishonest,' the girl persisted, 'it's dishonest to pretend not to see what must be staring you in the face.'

Pretending not to see things. A miscalculation there from this nasty piece of work. If only you *could* not see things, bat away those images that came at you. She'd had seventeen years of it. But Philip's infidelity – no, she wasn't going to allow any more of this.

'Get out of my house. You're not gaining anything by telling me your sick fantasies.'

'I'm doing it because I know he loves me.'

'You're not. You're doing it because you're just another greedy little girl who thinks she can nick any husband who catches her eye.'

But a doubt had crept into her mind. She stared silently at the girl's face, an alien mask with thoughts she couldn't read.

'My name's Daisy.'

'I don't want to know. You can be Lily or Poppy or Rosie for all I care. Now I'll show you to the door.'

After the girl had gone, Kate sat down again in

the silent kitchen. A feeling of poison, of suspicion lingered. Was it true that Philip was having an affair with this girl? Or had he only wanted to? No smoke without fire; the old saying came back to her in all its triteness and inadequacy. Had he slept with her?

New and painful sensations crowded in. Philip was so much *there;* her one fixed anchor in anxiety-driven days. Temptation might appear in the background – the fatally beautiful Imogen for example who must be after a new man now that her snarky husband had taken himself off – but Philip was too upright and honourable to take advantage. He never turned his head.

But he had now. She was beginning to believe the girl's story. For a girl with a blank, amoral face and silken hair. In those years after Laurent, had she lost sight of Philip, of who he was? On one level she'd tried to make it up to him, to cover up her guilt. She'd given him love – of a sort.

But she'd cheated him of what she owed to him. She'd withheld the truth of herself from him, and had gone on feeding her secret obsession for Laurent in a way that was almost wilful. There *was* a dishonesty in all this that had skewed every other action of her life. Above all, she'd kept the secret of Teddy, allowing it to sit in the corner of their marriage, her Pandora's box.

How much better it would have been if she'd confessed everything to Philip at the time! Had it been his very generosity, his worshipping devotion of her that had stopped her? She tried to tell herself that it had been impossible for her to throw it all back in his face, to hurt him so cruelly, only to whisper that it had been cowardice that had made her keep quiet. She'd traded on his affection for her own convenience.

She remembered the many letters she'd written to Laurent, the ritual tearing up of the sheets of paper, as symbolic as blood-letting from cut wrists. She'd promised herself she'd stop when they moved to Wharton. But she hadn't, not even in her head. Someone, deranged and controlling, was still exacting these payments.

She sat staring at the knots in the surface of the pine table, her eyes following each spreading whorl. The table had come with them from London, and Kate knew each irregularity by heart; the knife marks on one side (Jonah in a childish tantrum); the gradual warping of the whitening wood (years of scrubbing). She'd fed her family at this table; she'd helped the children with their homework. It stood incongruous in the middle of this designer kitchen with its granite worktops and fitted appliances, a silent reproach.

The girl's words came back to her, spoken with that deadpan insistence: *you can't want to cling on to a man who stays with you out of pity.* Was it possible Philip's love and loyalty was a thing of the past? Had she finally killed it off with all her getting and spending? She remembered Philip's tiredness, his withdrawal from her since they'd come to Wharton, the shortness of his answers. She'd put it down to commuting.

No, it wasn't that. He'd come to the end of being treated like a workhorse, being taken for granted. That's what she'd done. She'd worn out his love, and he'd gone to this girl for the comfort he hadn't been getting from his wife. She hadn't bothered to give it to him.

Something vital and living along the path of her

marriage had been lost, and she hadn't even noticed. She'd thrown it away.

But the family table was the same. She began to understand at last more of the nature of the man she'd married. His love for her had been on a higher level than hers for him or for Laurent.

There was pain as she thought of this – and stirring deep in her consciousness a new and scarcely formed feeling of unselfish, yearning love. She'd *used* Philip – yet she loved him. She knew that now, when it was too late.

The telephone began to ring, its shrill tones insistent in the quiet house. Kate picked up the receiver. Please don't let it be Philip. Then she remembered it wouldn't be him, for he'd told her he had an important meeting with the other partners in the firm this morning which might last most of the day. Something about strategy-planning, or was it streamlined management? She hadn't listened.

'Mrs Gidding?'

The voice at the other end was coolly authoritative. Kate didn't recognise it.

'This is Mrs Davenport, your daughter's head teacher. There has been a very serious incident involving the bullying of one of the girls, in which your daughter has taken part. We would like you, or Phoebe's father, if he's available, to come into the school this morning, as a matter of urgency, to discuss what has happened. At twelve noon. The reception staff will show you the way. Can we expect you?'

Kate assented, her mind numb. Phoebe – bullying! It was nonsense, of course it was. There was some stupid mistake. She would go to the school and have it out with the crackbrained woman.

She groped in her bag for her car keys and then remembered that Philip had left the car at the garage for its MOT test, on his way to the station. She would have to walk.

She went upstairs to put on some more make-up. Checking her face in the mirror, she thought how strange it was that you could look normal when you'd been hit with something so heavy and paralysing that the pain was only just beginning. She pulled on her jacket from the hall peg, threw her mobile into her handbag and hurried out of the house.

Inside, the telephone began to ring again.

# THIRTY-SEVEN

There was something ominous about the school assembly today but Ellen couldn't work out what it was. She sat tense in her seat, waiting.

Now that she'd been nearly two terms at the school, Ellen was used to the routine of assemblies. It was never the whole school meeting together; that would have been impossible, given how many girls there were to fit into the hall. Some days there was assembly for just the lower part of the school; on other days there wasn't any assembly at all and they had tutor periods instead which meant boring administration and stressy talks about hygiene or dropping litter from whoever was in charge of your class. Today, being a Monday, it was everybody except the sixth form.

Girls of all shapes and colours crowded into the hall. It always amazed Ellen how different everyone looked, even though they were all wearing the same basic uniform of pleated kilts, white shirts and navy jumpers. The *way* people wore the uniform was part of this. Some girls looked all groomed and ironed, while others looked as if they'd shrugged on their clothes straight from the crumpled pile of yesterday. There were rules about having your hair tied back if it was longer than shoulder length, but even that left a huge

271

variation because you could still have strands hanging down over your face.

Most girls in Years Seven and Eight looked as if they were obeying the regulations pretty well, but after that everyone pushed the boundaries out in one way or the other, with make-up, or jewellery or weird hairstyles. The sixth form all wore their own clothes and once Ellen had confused one of them with a younger teacher and made herself look like an idiot.

The more senior you were, the further back in the hall you got to sit. The seats at the far end were still being filled up with Year Elevens who always came in last, mooching in as if they shouldn't have to come at all since the whole procedure was no business of theirs. In one corner of the stage in front of her was a grand piano which was being played by one of the music teachers. She didn't have a soft and sweet face like Jane, but looked sour as if she didn't like the music she was playing and wanted to punish everyone. Nobody ever listened, because although you weren't meant to talk while everyone was coming in, there was still a lot of signalling and messages mouthed down the rows.

In the centre of the stage there was a semi-circle of chairs occupied by senior members of staff. They sat calmly, watching the hall fill up and alert to any sign of bad behaviour, wearing the composed and intelligent expressions they always put on. Today Ellen thought they looked grave, almost shocked, as if they knew this was not going to be an ordinary assembly.

It was much more drawn-out than usual; they'd been waiting in the hall for ages. Beside her, Clover was making faces and was just heaving her best *Hollyoaks* sigh when the teacher at the piano played a loud finishing chord, and Mrs Davenport the head teacher walked to the front of the stage. This was the signal for absolute quiet and it always surprised Ellen that she got it after a few seconds. Today it was just the same, but Mrs Davenport's face was unusually forbidding. Ellen sensed she was about to tell them that something awful had happened.

'This is a day each one of us will always remember,' she began, speaking in a steady voice that carried right through the hall and made Ellen feel shivery inside, 'because I have some very serious news for you, which I have been requested by the people most concerned to speak to you about at this assembly. Over the weekend, Millie Heath from Year Ten attempted to kill herself.'

There was a shocked drawing-in of breath around the hall and then a dead silence.

'By what appears to be a miraculous chance, Millie was found in time – and mercifully has survived. But she will be in need of special help for a long time to come. I have spent some time with her parents and with the police. Mr and Mrs Heath have asked me to talk to you all this morning, and in particular to those girls with whom Millie associated.'

There was a pause while Mrs Davenport's clear gaze swept over the rows of faces, as if seeking out particular individuals without betraying who they were.

'It appears that Millie was driven to such a desperate and despairing act by a feeling that she was trapped. That there was no way out of the deep unhappiness enveloping her, and that this unhappiness originated in school. I believe there is nobody here in this hall who will not be shocked to the core by what I am telling you. Some of you may want to write to Millie. You will be given time and help to do so during your tutor periods this week.'

Ellen sat petrified. Millie Heath! Wasn't that the poor girl whom she and Clover had seen crying in the road, the day they'd gone shopping after school and Clover bought her the scrunchies? That was last autumn; since this term had started she didn't think she'd seen Millie around the school at all. She put up a wondering finger to feel her plait. It was as if the whole thing was a nightmare and she must touch things to find out if they were real. In her head she saw Millie disappearing around a corner, hurrying away from the newsagents in her thick tights and an ugly anorak that looked more like a tent.

'This affects every one of us. Millie has something to offer our school that nobody else can replace. We have nearly lost it. Our examination of ourselves will be deep and painful. Our self-reproach must lead to a renewed determination to value each and every one of our community, and to treat them with kindness and respect.'

There were sounds of sobbing throughout the hall as some girls turned to their neighbours for comfort and put their arms round each other.

'All of you are old enough to understand that this leaves a deep stain on the school. Millie wanted her life to end because she was unable to endure the cruel and consistent bullying to which she felt she was subjected. To have such a thing happen in any school of which I am the head teacher is the greatest source of pain to me, and it is a grave indictment on us all.

'Bullying of any kind is not something we have to tolerate and nor must it ever be swept under the carpet or dismissed as inevitable in a school of this size. It is not. That both staff and pupils have allowed such behaviour to go unchecked is both unimaginable and unacceptable. But it has happened, and it must be faced up to by each one of us. There is not one of us who does not need to search our heart to ask what we could have done to prevent it.'

She paused, as if to allow her words to sink in. Ellen stared down at her bitten nails, feeling sick and cold. It was true. She and Clover hadn't done anything to help. They'd seen Millie crying, and had avoided that hateful group of Year Tens smirking over their mobile phones, and most likely sending Millie spiteful texts. They'd thought of themselves first, not wanting to get involved in hassles with Phoebe Gidding and the rest of them, like Char and Renny.

She'd had another reason for keeping quiet. She hadn't wanted to get on the wrong side of Phoebe because Phoebe was Teddy's sister. Phoebe might say things against her at home and Teddy would have to side with his sister. But now, what must poor Teddy feel when he knew about this! She couldn't bear it for him. He was so loving and kind, like the big brother she'd always wanted. He wasn't her boyfriend – those lying-in-bed-imaginings of him kissing her weren't going to come true – but Ellen knew she would never feel the same about any other boy. If only – but that was all too late. Sticky tears trickled down the scar on her face. She put out her tongue to try to lick them off and wiped her nose with her sleeve.

Beside her, Clover put out a comforting hand, her nails painted cupcake pink. You aren't allowed coloured nail varnish until you're in the sixth form, Ellen found herself thinking irrelevantly. It looks pretty against her black skin. Then she wondered how she could think of something like that when Millie must be still lying in hospital, and hated the way random and self-centred stuff came into your head.

'I want you to go to your classes now, but instead of your first lesson, you will spend the time thinking over what has taken place. Your teachers have been instructed to answer any questions, and to help you cope with your feelings. We must all work together to prevent such a thing ever happening again. I will be available in my room until the end of break, if anybody wants to speak confidentially to me. The police will be coming to the school to talk to some girls on an individual basis. All the girls in Year Ten will stay behind now, as I wish to talk to them on their own. The rest of you please file out quietly.'

For once, nobody jostled or joked as they got up from their seats and left the hall.

'We couldn't have done anything, we honestly couldn't,' whispered Clover as they trailed in shocked, silent groups to their classrooms.

'No, we couldn't,' echoed Ellen.

But she knew it wasn't true. She thought of her mother and the way she'd died. Granny had explained it all to her. He mother had tried to do good things right up to the end. Her mother would have saved Millie.

But Ellen hadn't done anything except go shopping when she'd seen Millie crying. She was certain that for the rest of her life she would remember this day, and how she'd passed by on the other side, like the people in the parable.

# THIRTY-EIGHT

At first, the head teacher's conference room seemed a blur of people, but as Kate moved forward to take a seat amongst the rows of chairs arranged in semi-circles, she saw Phoebe and five or six girls sitting silently together in the front. Behind them were half a dozen adults, who Kate supposed to be other parents. They were almost all mothers, which was presumably to be expected, even in these days of so-called equality. The fathers would all be out at work. Even to demand that mothers drop everything and come into the school like this was colossal cheek. Mrs Davenport had a nerve, hauling them in here without a moment's notice, as if the school needed parents to back them up.

She chose a seat on the end, and sat down, uneasy and out of place. Phoebe didn't look at her, apart from one white-faced glance as she came in. On either side of her were girls whom Kate recognized as Phoebe's friends, Renny and Char, but since they'd only been to the house on a few occasions Kate barely knew them. Phoebe preferred to socialise around the town's shops and coffee bars. None of the parents were familiar to her. Kate realised with a shock that she'd been so taken up with networking among Wharton parents that she hadn't thought to make friends with any of the mums from Phoebe's school.

Mrs Davenport's appearance was quite different from what Kate expected. She was younger for a start, and considerably better dressed. Kate decided immediately that she didn't like her. Almost certainly power-mad, wanting nothing more than to sit in judgment.

A glance at the faces of the other parents told her that most of them felt the same; apart from one mother who kept her eyes fixed on the floor, they wore an identical belligerent expression, as if to say their daughters couldn't possibly be at fault.

'Now that you are all here, I need to tell you that one of the girls in the school, Millie Heath, has tried to kill herself. Thankfully, she did not succeed. Following extensive questioning of the entire year group, it is clear that your daughters have been involved in the bullying of a particularly vulnerable fellow student. This has been going on since the beginning of the year, but abusive text messages to Millie on Saturday night appear to have been what finally pushed her over the edge.'

It was several seconds before Kate took in what she'd heard. Sharp thuds in her chest began to hurt.

'I told you, I didn't join in – ' Phoebe burst out sobbing and turned round to Kate, tears streaming down her face.

'You did. And all the other times.'

This was from one of the other girls whom Kate did not recognise.

Mrs Davenport's face and voice were expressionless.

'You were with the others and knew what was

going on. You didn't try and stop your friends, did you, Phoebe? You've already admitted you only went home earlier than the rest because you didn't have any money. That was after sending the first text to Millie.'

'Are you accusing,' Kate heard the words, but they seemed to hardly come from herself, 'the girls in this room of driving another girl to suicide by their treatment of her? Because I deny it. I refuse to believe my daughter has ever laid a finger on anybody else. She wouldn't be a popular member of the school if she were capable of such behaviour.'

'Bullying is very rarely a matter of physical blows, Mrs Gidding. Girls have the social skills to use psychological cruelty to a fine degree. Mobile phones and the internet have become one of the commonest means; they offer unlimited scope for taunts and pressure. All the girls in this room have been involved in this kind of activity, and so-called popularity has nothing to do with it.'

'The girl was a basket case to begin with, so it's hardly fair to pin the blame on teenage stuff. They all talk tough, this girl just couldn't take it.'

It was the only father present who spoke, and he did so with much of the aggressive pugnacity of an *EastEnders* character that Jonah was good at mimicking. Kate sensed the silent applause of the other mothers. They wanted a spokesman. She remembered reading about cases of violent children with equally violent parents attacking teachers when their children were excluded. 'He's no angel,' they always said, 'but he never means any harm, not a mite of trouble at home.' She'd treated such attitudes with contempt.

The girl had nearly died! Kate felt her mouth go dry,

her stomach churn. As Mrs Davenport went on speaking, her imagination plunged towards what had happened in that family's home and then sheered away. It was beyond her; the horrific discovery, the nightmare disbelief at what Millie had tried to do. The panic-stricken guilt, the desperate questioning, the search for someone to blame. Phoebe, Renny, Char and the four other girls.

'Teenagers can be sharp with each other within their own accepted limits – they can also be tremendously affectionate and generous-hearted to their friends. But they can adopt a pack mentality. The layer of civilisation in all of us is very thin; look beneath the surface and you'll find the impulse and capacity to be vicious is in all of us. William Golding's *Lord of the Flies* has been a set text for O Level and now GCSE for over forty years and we still haven't taken in its warning. When children, and I include teenagers, get together in groups they can behave in a way that would be inconceivable as individuals. They will be capable, given certain conditions, of the deepest physical and mental savagery, of unimaginable cruelty. Unless goodness and civilised values are consciously and consistently taught throughout a child's life, they will revert to the group's lowest common denominator at the least opportunity.'

'Then what was the school doing looking the other way?'

'We've done our best for her. Nobody can say any different – '

'Renny wouldn't hurt a fly – '

Mrs Davenport looked at the cluster of bristling mothers, and at the father who leant forward in his chair, angry red hands pressed against his knees.

'These moral values have to be taught in the home. By the time children arrive at secondary school, attitudes that have been unconsciously learnt for years are very difficult to change. We cannot expect to turn children entirely around, however hard we try.'

Mrs Davenport stopped speaking and looked into the distance for a moment, her face sombre.

'The girls in this room,' she continued, glancing at them briefly, 'are just the most culpable. They conducted a concerted bullying campaign, through manipulation and social exclusion. The human desire for power over others easily slides into cruelty, and here it was towards a girl who was less adequate than themselves to cope with the increasing pressures under which teenagers find themselves. The world today expects them to be successful on all fronts. This is not how human beings are made. There are always people who need the help of others. It's the mark of a civilised society how it treats minorities of all kinds, and that includes the weak and vulnerable.

'These girls may have thought – or wanted to think – they were just having a bit of fun, which then got out of hand. But to Millie Heath it didn't come across like that and she didn't take it like that. There's a saying that all teasing is a form of attack. That's an exaggeration, but we need to tread particularly carefully with people who may not be able to grasp the difference. All your daughters are capable of making the distinction. Do you agree?'

Nobody looked at anybody else in the dead silence. Kate breathed in the stench of fear from the bodies around her.

'I must make it clear that they are the ones who,

according to our internal investigations, were actively unkind to Millie, but there are many others who stood by and allowed it to happen. You may know the saying that for evil to triumph, it is enough for good people to do nothing. It's certainly appropriate in cases of bullying.'

'That includes you, then.' The father's voice was sullen.

'Yes, it includes myself. And it includes you as a parent.'

'Not much of a school then. Don't think we're staying, because we're not.'

Mrs Davenport didn't answer him directly. Her face softened slightly.

'There are girls – a few in every year – who work as a force for good in the school. They lead the rest, sometimes in small hidden ways, but they give us hope. Your daughters have not been among them. But that doesn't mean they are incapable of such qualities. They may yet, with help, grow up to be the sort of women who bring good to others. I hope and pray that one day the school will be glad to have them among its members, and proud of what they have become.'

Mrs Davenport rose to her feet and stood for a moment with her hands resting on the desk in front of her.

'Exclusion from school is not appropriate in the circumstances, but those of you who wish to take your daughters home for the rest of the day may do so. During the remainder of the term we shall be working closely with the whole year group to try and help them understand themselves and other people better. We shall expect them back in school tomorrow as usual.'

Kate and Phoebe walked home in silence. Kate, for the first time in her life, hadn't a word to say. What could she say to this daughter who'd all at once become someone she didn't recognise? Phoebe was her clever and successful daughter; a girl who knew where she was going. Slamming doors and screaming matches – there hadn't been much of that, not compared to other teenagers you heard about. She hadn't resented her brothers going to a private school. She was poised for an unsullied set of starred A grades in her GCSEs next year. Kate had already imagined the photograph in the local paper showing Phoebe and her friends holding up their results slips. Now all that went for nothing.

She must say something to Phoebe, dry-eyed and expressionless beside her. There was the rest of the day to be lived through. She must speak seriously with her and find out exactly what she'd been doing and why. On the corner by the church, the pollarded lime trees loomed over them with accusing fingers.

'I don't want anything to eat,' said Phoebe, as they went into the house, her voice cracked and brittle. 'I'm going to my room. Leave me alone, will you?'

Kate put down her handbag on the hall table. She heard Phoebe close her bedroom door. There was nobody to whom she could turn for comfort or support. Automatically she switched on the answering machine.

'Mrs Gidding, this is Gareth Ridsdale, Teddy's housemaster at Wharton. Teddy wasn't present for callover in the house this morning, and he hasn't signed in as being late. Could you please telephone me to let me know why he's not in school today. Many thanks.'

Kate flew up the stairs two at a time, and flung

open Teddy's door. One whirling look told her the room was empty. She began to breathe again, leaning against the wall, the madness of unreasoning terror slowly releasing its strangling hands from her throat. Her limbs felt weak and heavy. Sweat stuck to her shirt.

That girl Millie – and Teddy. A coincidence. There was no connection; there couldn't be.

You're not thinking straight. Put that right out of your mind.

Her eyes ranged over the untidy room. There were clothes in a pile on the floor. Kate couldn't tell whether they were clean or dirty; probably they were a mixture of each. Teddy never put anything away. Various open books and pages of lined paper covered with his writing were stacked higgledy-piggledy on his desk and every available surface, in among deodorant sprays, pens, dirty mugs and an empty cereal bowl. Kate started tidying up, making immaculate stacks of books and papers, her hands mechanical, her mind feverish, testing and rejecting various possibilities as to Teddy's whereabouts.

It wasn't like him to go off like this. He was moody and secretive at times, but that was being a teenager; there was nothing in it. She knew other mothers furtively searched their teenagers' rooms for signs of drugs, but she'd never needed to. Teddy had stayed on the rails and was both straightforward and reliable.

He was also almost seventeen. Having been brought up in London, he was competent with public transport and, in his own way, street-wise. If he'd felt like doing a bunk off school for the day and gone to check up on his old mates in London, Kate couldn't honestly blame him. It wasn't a major crime, but not something he should make a habit of.

This was the line she would take with him, when he appeared back later in the day. She would insist he make his own excuses to the housemaster; she wasn't going to tell lies on his behalf.

She told herself this, but as she did so, she knew it wasn't true. She would always tell lies for her children if it would do any good; she always had. She was on their side, for who else would be if she were not? She didn't blame Teddy. Just now she wished she was back in London herself.

Philip's words about Teddy not being happy came back to her. Could Philip have been right after all? And money, she thought suddenly, what was he spending his allowance on? He never bought anything so far as she could see. Had he been secretly saving up to go somewhere today? Recent television news images of runaway teenagers boarding planes flashed through her mind. His passport! She wrenched open the drawer of his desk, and saw it among the clutter. Not that particular nightmare then.

London. Was that it? A girl? No. Kate had seen no signs of any interest in girls. It was something she hadn't cared to admit to herself or to anyone else. But there had been a gang of friends in his London school and it was possible he missed them more than he let on. He appeared to have made new ones at Wharton, but they wouldn't be the same as those he'd known for a long time. She tried to convince herself this was the explanation – and almost succeeded.

She picked up a pair of jeans and a couple of sweatshirts from the medley of clothing on the floor and folded them up. They looked reasonably clean and could be put away. Pulling open various drawers she began to rearrange the contents, shaking out crumpled tee-shirts and pairing up socks. Teenage chaos. It would be starting with Jonah soon, and then she'd have three rooms like this.

Something was stuffed at the back of one of the drawers. She pulled it out and saw it was a photograph of a boy, dressed up in costume. Laurent. Laurent as a boy. It was unmistakably him. She stared at it for a long moment and with a shaking hand turned the photograph over. *Laurent Zinchenko, The Alchemist,* was written on the back. Nothing else.

She sat down on the bed, feeling unable to stand. I got what I wanted, my secret reward. My sons at the same school that Laurent went to. Oh God, what have I started?

It means he knows, a voice inside her head whispered. He's found this photograph, and has noticed the likeness. For there *was* a likeness, she could see it plainly. So must anyone. Not in the features or colouring; they were very different. It was all in the eyes.

She put the photograph down on the desk and walked away from it, wiping her sweating hands down her thighs. As she paced about the room, accusations crowded in on her. Why had she gone down this dangerous path of sending the boys to Wharton? To have indulged such self-destructive desires, to have taken such a terrible risk. Why hadn't she gone back to a shrink, any shrink, told him what was going on in her head?

But was it irrevocable? She stood over the desk staring down at the photograph, trying to see it as a stranger might. Was the likeness unmistakable or was it her knowledge that made it appear so? Would an objective person see any resemblance to Teddy? As she considered this, she thought perhaps they might not. It was only in the eyes. In every other way Teddy was so exactly Philip's son. There was even the clumsiness, and the idiosyncratic walk, with one leg and foot turning inwards more than the other.

Was it all her imagination? Eyes were the window of the soul, they said. Did she see in Teddy's eyes something that wasn't there, was it just a projection of her own guilt?

I must ring the school, she thought, suddenly remembering the housemaster's phone call on the answering machine. I'll say Teddy had a dentist's appointment and I forgot to inform them, so sorry to be such a vague mother and cause trouble, it won't happen again.

She pushed the photograph back into the drawer and replaced the sweatshirts over it. Then she went downstairs and telephoned Wharton school. As usual the school secretary was perfectly spoken and entirely courteous.

*Teddy isn't happy.* Philip, blaming her.

She fumbled in her bag for her mobile. She must hear Teddy's voice, know he was all right.

The number was unavailable. She sent a text.

*Teddy, please call me. Tell me where you are.*

# THIRTY-NINE

Teddy stared out of the train window, not seeing the fields and trees flashing past. He was aware only of feeling glad he was getting away from Wharton. At each stop, as passengers piled in and out, he stayed still and defiant, telling himself he could do what he liked with his life. If he wanted to be on his own, he had a right to be. Nobody was going to stop him.

It wasn't just the business of the photograph, even though that stank at the bottom of his mind, making him feel he was dragging through each hour, weighed down by knowledge he'd have given anything not to possess. Though it wasn't knowledge, not really. It might all be his imagination playing tricks.

The uncertainty of it; that was what made it such complete shit. If things were definite one way or the other, then you could bear them better, you knew what you were up against. You could set about dealing with it. But if all you had to go on were wild suspicions jabbing at your mind like those bloody magpies that stalked about invading their garden it was a whole lot worse.

He wanted to get right away from school as well as home. When Ollie had shown him the photograph of Laurent Zinchenko, did Ollie really think this guy with his mix of French and Russian names might be his father? Or was he trying to make trouble for the sake of a bit of excitement? He did that sometimes, as if he needed things to happen all the time, for him to be pulling the strings.

You never knew with Ollie. He was clever, and far quicker on his feet than Teddy when it came to thinking what to say. He was always ready with some off-the-wall comment or cool shut-your-face reply. Nothing ever fazed him.

But Teddy had seen that Ollie was by no means an open book; he kept areas of his life secret from everyone. Like how he never talked, or hardly ever talked, about his home. He put up a Keep Out fence, and Teddy had learnt that it wasn't any use trying to get over it. There was something dodgy about such reserve. He was hiding something, maybe something bad he'd done. If people didn't trust you, how could you trust them?

Just now he hated the power Ollie had over him. The more he went over Saturday afternoon in his head, the more he felt Ollie had set out to disturb him in some way, as if to gain some hold over him. And then he'd *kissed* him. A shot of awakened desire stole over him. How the fuck was he going to react when he next saw Ollie?

And then Jonah had cried. Teddy knew, obscurely, how much he relied on Jonah always being on top of whatever was going on. It was how things always had been, how they ought to be, in their family. Jonah crying was all wrong, but he felt entirely at sea about what to do with such an unexpected problem. As he sat slumped on the sofa with Jonah and Phoebe, he made up his mind he would cut school on Monday and give himself a break, clear his head. Then maybe he might see a way to sort it.

Now, sitting on the train, he wanted to be rid of the whole thing: his family, his school, Ollie. He felt like giving them all a big shove, knocking them out of his way. To be alone, free from all the crap that was being handed out to him; that was what he needed.

He put on his headphones to listen to Nick Drake and slumped back in his seat. Nick Drake had known about the mess in your head all right; he said it all in those haunting lyrics in a voice that drifted about in your brain. Had he meant to kill himself? Teddy began to brood over the question, giving way to the strange attraction of escaping into the mind and dreams of a man who had been dead for more than thirty years.

Getting off the train at Charing Cross, Teddy eyed the coffee stall before turning away. He needed to save his cash for when he was hungry later on. He had less than a tenner on him now he'd paid for his train ticket, and it was no good going to a cash machine when his account was down to nothing.

Where was he to go now, with the whole of London beckoning him? Somewhere that didn't cost any money.

Lose himself amongst the crowds where nobody could get at him.

A high building.

He hesitated at the station exit, watching the taxis sweep up. To the right, down the Strand, was his father's office. He felt a sudden longing to go and find him, to reassure himself he was there, that everything was all right. But then he remembered Dad had an important meeting today, to do with the future of the firm. Dad had said they might be merging with another firm, but this was top secret and Teddy must keep quiet about it. Disturbing him today would be way out of order.

He turned left, and crossed the road behind a milling mass of schoolgirls of around Ellen's age. Their bright, assertive faces and shiny ponytails pissed him off. He thought of Ellen with her lopsided plait and bitten nails and decided he preferred them. She was real, absolutely herself. Hadn't caught on about the iPhone. That made him feel good, whatever else.

He had loads of time. It wasn't even mid-morning yet. He could go into the National Portrait Gallery first. He might as well give in to himself. If he looked at other faces, lots of them, paintings and photographs, they'd fill up his head, they'd crowd out the one that lay hidden in the drawer at home.

He hadn't been to the National Portrait Gallery for years, not since Mum had marched him there to see all those Tudor portraits for his history project in Year Six at primary school. He remembered their pale faces with buttoned-up lips and cold, mean eyes. It had been a drag, but Mum had let him choose souvenirs in the gallery shop and then bought him an ice-cream afterwards, so it hadn't been all bad.

Thinking about it now made Teddy feel confused. Everything had been so simple in those days. His parents said the same things; they agreed about the important stuff and it never occurred to him they might not. Mum organised what happened from day to day, Dad earned most of the money and they both looked happy enough.

You knew who people were then.

Some bloody hope of that these days. You couldn't know what people were like underneath. Mum and Dad had secrets they deliberately kept from him. His friend Ollie might be laughing at him behind his back. Ollie got bored easily, Teddy had often seen how he got a buzz by tricking those around him into doing what he wanted. Maybe he was just playing around when he'd given him that kiss.

He swung through the heavy doors. Old stuff or modern? Modern, no contest. All those pictures from history made him think of his childhood and Mum and Dad. Now wasn't a good time for any of that.

Thomas Stearns Eliot, he read, stopping in front of a portrait like those cubist paintings where you could see the profile and the full face all at once with both of them looking way-out and weird. So those were his Christian names. He hadn't ever wondered what the T. S. stood for, and it was one of those useless bits of information that didn't do anything for anyone, so he wandered on. Various politicians and people he'd never heard of. A lady chemist with lots of hands moving amongst papers. She had a shock of untidy white hair which reminded him of Nora. Harold Wilson in a cloud of pipe smoke. A haunted looking guy with huge, luminous eyes: Derek Jarman who'd died from AIDS. Teddy shivered.

He stopped in front of a painting of Iris Murdoch, remembering how his mother had made the three of them watch the DVD of *Iris,* all about her early life and then her getting Alzheimer's. 'What's the point of a film about an old biddy who ended up watching the teletubbies?' Phoebe had grumbled.

It was kind of a cold painting. The leaves at the

front were the same as that tree in Ellen's garden, a ginkgo, she'd called it. He remembered the tree as it had been last autumn, tall and showering gold leaves on the grass around the wrinkled trunk. Soon it would be green and beautiful again with new, bright leaves, and those kids from the other house, Terzo and Sofia, would be playing there again. As he pictured this, such a flood of unhappiness poured through him he had to clench his hands tightly to stop himself from crying.

He was caught in a trap. There was no way out. He was gay and there was nobody he could talk to about it. His dad might not be his real dad. Mum and Dad looked like they hated each other. They would split up and they'd have to move again. No more Nora and Ellen looking out for him.

He'd had enough. What was the point of it all? He'd like to go to sleep and not wake up. He didn't have anything to live for, so he might as well be dead.

# FORTY

'We would like a jug of water, please, with ice, from a tap. There is no need for it to be from a bottle.'

Dorothy spoke with carefully measured firmness, for the waiter was only a boy. She believed in encouraging the young to go the right way, so long as they understood this to be the same as hers. He was probably on work experience, and hadn't yet assumed the evasive tactics necessary to a waiter's survival. No doubt a more senior waiter would deal with the important business of helping them choose between Saltimbocca alla Romana or Scallopine alla Bolognese, and explain the finer points of the specialities of the day.

They were having lunch in the new Italian restaurant which had opened up in the High Street, ostensibly to celebrate Dorothy's birthday, but in reality to provide an outing for Grace Whipple, who had become more twittery than ever since Mabel's death. Dorothy's sidekick crony Mary Silcox made up the foursome, and Jane, who was fond of her mother's friends, had suggested it would be fun to try out Luigi's.

It might still be Lent – that season of self-denial which doesn't always quite work out like that – but it was almost over. Easter was less than two weeks away, and soon they would be singing *Jesus Christ is risen today*. Jane thought of Nora admitting to feeling tired of singing alleluia too many times. It was to be hoped the vicar would make sure that the hymns he chose for the Easter service did not *all* have it at the end of every line.

Dorothy, who was always generous – and liked her generosity to be recognised – was paying for all of them. It made her happy to see her friends and daughter enjoying themselves, and to know they were doing so at her expense and under her guidance. She drew a dignified breath and leaned impressively across the white tablecloth.

'I do not believe in pandering to this modern fad for drinking water out of a bottle. It's nothing but a racket. I've heard that some of it is years old, absolutely stale and not good for anyone's health. But people will believe anything nowadays.'

Jane sighed inwardly. She was devoted to her mother, but in public places Dorothy's insistence on having exactly what she wanted took away something of the enjoyment. Had it been disloyal of her to give the waiter a sympathetic smile? She remembered many similar occasions when she'd shrivelled up over her mother's sublime disregard for the possibility that other people could hear her comments or understand them if they did. If only her voice was less carrying!

At the next table a husband and wife studied the menu with too much concentration, and addressed each other with the indifference of people who have already spent too many hours in each other's company and have nothing left to say or be.

On the other side, a woman with earrings in the

shape of parrots sat alone, writing occasionally in a notebook. Was she an impoverished poet or novelist, driven by circumstances to write in the warmth of restaurants? Jane remembered a story about a certain well-known author said to have written her first bestseller in a café. This woman might believe that here was the secret to published fame.

Or she could be one of those diligent women, perhaps recently widowed, divorced or facing empty-nest syndrome, who had enrolled in a creative writing class and been told by the tutor to observe people in natural situations. Look for a distinctive physical characteristic and expressive body language, Jane imagined the tutor advising, eavesdrop on conversations and place your characters in a situation of conflict which they must struggle to resolve. This poor woman was in for a disappointment.

None of the other customers in Luigi's looked like pensioners, which may have explained the restaurant manager's attempt to seat their party at an undesirable table in the gangway to the cloakrooms. He would be adept at summing up at a glance who could be palmed off with an inferior position without complaint, and who must be shown with smiles and a flourish to the superior tables in the window. But he had reckoned without Dorothy, who had spurned the suggested table with a dismissive gesture, and surged forward in full sail to a more comfortable one. Life yields to the conqueror, she might have said – it was one of her favourite maxims – and Jane had to admit that on occasions it obviously did. She herself, and no doubt Mary and Grace, would undoubtedly have been stuck with the table by the lavatories, too feeble to protest.

'The cubicles in the ladies are ridiculously small,' reported Mary, who as a churchwarden had developed an interest in these necessities and considered it her duty to research them before they started eating. 'I found myself having to squeeze right against the bowl – almost touching it, *not* very nice – before I could close the door.'

'It's a good thing you've kept your slim figure,' said Grace. 'A fat person might find it a little awkward. They ought to take these things into account, especially as people are getting so much larger.' She cast her eyes anxiously around the restaurant as if to locate any overweight customers whom she should warn about possible hazards in the lavatories, before realizing with an apologetic flutter that Jane could be included in this category.

'No doubt the conversion of the building was planned by a man,' remarked Dorothy. 'There are never enough female facilities in theatres and public places. I suppose they forget that women take longer, or need to go more often. The queues are often scandalous. I always mean to write a letter of complaint.'

'I was once told there's an old Jewish prayer or saying, about thanking God for not being born a woman,' Jane said, a picture of a snake uncoiling itself into a queue of women stretching out in her imagination. 'The loo problem might come into it.'

There was a pause while all four women contemplated this possibility.

'I have often had some very pleasant conversations with other women in cloakrooms,' said Grace, breaking the silence. 'A woman offered me a spray of her perfume once when I was feeling upset that I'd forgotten to bring any in my handbag. It was Elizabeth Arden's Blue Grass – such a favourite when I was young.'

'I love these random encounters with complete strangers,' said Jane. 'They're doses of happiness given to you by surprise – and often just when you need them. It's like when the train breaks down. Or even when it doesn't … '

Luigi's was full of women meeting each other for morning coffee or lunch. All varieties were there. Young mothers consoled each other for sleepless nights as they spooned up frothy cappuccinos, their babies and toddlers in vast all-terrain buggies blocking up the spaces between the tables. Forty-something women on diets gorged forbidden pasta in rich sauces, laying bare their lives to identikit friends. Will my bulimic tendencies increase? Will my husband leave me for another woman? Don't miss next month's thrilling instalment on my cellulite treatment. Jane imagined all these exchanges being made, despite the close proximity of the tables to each other. Women were hungry for communication and needed to confide their indiscretions, though these might range from the illicit consumption of a forbidden Mars bar to the pains and pleasures of extramarital forays.

Did going to the pub perform the same function for men? Jane tried and failed to imagine Austen in such a setting, at a boys' night out. Instead, she began to picture the two of them here at Luigi's, having a romantic dinner. Asparagus with Parmesan, the butter gleaming on the spears. Then some classic dish like Risotto con Porcini, drunk with Chianti glowing red in the glass, and finally rich, dark Italian coffee and tiny almond biscuits. They would linger over the food, and plan other meals they would have together, even ones she might cook for him. They would talk of the places in Italy they had been to and which they would like to introduce to each other. What would it matter if no Italian had ever said *ciao bella* to her?

If she had Austen for her own, if she was beautiful to him, it would be more than enough. They would finish each other's sentences and his bear-like, gentle hand would touch hers across the table. They would be the last to leave, and afterwards they would laugh about how Luigi himself had finally advanced apologetically with their bill and an offer to fetch their coats.

Last week she'd gone up to London to have lunch with Stephen and Beth. Summoning up any enthusiasm was hard work, but she'd scolded herself into making the effort.

She was glad she had, for the day had been quite different from what she'd expected. She was welcomed as a dear friend; the other guests were familiar faces from the past and included a delightful unmarried curate, with whom she had a very satisfying conversation about the hymns they either loved or hated. What did it matter if some of their favourites were of questionable theology? She wished Nora had been with her.

She saw Stephen and Beth exchange pleased glances. It was difficult not to have a secret laugh at their kindly matchmaking efforts. He was, as her mother might say, the kind of man who was unlikely to marry. While she could imagine a pleasant friendship developing between them after today, she guessed that if he ever married anyone at all it would be another man and hoped it would be someone who deserved him.

She found herself wondering how Stephen and

Beth would react if this happened and decided that it was better not to expect too much of them. They'd joined in the jokes about the funny little ways of church-goers all right. But if only Christians could agree to disagree – and be nice about it!

All around them, waiters brandished tall pepper pots and lurked menacingly with graters and Parmesan cheese. Despite her dismaying experience of the morning, when she'd been handed a leaflet by a teenager in the street which turned out to be for a weight-loss programme, Jane dipped her third slice of ciabatta bread into the dish of flavoured olive oil. A romantic dinner with Austen was something to dream about, but this was reality: four women enjoying each other's company, and the joy of eating food for which they had neither shopped nor cooked.

'It's only women who fully appreciate this luxury,' said Grace, breaking into her thoughts. 'Men take it for granted, regrettably even the best of them.'

'And what will you four ladies have to follow – some Tiramisu or Cassata Siciliana maybe?'

'I'm not sure what to make of the way he said the word *ladies*.' Mary looked with indignation at the waiter's departing back after he'd taken their order.

'He made it clear that if we were in a piazza in his native Rome on a hot summer's evening he wouldn't be pinching our bottoms,' laughed Jane. 'Women of thirty-plus, and some of us with waistlines to match – *we're* not worth more than the offer of predictable puddings, and perhaps a caressing Mediterranean manner with the bill.'

Austen wasn't the kind of man whom waiters and barmen served ahead of others. She'd never liked men like that. Austen was *her* kind of man. Could she invite him to supper – just him? When her mother was safely out of the way at her Bloomsbury Group class. Still there was the familiar weight. She pictured Dorothy's stalwart figure by the wardrobe, heard her trenchant tones telling her what to wear …

'I so wanted Ellen to find a special friend when we moved here,' Nora had said to her yesterday.

'Clover?'

'Yes, there's Clover, and of course there's Teddy too – I hadn't quite envisaged a best friend in the shape of a boy. He's the very dearest of boys, isn't he? It's you I'm thinking of – it's privileged our family is, finding you, with your loving and generous heart. *God is his own interpreter, and he will make it plain,*' concluded Nora, resorting to a favourite hymn to explain her meaning.

But Jane needed God to make things plain to Austen.

She licked a spoonful of froth from her cappuccino. A small voice inside her whispered that he did love her … Why were clever men so stupid? Hadn't he learnt anything from all that human passion in Greek literature?

She thought of the perplexed longing in his eyes. It *couldn't* mean anything else.

Men must work and women must wait. Jane turned the words over in her mind. Was it suitable for a woman in the twenty-first century to remember such sayings? Shouldn't she be the sort of woman who kept men waiting for *her*? She bent her head over her cappuccino as if acknowledging this impossibility. Nor did the quotation sound quite right. She'd muddled it with something else. Women must weep, not wait; that was more like it. However, they might well come to the same thing.

But must she sit about waiting or weeping? After all, life did yield to the conqueror in the matter of vanquishing ruthless restaurant managers. Could the same rule be applied to what Winnie Pumfret would call landing her man? It was about time she took the initiative, and did away with that woman who sat meekly at tables in draughty gangways next to the lavatories.

Not an invitation to dinner but something else. *There is a tide in the affairs of men which taken at the flood leads on to fortune* ... what was the rest of the quotation? Something about being bound in shallows and miseries. You ought to be able to rely on Shakespeare.

She could feel a rosy blush spreading across her face and neck. Nora's words on the day of Mabel's funeral came back to her. *There's only one thing that you'll regret – missing the passing of your lives together.*

Soon it would be a whole year since she'd first seen Austen on the train as she was coming back from Stephen and Beth's wedding. *He may never ask, you know ... you might have to instead.*

'You look as though you have some secret you're keeping from us,' said Grace, smiling at Jane while Dorothy paid the bill. 'Perhaps you're in love.'

'It's to be hoped she is,' said Dorothy surprisingly, punching in numbers with a majestic air. 'All young women – and Jane is still that – should be in love. It is the proper order of things in the spring.'

# FORTY-ONE

'Are you all right?'

Angelo spoke roughly. He didn't want to talk to anyone. He'd come to the National Portrait Gallery for his own reasons. He wanted to look at faces to find the one he was looking for. He was chasing an idea; emerging, half-formed and still eluding him. People got in the way when he was like this.

But the boy looked in bad shape, standing there as if he'd had some kind of shock. Angelo stared at him reluctantly, and then realised he was the boy from the next door house down at Wharton. The older, clumsy one he'd seen loping off with his bright-eyed brother to the public school. Teddy, or was it Eddie? Hell and damnation. He didn't want to find himself playing Good Samaritan to this boy – or any other boy come to that. It wasn't his line of country.

He put out a hand almost angrily.

'What are you doing here anyway, all by yourself? Aren't you meant to be at school?'

No answer from Teddy or Eddie who was now turning away to rub his face on the sleeve of his school jacket. Angelo touched his arm.

'Come and have a drink. No, not that. How old are you? Sixteen? Something to eat then. In the place here, as long as it's not too full of arseholes and old trouts.'

He turned to lead the way and found the boy was trailing behind him, forlorn in his adolescent gracelessness. What the hell was he letting himself in for? He was the last man to help anybody; he was a man afraid of loving his own children.

'Look,' he said. 'Teddy, is it? Yes, well. I hardly know you from Adam, and you don't know me, for which you can thank your stars. But you can't stay there blubbing in front of Iris Murdoch. Even if the thought of reading one of her books is enough to excuse it.'

'My mother likes them.'

Tears streaming down his face in public and still the boy thought he had to say the polite nothing!

'Does she, indeed? So do I. The ones I've finished. But have you ever known one author praise another without a snarky comment tucked away at the edge?'

In the café he bought a couple of filled baguettes, coffee for himself and a coke for Teddy, and they sat down at a table in the corner.

'Okay. I've got an hour. Or if the coffee's isn't as foul as I'm expecting, two. No more. You tell me why you're here and if you want to, what the matter is. Then you'd better get on a train back home. You've probably got everything wrong. You look like the sort of young fool who'd make two and two add up to five.'

'I've got some money.' Teddy dug in his pocket for his wallet, dropped it on the floor, and retrieved it.

'I've just been offered something I'm not going to refuse by my Italian agent. I can afford to waste the odd pound. Get on with it, or it really will be wasted. You'll never see me again most probably, and so you can say what you like.'

'Aren't you coming back then?'

304

'Back? Back where? Oh, you mean Wharton. No, I shall go to Italy.'

Angelo's mind slid away from Teddy as images of what his future might be flashed across his brain. He stared sombrely at the boy in front of him, feeling a strange revulsion at the certainty that he could and would recover from the wreck he'd made of his marriage. In time he would forget.

Paola would be sleeping with other men now. Why had he lied to the police about who was driving the car on that day of judgment? Not for love of her but to save her from the onslaught of the law. That deception was a lesser crime than everything else.

Had it been for Imogen, the child wife he'd misused with the same absence of conscience as those who had misshaped his own childhood? Perhaps. He'd loved her – once.

Not that any of this led anywhere, or even mattered now. A violent and abusive childhood had showed him how strong the human will is to survive. As an adult he'd brought havoc and tragedy into other lives, but he knew that in the end the instinct to get on with the business of living would triumph over his grief. He would have other relationships, and he would write.

There was something cruel in the acknowledgement of this truth; a mix of horror and despair rose up in him as he foresaw how he would become at ease with himself, would forget what he'd done.

The familiarity of his surroundings all at once felt stifling, like too many bed-coverings on a summer night. There were the same arts students in predictably paint-stained and torn jeans, earnest Japanese tourists trying too hard, middle-aged women from the Home

Counties in soft lace-up shoes standing very near to the paintings, as if this would somehow be of greater benefit. Then when they felt that sufficient good had been done to them – and their feet began to hurt – they would come thankfully into this café in search of a reviving cup of tea and a cake. They would buy postcards from the shop, which they would put up on the mantelpiece at home to remind them of their day of culture. In the train they would long to put their feet up on the seat, only they would never dream of doing anything so inconsiderate. Instead they would enjoy thinking about their nice collection of postcards which secretly gave them more pleasure than looking at the paintings themselves.

'Yes,' he found he was saying, the sour taste of bitter humour twisting his words, 'think of it as doing me a service. Who knows, I might serve it up in a book in another ten years. It's all right. You won't recognise yourself. People never do.'

'Telling it item by shit-filled item is the best way,' he went on, brooding over his coffee, and almost forgetting to whom he was talking. 'Then you can cross things off, and get rid of having to think of them, like a woman's shopping list.'

'You won't understand.'

He thrust down his coffee cup savagely.

'That age-old cry. Don't bother me with it. I wouldn't say if I did. Don't you know that when people say they understand it usually means they're tired of listening? Get on with it, will you?'

# FORTY-TWO

*You won't be surprised to hear that Conor's been spotted with an eligible widow on his arm. Stella Carberry's evidently besotted. She's been quick to snap him up, it's not six months since her husband dropped dead and she only moved to Dublin in January. We're all anticipating news of further developments …*

Nora stopped reading. Being able to keep up so easily with her old Dublin friends by newsy email exchanges had made her feel that some essential part of her was still living there. Sitting here at the kitchen table with her laptop and a cup of coffee beside her, the April sun slanting through the windows, she'd been transported in her imagination to the city she loved – and where Conor was. She should have known that sooner or later she'd be reading words like these.

Her love for Conor spanned more years now than the length of her marriage to Everett. Now it looked as if he was going to be claimed by this Stella Carberry.

She got up to pour some milk into Semolina's saucer, and watched the cat uncurl himself, rise slowly to his feet and saunter with dignified mien to drink it.

*You didn't say anything about Austen in your last email, is there something you're not telling me?*

Nothing more about Stella Carberry. Nora closed her laptop. Picking up her coffee cup, she loaded it into the dishwasher and wiped away the breakfast toast crumbs from the worktop, thinking all the time she was a fool. Another illusion lost, a silly, idle daydream more fit for a schoolgirl than a woman in her sixties. Now it must be swept like those crumbs into the bin.

She'd indulged herself with the thought that one day they would be together. She had in effect told him there was no possibility of her returning to live in Dublin in the immediate future, but she knew now that she hadn't meant him to accept this. Deep down, she'd hoped – had *believed* – he would wait. She'd pictured a retirement with him by her side, a time when Austen was remarried and Ellen part of a proper family again.

Was his former wife indignant at being replaced with such insulting promptness? Finola had only left him in the autumn. Or was she so happy and engrossed with the man she'd run off with that she didn't care? Let him get on with it, she might be saying, let someone else bear the burden of a husband who's married to his work and never notices if his wife is there.

Nora wasn't convinced. Finola would be rattled, her pride dented. She was only human after all, as people always said, though it seemed a tired enough excuse, not really an excuse at all.

Stella Carberry. Nora tried to imagine a gentle and pretty woman who needed a man by her side. The kind who would never think to contradict or laugh at her husband, even in private, but would nurture him into his old age. Having a woman so openly devoted to him and eager to put him first must have been irresistible. He was a warmly affectionate man; he must, like Captain Benwick in *Persuasion,* love somebody. Stella

Carberry was available and he was turning to her, just as Captain Benwick had turned to Louisa Musgrove.

She'd hurt him by her refusal to return to Dublin when he'd asked her to. If he really had asked. He hadn't sounded very encouraging. But what if he'd needed *her* encouragement? She'd been too proud to give it. He might have no idea that she loved him. She'd always been so careful ... How could she tell him of her feelings in her reply to his letter last year when his own words had been so cautious and so capable of varying interpretation – and this possibly deliberate?

Now it looked as if she was losing him to a woman he'd met just a few months ago. *Pride and Prejudice* again, and at their age. There was no excuse.

A woman should always show more love than she actually feels if she is to secure her man. Charlotte Lucas wasn't exactly to be relied on when it came to marriage, but she had a point. Conor hadn't taken her up on her suggestion that he might visit Wharton. The chatty emails they had taken to exchanging were hardly those of two lovers. She should have given him a definite promise, suggested a long distance partnership for the present. Men weren't as good as women at waiting. Hadn't Anne Elliott said it was women who went on loving longest when all hope had gone?

She threw away the rest of her coffee and gave the sink a vigorous scrub. Maybe Stella Carberry wasn't pretty and gentle at all, but a woman on the make, out to grab a man, any man. Conor might be just one of many men within the range of her arrows. If she couldn't wing him, she'd aim for someone else.

If only she'd still been in Dublin! One shouldn't expect too much of men, even the best of them could make a muddle of things and get in a mess. Was this it, was this why he'd said nothing about Stella Carberry in his emails?

There was probably a whole collection of spare women ready to console Conor. Literature was full of rapacious and alluring widows, working out their designs on men. Then she remembered she was a widow herself, and that was the trouble, she wasn't designing enough.

When you came down to it, was it any use turning to literature to make excuses for men or even to understand them? In novels people conveniently died. In real life it would never be the right people. Then she remembered Everett's dying had meant she was able to step in and be all she could be to Ellen after Verity was killed.

How much less painful it would have been if Finola had never left Conor! Easier to be allowed to feel she would have been Conor's choice if only he'd been free … She had, after all, been a happy widow, relishing her escape from living with a man who had drunk himself to death immersed in his books of philosophy. Her love for Conor hadn't been a distraught or desperate one, it had been a secret light, sustaining her with its warmth down the years.

If it was really true that he was going to marry Stella Carberry she could still have his friendship – if he wished it and his new wife allowed it. Their friendship might even outlast that other kind of love.

*Not for ever in green pastures, do we ask our way to be,* she hummed under her breath, not altogether tunefully. A hymn written by an annoyingly good person, as Ellen would say.

She was prepared now for his next email. He might tell her himself how he had met somebody and how she was becoming important in his life. She had time to compose suitable responses, to affect a joy and warmth that wouldn't falter.

*But the steep and rugged pathway may we tread rejoicingly.* The words and tune of the hymn continued to swim about her head. Had the writer really believed what he'd written? Did anyone honestly rejoice in the steep and rugged pathway? Maybe if you pretended you did for long enough, the wish worked its way through to the heart and became true.

Rejoice with those who rejoice and weep with those who weep. It was easier to do the second than the first, though why this should be so eluded her.

# FORTY-THREE

Teddy waited.

After so much crying, shite embarrassing at first and then surprisingly okay, he felt limp and drained over his whole body. His mind felt exhausted too, as if the pouring out of everything in his head had emptied it of energy.

Now Angelo had gone to the gallery's bookshop, but only for a few minutes. He'd said they might as well walk back to Charing Cross together as he had to get the Tube somewhere.

Talking to Angelo Arzano had been like looking through a telescope the wrong way. Everything that seemed so big to him was a small part of the landscape to Angelo's way of thinking.

'Your father's with your family, isn't he? Your parents are married and living together? So what if they give each other a hard time on occasions? That's what human beings do. They love you. They make that pretty plain, don't they? As for not being your father's son, I never heard anything so dick-brained. You're practically his clone. You can see it a mile off.'

'Can you?'

'Clumsy git, aren't you? Arms and legs all over the place. Much like him. I ought to know. I'm in the business of writing about people; mind, soul and body.'

Angelo's critical gaze flickered over two spreading women unloading their trays of tea and carrot cake.

'Usually writing them off. What if you are gay? It's not such a big deal. It'll be compulsory before too long. *They're taking him to prison for the colour of his hair* – be thankful you live in these enlightened times. Be proud of who you are. Get on with being interested in the world as it is, not how you'd like it to be.'

'It's other people, more than me. Ollie. Winding me up.'

'So friends aren't perfect, so people aren't always the faultless characters you first dressed them up to be. But that doesn't make them worthless. It means you've asked too much of them, you made a mistake. You've got a family whom you obviously love; I'd say you're in luck. It's one hell of a lot more than most of us can boast of.'

A self-mocking smile flitted across Angelo's face for so brief a moment Teddy wasn't sure afterwards if it had been there at all.

'Hasn't it occurred to you that Ollie is jealous you've got a dad to be proud about and his own is a creep he's ashamed of?'

'He's never said anything against his dad.'

'Exactly. Tad slow on the uptake, aren't you? *I gran dolori sono muti*. Great griefs are mute. A heap of crap most likely, but worth bearing in mind.'

Teddy struggled to understand.

'D'you mean even friends want you to have problems because they do too?'

'Every man for himself. You've had it soft. Nobody

313

trying to push into your nappies. You can be grateful for that if nothing else.'

'Is getting your head round the harsh stuff about people what you write about?'

'Why not? And what I can't get my head round. Why read – or write – about what's already obvious or you agree with?'

Because it's less hassle, Teddy thought, but decided to keep to himself. He looked down at his coke which he'd almost finished. He'd better leave a drop or it would look as though he wanted to be bought another.

'Pushing things out further, not staying within the limits of what's understood and been repeated too many times. Digging out what powerful men thought they'd buried. That's what it's about – or partly about. A ruthless business. Cruel at times because you can't afford to be merciful, it gets in the way of the truth.' Angelo stared with restless eyes beyond Teddy, as if seeing something in the far distance of his mind.

'I don't think you're cruel.'

'You haven't thought at all. Writers can't go on writing out of their own pain. They run out. So they use other people's. We're like carrion crows, feeding with desperation on torn flesh, and we're detached because we've learnt to care more for our writing than the human beings around us.'

The terse, snapped-out comments joined up in Teddy's mind and toppled things over in his head, like a row of skittles in a bowling ally. One after another, his thoughts fell flat, only to feel quite a different shape when he tried to pick them up again.

At the barrier to the platform Angelo turned away abruptly. A casual wave, and he hurried away without a backward glance. He looks pissed off, thought Teddy, as though he couldn't care less, but it's weird how he bothered. It's not as if he's ever shown any interest in anybody in Wharton. The only times I saw him he looked right through me, or gave me that superior shrug like I was a complete knob. Then he appears out of nowhere and gives me lunch and is cool over the heavy stuff.

Loitering down the platform and choosing a carriage, he thought about Angelo and how he'd got him wrong. Or was it that people weren't just one thing or the other but could change, and show different sides to themselves? So that the person you thought was always kind could go way out of order, and the bad-tempered shit might, at times, not be shitty at all. And, above all, the person you'd have put down as the shittiest of the lot, was the person you found yourself pouring out all the junk inside your head to.

Even Mum, who you'd have thought would have been sycophantic over Angelo Arzano (she was always wanting them to meet famous people, going on about how it would be useful for them) had snapped that he was 'one of those pretentious literary pseuds who thinks he doesn't need to keep the rules' when Angelo had turned down her invitation to drinks one evening. Phoebe, who'd started off admiring his amazing looks, had dismissed him as a waste of space. After that, none of them had bothered thinking about him again, or even noticed when he'd left to live in London.

The unexpectedness of people – how come he'd never thought much about how extraordinary and different they could be? It was something that might send you off balance sometimes, but at other times …

315

A chance meeting has changed my life. I may never see Angelo Arzano again, and yet that won't change what's happened to me. We had today.

Teddy leant back in his seat. Not everything made sense, but he was too tired to care. He was going home. Tomorrow he'd shove that photo back where it belonged. He shut his eyes. His thoughts began to slide into a dreamy tangle.

'Teddy. We need to get out here. The train's coming into Wharton.'

It was his father's voice. Teddy opened his eyes, still half-asleep. He struggled to his feet.

'Dad? What are you doing here? Why aren't you in London?'

They climbed out of the train with a smattering of other passengers. Behind them the doors shut and the train moved off, leaving them together on the quiet platform of the afternoon.

'I came to be with you. I *wanted* to be with you.'

Teddy turned away his face as he hoisted his rucksack over his shoulders and fiddled with the straps.

'How did you know where I was?'

But even as he asked the question he knew the answer. It was why Angelo Arzano had quizzed him about where his father worked. He must have made a call on his mobile to Dad's office while he was in the gallery bookshop. He'd betrayed him, the sneaking bastard. Saying one thing and doing another, going behind his back, as if he was a stupid kid.

'You had an important meeting today. You told me you did. You ought to be at it.'

'Meetings aren't as important as sons.'

Teddy clung on to his grievance.

'If you knew everything, you wouldn't think so.'

'I would always think so, whatever I knew. You're my son. Nothing else is as important as that.'

They walked in silence to the station exit and the row of waiting taxis. Teddy looked down at the painted lines on the road without seeing them. Why couldn't he let stuff go? He knew underneath that Angelo wouldn't have told his dad anything except that he was on a particular train. Teddy felt quite certain of this. Was that a betrayal? A sensation of something like gratitude for what Angelo had done edged into his mind, barely acknowledged.

Apart from anything else – though was anything *ever* apart from anything else? – his father was with him, standing beside him now on the dusty, chewing gum-splattered pavement. That was something; perhaps it was everything.

'Will it matter,' he said, saying the words with some difficulty, 'will it matter about you leaving the meeting?'

His father didn't answer him directly. Instead, he said, eyeing Teddy's rucksack, 'Is that very heavy? If not, how about we walk the long way home? Time to talk on the way. Unless you want to clock in at school, though I suppose there's not much of the day left. Probably not worth bothering.'

'I didn't tell them I wasn't going in. I just didn't go.'

'Yes. I gathered that was it. I rang Mum an hour ago. She told your housemaster you had some appointment and she'd forgotten about phoning earlier to say you'd be absent.'

'She didn't have to do that.'

'No. But Mum would always try her best for you. You weren't answering your phone. She was worried about you.'

He hunched a shoulder.

'Was she?'

His father put an arm around him. For an instant, Teddy stood rigid as a statue, wanting to draw away. But then some new understanding told him that his father was as much seeking comfort as offering it. The old picture of his dad as up there and him down below tipped sideways. In some strange, uncertain way they were meeting on a level, both with needs wanting to be met.

A faint feeling of responsibility stirred in him. Or was it the wish to protect? He remembered what Angelo had said. Whatever might be the truth of it all – and some small part of Teddy still doubted – his dad was the person who'd always been there loving him and that meant he *was* his father in every way that counted. He leant against him for a moment, feeling some inexplicable shift within himself.

'Let's go home,' he said. 'Mum'll be waiting for us.'

# FORTY-FOUR

Kate took out a block of Pecorino Romano cheese from the fridge and pulled open one kitchen drawer after another looking for the grater. On the rare occasions she allowed the children to unload the dishwasher for her, they never put things back where they belonged but flung them into the nearest and most convenient space. She restored the cooking knives to the exact order they needed to be in, and lined up vegetable peelers, mashers and the garlic crusher in soothing rows.

Philip had given her only the briefest of explanations when he and Teddy arrived home in the late afternoon. Then he'd gone immediately into his study and closed the door, while Teddy hesitated and mumbled his thanks for covering for him with the school.

Once, Kate might have pried; now she let it go. What was bunking off school for a day compared with what Phoebe had done? She watched him pick up his mug of tea, switch on his mobile and make for the door, murmuring he needed to catch up with mates from school.

'Hi, Ollie, how's it going?' she heard him say as he trailed up the stairs, almost certainly spilling tea on the carpet. (But what did stains matter now?) 'Yeah, I'm good, thanks …'

She poured a cup of tea for Philip. Usually when he got in from work he came straight into the kitchen for a drink while she was cooking. Today he'd shut himself away, leaving her uncertain of how to respond. She stood vacillating, the cup in her hand, but then she heard the study door open so she put it down again. He came into the kitchen and sat down at the table, where the girl with the viridian eyes had sat this morning.

'Teddy seems okay.' She kept her voice neutral, leaving her words as either a statement or a question. She must deal with one thing and then another in considered order. That way she wouldn't break down.

'Just about. A misunderstanding.' Philip glanced at the cup of tea as if it was an irrelevance and continued to sit in silence.

They might have been strangers. Philip must know everything now. The two of them were sharing something in which she as Teddy's mother had no place and never would have.

For something to do, she started to chop tomatoes and then peppers for the family's supper, though it was far too early. As she brushed away the stalks and seeds she thought that whatever Teddy had made of the photograph of Laurent, she must wipe her discovery of it out of her mind. She must forget her visit to Teddy's empty room and how she'd stood there with Laurent's face staring up at her. Some things were better left unsaid if families were to survive.

And it was as it should be. After all the wrong she'd done them both, after all she'd taken from Philip, it must be in her to be glad if Teddy turned to him instead of to her for comfort. Didn't she owe that to the man she'd married, for the deceit which had begun so long ago and culminated in the final dishonesty of sending the boys to Wharton? In the face of losing Philip's love, everything she'd striven for and gained shrank into irrelevance.

But now she must tell him about Phoebe.

'Philip – something awful has happened at Phoebe's school. I had to go there – and I couldn't say anything to you when you rang about Teddy.'

It wasn't a good time, but it never would be. She watched the shocked disbelief in his face change to a weary sadness, his tea growing cold on the table in front of him.

'Where's Phoebe now?'

'In her room since I brought her back. I took her up some tea and tried to talk to her. She wouldn't answer.'

'I'll go up to her.'

They ought to have been comforting one another over what had happened today, but instead they were talking across a vast gulf. How could she pour out all her confusion and bewilderment when Philip was withdrawing from her like this?

'Maybe you should wait until later,' she said, hearing the unwillingness in his voice. 'Recover from your day first.' She hadn't meant to sound sarcastic, but she felt Philip register the implied rebuke. She hurried on. 'All she said to me was that she wanted to leave Wharton and go back to London.'

'Is that what you want to do?'

Yes, one part of me does, she wanted to say, but I know it's the mean, proud, cowardly part. I don't want to face anybody after this. The thought of people knowing what's happened – anything would be better than having to see the judgment in the faces of Wharton parents. No wonder Phoebe wants to run away. She's like me and I always thought she was so different … And yet for me it's even worse, for the mother is always to blame. Every wrong a child commits is laid at the mother's door.

'I still can't take it in,' she said. 'She's had everything, been given everything – '

'Yes,' he said heavily. 'Yes, she has. We missed something more important.'

'You mean *I* did – thank you for not saying so.'

'Kate, don't be like that – '

'Unless goodness and civilised values are consciously and consistently taught throughout a child's life … '

'What's that?'

'Just something Phoebe's headmistress said.'

'If this had happened last week,' Philip said levelly, not looking at her, 'we might have done whatever you wanted. Even gone back to London. But today was the partners' meeting.'

She hadn't given it a thought. He'd have missed half of it because of Teddy, but what was that compared to everything else? Philip always thought he was indispensable at work.

'I had to pull out early, but enough had been said to jolt me into making a choice.'

Kate stared at him. That girl. So it was coming.

'About?'

'I'm going to look for an opening locally here in Wharton. The firm isn't getting in enough work. It needs to slim down, to shed some people. I decided I want to be one of them. I resigned from the firm with immediate effect.'

In the silence, she was aware only of a relief so

sharp and overwhelming she was unable to speak. Of all the things he could have said he'd decided to do – Kate shut her mind to the girl's visit this morning – this was the most unexpected. Philip had always worked for the same firm. Not for him the modern practice of switching, of looking for the next career chance, of getting more money; he was loyal to the point of obduracy.

'Kate?'

'Why should you have to go rather than anyone else?'

'I've seen the writing on the wall for firms like ours for a long time. We're not aggressive enough, at least not for a London firm. It isn't enough just to do a good job nowadays. You've got to sell yourself all the time, market your image. I'm not much good at that. And I don't want to be.'

Kate struggled to take in the implications.

'Does that mean a big drop in earnings?' She immediately wanted to unsay her words. She sounded grasping, the last thing she wanted Philip to think her.

'I won't have to commute. I can't expect you to understand, but seven months have been more than enough. I'm tired all the time from being packed into a damned train and I see almost nothing of the children.'

You don't say you mind about seeing almost nothing of me, she thought bitterly. He hadn't left her out deliberately to punish her, she knew. That would have been easier to bear. But Philip never indulged in small-minded pettiness. He'd spoken as he felt, and she endured all the silent pain he unconsciously inflicted.

'Will it be easy to find something in a local firm?'

'It should be in a prosperous town like this. No

shortage of clients. High rates of divorce, money squabbles, child access disputes.'

He's been thinking about all this and making these decisions without a word, thought Kate. I never noticed how much he hated commuting or that he was so disillusioned with his job. I never asked him.

'So it's all settled?'

'If you mean, have I made up my mind, yes I have. I'm sorry, but I haven't been able to talk about it with you. It's something I've had to battle out for myself.'

He didn't sound at all sorry. People always followed the *I'm sorry* with the *but* which made it meaningless.

'Do *you* mind?' he said suddenly, looking at her properly for the first time.

She met his gaze for a long moment. There was something in it she didn't understand. She tried to speak and failed.

'I should have tried harder,' he said, but quietly, as if to himself.

They watched each other across the spotless hygiene of the kitchen floor.

The garage never rang to say the car was ready to be collected, she thought irrelevantly. It may rain tomorrow and Philip will have to walk to the station and he'll get wet. I must phone them first thing in the morning. But what if one of the children is taken ill in the night? I won't be able to drive them to hospital.

She began picturing the frantic ringing for a taxi which would be late or not able to find the house, all the time knowing in another part of her brain that she was mad to be escaping into hypothetical difficulties when there were so many real ones to deal with already stacked up around her.

She couldn't bear it any more. She leant against the worktop, holding her eyes hard open to stop the tears. Why couldn't she throw herself into Philip's arms as a wife ought to be doing at moments like these?

The morning's encounter burned flame-like across her mind. The girl called Daisy stood between them, taunting her. Before today she'd never considered the possibility of Philip being unfaithful, at least not in the physical act. She knew his fastidiousness, his dogged sense of principle. She would never know how often he had slept with Daisy – only that she could never ask him.

Nor could she ask him for comfort. He wasn't offering it, not to her.

'I'll leave you to it then.'

The untouched cup of tea lay abandoned on the table. She heard his step in the hall and then the study door closing again. He's gone to escape among possessions and comforts that have nothing to do with me, she thought. The peeling Agatha Christie paperbacks, the grammar school photograph, the cricket bat with its black thread fraying off the handle. At this moment they mean more to him than I do.

She began to slice mushrooms, so fresh that the knife cut through them cleanly, the blade sliding through the white flesh. *I should have tried harder.* What had Philip meant by those words? He'd given up on her, found her out. He was only staying with her out of pity, because he was a good man and stiff-necked with it ...

She piled the mushrooms into a bowl and started off on what she usually thought to be the disproportionate amount of work and washing-up involved in making lasagne. But it was something that she'd always done well, and it came as a relief to her trembling brain and hands. As she pushed the heavy Le Creuset dish into the oven she was certain of one thing.

The horror over Phoebe's part in Millie Heath's attempted suicide, and the blow to her pride in her children, and her own role as a good mother: none of this could be faced if Philip left her. She couldn't imagine how she was to go on living. Without him she'd be lost in the terror of the obsessions that pursued her, because they would, she knew they would. They might change over time but they would always be there. You never got shot of this illness.

She went slowly over to the window, looked unseeing into the garden. She could hear Philip's footsteps going up the stairs. He doesn't know! He'll never know! I'll work full time, suggest we move to a smaller house. I'll do anything, whatever it takes. But we can't take the boys away from Wharton, we can't do that to them, not now.

The light was going. She stared out into the dullness, seeing only the punishing path ahead. Days, months, years in front of her when she must try and affect a confident innocence she didn't possess; pretend she hadn't seen into Philip's mind; didn't know she was a thing to be endured out of a misplaced obstinacy. She must play the part of the unsuspecting wife, who for the sake of her marriage doesn't see what's staring her in the face. She and Philip would dissemble, play a part, and perhaps in the end they might come to believe that all was as it ought to be between them. This long, dreary striving to be something she was not, and to recover something which she knew was lost, felt infinitely harder than giving up Laurent had been.

But nobody would ever guess. That anybody at all should learn of her humiliation was the worst of all. If she could hide it from everybody she would be able to hide it from herself, from the real hurting person that nobody would ever see.

Soon Jonah would be home from school. The bright star in the family. Her vivid, sparkly boy, so inexplicably like Laurent must have been as a child. A fierce surge of protective love flooded her; he must be shielded from all knowledge that hurt him. She would be successful in this, if nothing else.

'D'you want me to do that for you?'

It was Teddy, hovering in the kitchen doorway, unsure of his welcome.

Drops of blood stained the mound of yellow flakes. She'd grated the piece of cheese too near its end. Kate ran her stinging finger under the tap.

'It's all right thanks, I've nearly finished – '

'I always offer to help just too late – '

He held out some squares of kitchen roll. How like Philip he was in those quick reflexes of conscience, the deep pervading anxiety to please! He might do the wrong thing to help – fall over his feet and break things – but he would rush into it unasked. Her heart ached with love, with guilt.

'It doesn't matter … you don't … you're like Dad, you always rescue me at exactly the right moment.'

She spoke slowly, as if testing her own words, trying to dissolve the clouded thinking that had obscured what now seemed so simple. How could Teddy be Laurent's son when everything about him was so like Philip? Had she made her own punishment by imagining a likeness to Laurent all these years? Had she not punished them all?

'Mum?'

She wrapped the kitchen roll round her finger, washed clean of blood, and smiled into his eyes.

'Nothing is ever too late, darling. I can hear Jonah coming in. Could you tell everyone that supper's almost ready?'

*

Philip remembered a phrase from an article on Nazi Germany, about nations sleepwalking their way into sin. He thought of this now as he sat on Phoebe's bed. The collective, insidious slide could go unnoticed within families. How was it possible that his beloved daughter had gone so wrong? The signs must have been there and he hadn't seen them.

'If only we could go back to London where everything went well for me,' Phoebe repeated. She had begun to cry again, but weakly, as if worn out by so much misery.

'Yes,' said Philip, feeling only an immense love and pity for her and hardly thinking of what he was saying. 'We all long to go back in life, but it isn't possible. We have to go on.'

'But don't you see I *can't!* This morning at school and Millie – I never, ever meant – I never thought – '

Philip tightened his arms around her.

'Of course you didn't. We never do think – or think enough – of the consequences of what might be small choices at the time. Other things seem more important. If you've learnt this, then that is something, in all this terrible sadness.'

'But it's still my fault. I was with the others on Saturday. I didn't say anything to stop them.'

'By the grace of God, Millie is still alive. You've been given another chance.'

'But I'll always, always have it with me, there'll never be any end to remembering.'

Philip felt a great shudder go through her. When you were young you believed you would never get over things. Grown-ups who told you otherwise weren't to be trusted. And in this case it was right in one sense that Phoebe *should* never get over it. None of them should. She'd played a part in nearly destroying another life. He must choose his words carefully.

'All you and I know is that you've learned one of the most important lessons in life. To pay attention to the feelings and needs of others, and to remember that in looking for their happiness you'll find your own.'

Was she listening? Were the young able to even hear these things, let alone begin to act upon them? He'd neglected to show his daughter something of those ideas by which he'd sought – and yet failed – to live. These things were so sacred to him as to make it seem impossible to speak of them even to his own wife and children. He sat heavily, hearing his own heart, the pain of helpless love pressing in on him.

'If we look for happiness too directly and solely for ourselves, we shall have an unhappy life,' he told her. Who had said this, or something like it? He couldn't remember. Had he or she learnt the hard way, as human beings usually had to, through misfortunes and mistakes, tragedies and tears?

'Don't ever feel,' he continued, stroking the shining hair falling across her face, 'that every single one of us hasn't done things of which we're bitterly ashamed.' For one hideous moment he found himself remembering the silky sheen of Daisy's hair. He thrust away the image with an effort. 'We're not so different, any of us, and this means we'll see things through together, as a family, here in Wharton. By sticking beside each other, we'll get through it and have happy times again.'

'Dad?'

She moved her head slightly against his hand.

'Yes?'

'Do you really mean that? About sticking together? I thought – I know Teddy and Jonah thought – '

'If you or Teddy or Jonah ever thought for one moment that I could ever stop loving any of you, or Mum, then put it out of your head once and for all.'

Philip wrenched his mind away from the pain. What had he and Kate done to the children through their blindness and mistaken choices? Gently, he turned Phoebe's ravaged face to look at his.

'You must believe this and trust me. There are ups and downs in relationships because of all kinds of things, but that doesn't mean there isn't the deep, accepting love underneath. Okay?'

He sensed rather than heard her assent, a tiny whisper. He felt very tired. From the kitchen, he could hear Teddy calling that supper was ready.

'Come down with me now,' he said. 'I made an exciting decision today at work. Mum knows already but I want to tell you three all together.'

# FORTY-FIVE

'They won't find it embarrassing to get married, will they?' Ellen looked down admiringly at the nails she'd managed at last to grow to a length that impressed even Clover. 'I mean, then they'll be Jane and Austen.'

'So appropriate,' murmured Nora, half-shutting her eyes in pleasure at the delicious caress of May sunshine on her face. A tea tray with mugs and the remains of a misshapen lemon drizzle cake rested on a low table between the luxurious garden loungers recently and surprisingly bought for them by Austen.

'But people might think it's ridiculous and laugh,' persisted Ellen, who was lying on her stomach and thoughtfully arranging fallen blossom petals into an intricate pattern on the grass next to her.

'Do you think they'll mind if people do?'

'They probably won't notice. They're not very good at seeing that sort of thing. I suppose that's why they've fallen in love. Actually, I was thinking more of myself.'

'For what do we live, but to make sport for our neighbours, and laugh at them in our turn?' quoted Nora.

'I might have guessed you'd spout *Pride and Prejudice* at me. Mr Bennet isn't exactly to be relied on, since he married such a silly woman.'

Nora sat up and eyed her granddaughter.

'How do you know they're going to get married anyway?'

'Oh, I just *know*. Lots of reasons.'

Nora found her eyes blinded by sudden grateful tears.

'Mummy would be pleased. Jane is a loving and giving sort of person, just like she was.'

'Granny, I've just had a brilliant idea. We could give them a hint to choose *Come down, O Love divine* at their wedding!'

'To make it up to poor old Bianco da Siena, you mean? You don't want to have him repenting of his crimes in our final episode?'

'Jane's definitely not a wicked stepmother,' said Ellen, with something like regret in her voice. 'Things are *never* like they are in books.'

'Sometimes they're better.'

'Yes, and now I come to think of it, Jane's like Cousin Helen in *What Katy Did* – d'you remember, you read it to me when I had chickenpox – there was something about taking hold of people by their smooth handle? Making people nicer somehow by the way you speak to them? Jane gets hold of people in that way.'

'I'm thinking you wouldn't get a Cousin Helen in a children's book these days. Publishers disapprove of characters like her. It's grand to know we've got one in real life.'

This was a happy thought to Nora, whose tendency to think of fictional characters as living people had so often led to confusion.

Ellen glanced back at her nails, painted in sky-blue varnish, given to her by Clover. They really did look what Granny called fetching, saying the word jokingly in inverted commas; she was never going to get her head round fashion. But Dad didn't seem to notice things like that either. This was both good and bad, depending on which way you thought about it.

'I did do something mean to her once,' she said, in a sudden burst of confidence. 'I screwed up a postcard she sent to Dad and never told anyone.'

'Only a postcard?' said Nora, laughing. 'You could have been more imaginative than that.'

'And I lied about Dad having another girlfriend.'

'I don't think you can have been very convincing.'

'It wasn't funny *then*. Clover was wrong about her in one way but right in another. Of course,' Ellen's mind sheered off into a different direction, 'sometimes it's better *not* to see things. Or pretend not to. Like the maid in *Miss Marple* stories, she's always getting the chop for seeing what she shouldn't.'

'You must be glad you don't live in a cosy English village with murders in vicarages and crusty colonels in country houses. We can't expect anything like that to happen in Wharton, though Winnie Pumfret might find it very exciting if it did.'

'No, and the poor maid doesn't always understand what she's seen, so it's completely unfair,' said Ellen sorrowfully. 'You don't think we'd better hurry Dad along a bit? Jane might get snatched up by someone else. I bet there are other people after her. Dad ought to get on with it.'

Yes, men ought to get on with it, Nora agreed silently. It's no use sulking when life doesn't go the way you want.

The long-rehearsed relinquishment gave a little twist of its knife in the old wound. She might never

333

live with the person she'd loved for so long, never be able to tell him how much she loved him …

God was giving her over and above what she had prayed about during the long years since Verity had died: the safe-keeping and happiness of her son and granddaughter. Wasn't this infinite compensation for the one missed joy in her life? Save me from the selfish need to possess, which is always there, creeping like knotweed into the mind's compacted earth.

*Come down, O Love divine, seek thou this soul of mine* … the hymn of Ellen's villain. Didn't it say it all? *And so the yearning strong, with which the soul will long, shall far outpass the power of human telling* …

Out loud she said, 'We shall have to think of something.'

A secret waft of wind blew off a cloud of blossom from the cherry tree. In the late afternoon sunshine the petals lit up, glittering like a shower of golden coins; largesse scattered among the populace, thought Nora confusedly.

I don't *know* that he is involved with Stella Carberry. The gossip might be all wrong. Less than a week since his last email and nothing about her in that. Why am I so mistrustful? If he's the man I've known all these years he'll have understood me. He'll have waited …

'Our surname's not ridiculous. That would be worse,' said Ellen, looking for and finding consolation. 'After all, it could be Shufflebottom or Clutterbuck or – ' she paused, trying to think of more undesirable and undignified names. A thought struck her. 'What will Jane's mother do without her? Will she mind being left on her own?'

'Her friend Grace Whipple could go and live with her,' suggested Nora. 'Since she got that unexpected legacy from Mabel she's been wondering about moving to somewhere with a garden, but she's not exactly fitted to live alone. Dorothy might enjoy taking Grace under her wing and would rule over her kindly.'

I *will* jump on that plane to Dublin …

Ellen considered the picture of Dorothy and Grace living together. Her life with her grandmother had accustomed her to spending most of her time with adults. She liked old ladies, bossy ones like Dorothy and ones who made you think of quivery white rabbits like Grace. She decided the picture was a pleasing one.

'Old people *ought* to team up more and band together against know-all social workers, or even their own relatives,' Nora went on, her fancy extending to streets full of such households. They could be rather splendid in their way. It was even possible to imagine living in such a set-up in her own old age if Conor died before her … She pulled herself up. He hasn't agreed to anything yet, she told herself sternly.

Ellen looked up from her pattern.

'But *we'll* still live together, won't we? I mean, if – when – Dad and Jane get married. I do want them to, but I couldn't *bear* not to have you.'

'I might find myself an old gentleman to keep me company and have a little house just round the corner – and you can come to tea with us every day and eat cakes that have sunk in the middle.'

'An old gentleman? Granny! You don't mean Brian Goodacre from church? You could do *much* better than him … I could plan something.'

Nora leant over and dropped a kiss on Ellen's head. 'Back to your earlier point. When shall we kidnap Jane and arrange a Hyacinth Bucket candlelight supper?'

# FORTY-SIX

Seated at the organ in the Wharton school chapel, Jane remembered reading somewhere that Elgar had been inspired to write one of his *Enigma Variations* by seeing a dog struggling to escape from a river. As she played, she thought of Terzo and how she'd brought him the puppy. Now he'd started at his school with Sofia, and was no longer the silent child of last summer.

But Jane sensed that the loss of his twin would continue to affect Terzo at some deep, uncharted level. Something would remain missing in his consciousness, an unspoken grief for a bond that he couldn't remember and yet had been severed. He'll always be like this, she thought, needing to withdraw into an interior space, whether or not any further memories of his earlier life and the accident came back.

He was, after all, the child of his father, with whom he might – or might not – keep up some kind of relationship. She tried to imagine what form this would take, but remembering Angelo's bleak face as she'd first seen it when she stood on the doorstep, she found herself unable to imagine the future with any certainty. Terzo had his mother and Sofia, as well as capable and involved grandparents. Angelo must find his own way back, in his own fashion, in the years to come.

I never got round to reading *Priest and Victim*. But now Angelo Arzano has gone to live in Italy he is sure to write another book, and my mother and I could read that instead, which will do just as well.

Yet even as these thoughts flitted across her brain something of shame crept over her. It *wouldn't* do just as well. She hadn't made the effort to face what was uncongenial and frightening about human beings, the sexual evil that Angelo had experienced and exposed. He had suffered in the telling and for the notoriety his book had brought him. That shouldn't go for nothing, especially not with people like her, lucky enough to have had an unsullied childhood.

She heard Ellen and Nora's voices again all those months ago on their way down to the church questioning the title of Angelo's book. Why had he in truth chosen it? Could it be that he was one of those who go down the path to their own self-destruction, knowing that redemption is not for them – and yet it is that which redeems them? Tears – for Angelo, for Imogen, for their dead child – blurred the pages of music in front of her.

She lost her place and repeated the phrase. In another year, Jonah would begin playing on this organ, after he'd taken his grade eight piano exam. He wouldn't be taught by her for she played the organ for enjoyment only – and not at all well – while he would have lessons with Wharton's director of music. Only the most talented musicians among the boys were allowed on the chapel organ, but Jonah was undoubtedly one of them. She hoped he would still continue the piano with her, for otherwise she would miss him. Strange how a boy who could have been so full of himself and the wealth of gifts heaped on him remained so free of conceit. He had a mother who might well have ruined him – yet here Jane caught herself up. Kate had changed.

In the beginning, when Jane had gone to the Gidding house for Jonah's lessons, Kate had been business-like and a shade patronizing. Now her manner was subdued and carefully considerate, as if she had sustained a shock, though it was possible she was merely preoccupied with the French coaching agency Jonah had told her she was setting up. There was no doubt that Kate would be highly successful in the venture. More successful perhaps than Philip might be in the local firm of solicitors he was joining, but Jane was sure he wouldn't mind. Other men might be more ambitious, but Philip was of a different mould. He looked happy where he was within his family. That was all that mattered.

Kate was in some ways profoundly dislikeable, but creeping over Jane was the feeling that she was at the same time admirable. Complex and difficult characters like hers and Angelo's were disturbing or even unattractive if you were looking only for niceness. People should be something more, although she wavered as to what exactly this might be. She'd discovered that she wanted to get to *know* Kate. That was a start.

It looked as if there was no end to the unlikely friends that life might offer you, but each one of them would add to its richness. There was always a hidden mutuality if you cared enough to see it, an unexpressed sense of belonging. Jane stumbled over the word sympathy and instead arrived at dependence. Hadn't St Paul said everyone needed one another?

The lump of jealousy of Beth that she'd been carrying around all year had somehow disappeared almost without her realising it. In its place was a consciousness of gratitude that she could count Stephen and Beth as her friends, even if they did speak in a religious language that wasn't the same as hers. The goodness of other people – in the end, in the whole scheme of things, it was that which lifted you up into a happier, light-filled way of living.

She remembered the flower festival last summer, the passionate, alluring scent of the roses she'd arranged, mingling with her own feeling of inadequacy. Yet it was that afternoon she'd met the Arzano family and then Nora and Ellen. St Paul might have had his failings – being only a man, Jane could almost hear Winnie Pumfret's cosy voice – but you had to admit he came out with things that stayed to haunt your mind all your life.

Her thoughts strayed to Phoebe, remote in her teenage world, with interests and aspirations apparently alien to her own. Last week Phoebe had waylaid her and asked if she knew of someone who taught the mandolin, as she wanted to learn. Her friend Millie – she gestured towards the fragile and serious-faced girl standing beside her – had asked her along to a music group. Phoebe needed to be able to play something, but there were plenty of guitars and drums in the group already and so they'd hit on a mandolin.

It was unusual for a fifteen-year-old to take up an instrument without being pushed into it by parents, but it was Phoebe's choice and this was the important thing. It might grow and bring lifelong joy and consolation, and didn't every human being need these? So even there it was conceivable that a relationship of a kind might emerge, for underneath the defensive exterior Phoebe was like everyone else, sometimes misled and getting things wrong, but trying to find her way through life and what it all meant.

It struck Jane that the site of the old Victorian house, which throughout her childhood had appeared to her such a bastion of solid family values, now contained three families with a very different way of living. But what lay underneath hadn't altered, for families could come in endless variations, and join forces in new and creative ways.

What was she waiting for? She played the final lines, stuffed her book of music into her bag, and stood up to go.

It was in that moment she saw Austen, standing alone in the centre of the chapel.

*

Austen came out of his classroom and then wished he hadn't. Out of the corner of his eye he could see the maroon upholstered shape of the deputy headmaster's wife emerging from the far end of the quad. Sue North came under the heading of alarming women, and was therefore to be avoided. He waited a moment to see which way she was going. Towards him. He retreated.

A few minutes later and the coast was clear. Afternoon school had finished and the buildings were quiet. Most of the boys would be on the cricket field or athletics track; a few would be pretending to play tennis, still seen as the slackers' option. Masters like himself, who weren't involved in any of the sporting activities

340

of the school, were closeted in their classrooms or the Common Room preparing lessons and marking work. It was, he thought, a perfect moment for going to find Jane in the music department.

Casual enquiry had told him she finished at just this time today. Couldn't he meet her and suggest ... but he was not quite sure what to suggest. A cup of tea somewhere? A drink? It was still too early. A walk past the playing fields and into the country?

That would be best, he decided, thinking of the blossom-smothered hedgerows and the endless mesmerising greens of the spring trees. In such a setting, safely away from other people, he might be able to say what he wanted. He would feel less inadequate, and walking next to her would make it easier to take her into his arms. He quickened his step.

Even now he feared he'd misread the signals. He got these things wrong so much more than other men! Yet he knew he couldn't go on like this, churning with doubts and regrets that he hadn't brought himself to try his chance with Jane. He thought of her face, the way her transparently honest eyes looked into his. She was beautiful and she was infinitely dear to him. There was no reason why she should return his love, but if by some grace of God she did ...

When Verity had died he'd told himself that the profound, undeserved happiness he'd been given in their marriage would never again be his. Tears would always be at the heart of things for him; he couldn't live in such a way as to put his loss behind him. It was a weakness; he knew that. He owed it to others and to himself to be as other men. But he had nothing to offer another woman.

Then had come the day he'd travelled down to Wharton and found himself sitting opposite a woman who made him feel that his life could be different … He remembered the sudden yearning to speak to her, how he'd felt as if talking to her would be like coming home.

But she'd have been disappointed in him. He was sure of it after the tea party when he'd met her again so unexpectedly; he knew he'd been tedious and schoolmasterly. He'd only asked her to have a drink with him on the way home from school on that miraculous September evening because he couldn't avoid it and he was sure she'd refuse.

But she hadn't. She'd become the close friend of his mother and daughter. In the chapel, catching sight of her absorbed in Mozart's Requiem Mass, something had happened … but he didn't know it then. Not until he watched her at the piano before Christmas playing *O Holy Night*. He whispered to himself that he didn't have a right to such happiness; it couldn't be expected, much less asked for in those quiet moments when he tried to think about the whole business of loving and living.

Inside the music block, muffled notes from pianos battled with cellos, clarinets and the melancholy tones of a tuba. Austen peered round the door of the little room where Jane taught, and found it empty.

His face twitched. He was too late. He'd missed her, and it was his own fault. She'd probably left as soon as her last pupil had finished. He'd dithered too long, just as he'd done when he'd first seen her.

The chapel doors were open. He'd go in there before he went home.

The chapel appeared empty but he could hear the organ being played. The music scholars came in to practise at all hours.

Underneath the gold stars of the painted ceiling he stood listening to Elgar's *Nimrod*, waiting for the triumphant climax.